Lauren felt her
remember where I par
furious at myself for be
you didn't hear me swearing."

"You can go now—the light's green. I thought you were drunk. Wait a minute. Who were you talking to?"

"Nobody. I pretended there was a crowd of us to scare off those ruffians. Shoot! I almost went through the stoplight." She braked and the car lurched.

"Ruffians?" The professor turned, and his crooked smile showed off his full lips and his white teeth. "It worked," he said as the smile spread. "I never would have thought of it."

"When I was a kid I used to imagine I could save someone. I can't believe I actually did it. It was horrible watching them beat you up. God, my hands are still shaking."

"Whoa, turn here! This is my building. You can let me off at the next corner."

She stopped the car in front of a fire hydrant.

"Thanks," he said, as his huge hand engulfed hers. His thick fingers were surprisingly warm. "I'm glad you showed up." His eyes sparkled in the glow of the streetlights.

"You're welcome."

"I hope to find a way to show my appreciation." He still cradled her hand. The smile was intimate, as if he had been saving it just for her. Before she could react, he touched his lips to hers. Astonished, she didn't think to push him away, and the kiss went on, sweet and soft like summertime on the beach. No pressure, simply a waft of pleasure radiating from her lips all the way through her body. Stopping her breath. Stopping time.

"Merry Christmas, Lauren," he whispered to her cheek. "Thanks for scaring off the bad guys."

Buried Heart

by

A. Y. Stratton

Buried Heart

COPYRIGHT © 2009 by A. Y. Stratton

Cover Art by *Rae Monet*

The Wild Rose Press
PO Box 708
Adams Basin, NY 14410-0706
Visit us at www.thewildrosepress.com

Publishing History
First Crimson Rose Edition, 2009
Print ISBN 1-60154-572-X

Published in the United States of America

Dedication

I dedicate this novel to my husband, Freddy,
who has made my life a great romantic adventure;
to Margy, Diane, and Rick, our kids, who grew up
nicely in spite of their embarrassing mother;
to my faithful readers Marion, Marjorie, Vicky,
Patsy, Barb, Karen, and Jill;
to the members of
the Wisconsin Romance Writers of America
for their support;
and to the critique master Ian Leask.

Prologue

A village in the Yucatan, 1562

Deep inside the cave, Brother Guillermo
stumbled on shards of clay and collapsed against the
bottom step of the Temple of the Serpent. He let his
eyes adjust from the unceasing glare of noon to the
flickering light of smoking torches, glanced around
him at the vast, conical chamber and shivered. The
niche Guillermo sought must be high and out of
sight. He must hurry, or his absence from the fires
would be noted. Death would catch him.

With his dangerous prize tucked beneath his
arm, he gripped the first ledge and clambered past
the eyeless stone warrior with the bulbous lips and
clenched teeth. Righteous fury drove him up the
next wedge of stone past the blood-red fangs of the
serpent and higher into the darkness, sweat blurring
his eyes, torch smoke stinging his throat, decay
polluting his lungs. He scaled the third stone step
and paused to listen. Bats whirred and dipped at his
head. That was all.

After a year of living so far from his home in
Seville, Spain, Guillermo had befriended a local
priest who helped him learn the native language. In
secret, the priest had also shown Guillermo sacred
documents. As Guillermo's new friend narrated, the
strange symbols painted on folds of tree bark
disclosed astonishing scientific discoveries and
violent, bloody battles.

The sessions ended abruptly after Bishop de

Landa, representative of His Holiness the Pope, decreed the blasphemous works destroyed. Earlier that morning Guillermo had followed orders, flinging manuscripts into the torrid flames, his mind an angry sea. Was it the devil that made Guillermo's hands rescue a scroll from the pile? No matter. Once he had slipped it beneath his cloak, his path was set. Perhaps his fate was too.

Feigning illness, he limped back to his cell and then veered toward the caves where the natives had worshipped their gods long before Spain arrived from across the sea.

A shout nearly caused Guillermo's sweaty hand to slip off the ledge. His pounding heart muffled all sound as he shrank behind the mammoth head of a feathered monster and fumbled along the rough walls for an opening large enough to hold the precious folds of paper.

His fingers detected a cavity below the serpent's claws, and Guillermo whispered his prayer. "Lord, help me do your will!" The folded parchment slid in so perfectly he knew the Lord had answered.

Below him, howls of fear ricocheted off cavern walls. Guillermo flattened himself against the temple step to keep from falling. Hosts of natives burst through the narrow passageway and spilled into the courtyard below. Behind them soldiers exploded into the cavern. Armor clanking and swords slashing, they skewered bodies and hacked off arms and legs, hands and heads, painting the ground with blood.

The soldiers roared into the next passageway. In the sickening silence, Guillermo sobbed and asked God to bless the dead and forgive his compatriots.

A soldier's shout distracted him. He missed the last step and fell to his knees. "Look, there's one hiding over there!" Before Guillermo could rise, the heat of a blade singed his neck.

Chapter One

Milwaukee, Wisconsin, December, present day

Lauren Richman elbowed her way out of the circle of professors, stalked across the meeting room, snatched up her coat from a chair near the entrance, and squeezed through the crowd into the frigid night.

The air stung Lauren's nose and snagged her breath. At the street, a gust of snow blasted her cheek. Ignoring the do-not-walk sign, she crossed and leaped over a bank of slush onto the sidewalk. At the entrance to the University of Wisconsin-Milwaukee's parking garage she finally stopped long enough to zip up her coat and wrap her wooly scarf around her head.

Lauren mumbled the words she should have said to Enid's face at the reception in the annoying woman's honor and trudged up the stairs to the second level. Why had she stood there like a goon while Enid exposed Lauren's humiliating childhood to the gaping, giggling gossipmongers?

For some reason, every time Enid sipped one too many martinis, she would slur into embarrassing reveries of Lauren's parents' "ideal karmic connection," rhapsodizing over her mother's "lush beauty" and her father's "appetite for life's juiciest boughs."

Lauren's mother would have agreed that lush karma and juicy boughs were "bullshit," not exactly a poetic word, but at least an accurate one. Her

3

parents had competed with each other, as if life were the Olympics and they were the stars of every event. Even in death, they raced to the finish. Each time her father "mentored" another young artist, Lauren's mother retreated into a cocoon of grief.

Long before she'd ever had a crush on a guy, Lauren had promised herself she'd never let a man treat her like garbage. So far, she had succeeded. The sad thing was, Lauren had been so good at avoiding her parents' faults that her only outstanding accomplishment at the no-longer-ripening age of thirty-three was a stack of grammatically correct annual reports.

What she yearned for was not an explosive love affair like her crazy parents', nor even five more clients and a fully paid credit card account. What she needed was a quest that would fire her heart and her soul, something like Dr. Hernandez, the cocky archeology professor, had described at the reception. Goose bumps pricked Lauren's spine as she imagined herself tracking down a document lost in the rain forest for hundreds of years.

Lauren glanced down the line of cars where she thought she'd parked her trusty blue Neon, but it wasn't there. "Where the hell is it?" she shouted and stamped her cold feet until the echo of her voice faded away.

It was Enid's fault she'd arrived late to the event and Enid's fault she couldn't find her car. Instead of paying attention to where she parked, Lauren had been worrying whether Enid would be happy with the latest rewrite of her evening's speech—and whether she'd get the printout to the bossy woman before the ceremony began.

Had her car been stolen? Lauren steadied her breathing and forced herself to tramp around another loop of the ramp.

The dim lighting painted the garage a creepy

yellow. Lauren seemed to be the only one around. A shiver rippled down her neck. Just the week before two students had been robbed at gunpoint and another was raped in an alley not far from campus.

She picked up her pace and rounded the next loop, listening to the clacking of her high-heeled boots. The blue Neon was nowhere in sight.

Below her two men laughed, harsh, staccato barks that reverberated through the cold concrete. Lauren's heartbeat blipped in her throat. She could hardly swallow. If she didn't spot her car soon, her toes would be completely numb.

She heard footsteps and looked around. No one was in sight. Of course, there was nothing to be afraid of, as long as she remembered what she'd learned in her self-defense class: keep aware of the surroundings, keep the keys in hand, and proceed quickly to the vehicle. If she could find the damn thing.

With a wash of relief, Lauren spotted the front end of the Neon. Beyond it, a man in a leather jacket banged through the exit door. Lauren sprang back and dropped the car keys. Instantly two men in black knit hats exploded from nowhere and toppled the guy in the leather jacket.

Lauren snatched up her keys and scurried between two cars, fear thudding in her chest. Shouts careened off the walls. A fist smacked against skin. Someone swore in Spanish. Punches and expletives jammed the air.

Lauren peeked around a bumper and reached in her pocket for her cell phone, but it wasn't there. In the dim glow, she watched the victim, still on his feet, slam his elbow into one guy's nose, then whirl, and smack the other guy in the neck. With a howl of pain, one attacker rammed his head into the victim's belly while the other one jumped on his back and all three collapsed to the concrete floor.

Abruptly the noise stopped. Lauren snuck another look. The attackers held the victim face down across the hood of a car with his arms stretched behind him. They asked him where something was, tesoro, treasure, and then smashed his face into the hood of the car.

Lauren's knees shook, and she clutched the door handle of a salt-smudged Honda to keep from falling. The poor guy getting bashed up looked familiar. Was it that archeology professor who was talking to Enid? She had to get help, but her Neon was still at least ten slots away with her cell phone in it.

"Come on, primo, tell us, where is it?" a man growled. Something metal glinted in his hand. Was it a gun?

If Lauren interfered, she could get hurt, but no way was she going to stand around like a pathetic jerk and let someone die if she could prevent it. She took a deep breath, stamped her feet as loudly as she could, and hoped the echo would magnify the impact.

"Hey, Chuck, Jerry, here's the car!" she shrieked. "I told you it wasn't down there!" She stamped until her feet stung. "Hey, you guys, up here! I can see it. Listen!" She pressed her car's panic button, and the blare ricocheted like a tornado siren.

Lauren watched the attackers clatter down the stairway, and a wave of triumph washed over her. Her idea had worked. She'd scared them off! The poor victim was still alive. As her car alarm blared on, a car started on the level below and squealed away.

"You all right?" When the man didn't answer, Lauren hurried over and found him leaning against the door of an old Jeep Cherokee with his hands over his face. He stood up for a second and staggered. It was the professor, and he looked awful.

"Whoa!" she said, "Maybe you should sit down."

"The cement's freezing." His dark eyes flashed with fury. A purple lump blossomed on his cheek and blood dripped from his chin.

"Can you make it to my car?"

"Turn that damn sound off, will you?

"Sure. Sorry." She clicked off the car alarm. Dr. Hernandez gripped the fender and tried to take a step. "Lean on me," she said, and slid her arm around his waist.

"Thanks a lot." He slurred the words and then stumbled, nearly pulling her down.

Lauren settled him gently into her car, and then hustled around to the driver's side, started the engine, and began to call 911 on her cell phone.

The professor snatched the phone out of her hand and turned it off. "What're you doing?"

"Calling the police and an ambulance."

"I'm fine. Don't need to be the big news all over campus."

"But those men attacked you!" She punched the steering wheel. "You can't just let them get away with it."

"You have something I can use on my knee? It's bleeding like hell."

She dug into her purse for a pack of Kleenex and handed it to him. "There's blood on your chin too."

"It's not my blood," he said with a low chuckle. "I broke that bastard's nose."

He turned on her dome light and dabbed his knee. Lauren could not believe that the professor she'd listened to at the reception was in her car. Enid had described him perfectly: short, stocky, dark, and handsome, with hair as thick as a horse's mane, a chiseled profile, and splendid lips."

"You're Luis Hernandez."

Dr. Hernandez flicked a glance at her and nodded. "And you? Who are you?"

"Lauren. You don't know me. I, uh, was with a

friend and saw you at the reception tonight. That gash looks ugly. You should see a doctor. Did they rob you?"

"Nope. Lauren what?"

"They didn't take your wallet?" No way was she going to give out her name. Even if the guy was charming and smart, he could be mixed up with those men who jumped him.

"Guess they weren't after money." He stopped dabbing his knee and blinked at her. "What friend?" He started to smile, but winced instead and fingered his jaw.

In the dim light, Lauren watched him clean his wound and tried not to stare at his amazing dark eyelashes. "Do you owe those men drug money?"

He plucked out another tissue with his big, cut-up hands and dabbed his nose. "I owe money to lots of people, but not for drugs." He leaned close and rested his eyes on her. "I have only one vice." Still watching her, he laughed and opened the car door. "Now I better get home."

"Are you sure you can drive? You're in bad shape."

"I'll take it slow. Thanks again."

Twitching with curiosity, Lauren watched him limp to the Cherokee and lean against the door for a moment. When she put the car in reverse, she saw him staggering back.

"Second thought, I'll take that ride," he said and hefted himself into the front seat.

She glanced at his car as she backed out and saw why he'd agreed to let her take him home. "They slashed your tires!"

"Unfriendly bastards, wouldn't you say?"

"The hospital is a few blocks away."

"Never mind. My ribs are just sore and the knee's okay. Take me home, thanks."

"I know I'm being pushy, but you need to see a

doctor."

"You're correct—you're being pushy. I want to go home."

She inhaled to keep from saying more. "Which way?"

"You know the new apartments on Wisconsin Avenue near Marquette? Wait, now I remember, you're the pretty woman with Dr. Godwin."

"On the other side of the Convention Center?"

"I noticed your lips."

"My lips? Um, how do I get there? Do I go past the Grand Avenue stores?"

"If you want. Maybe it was your smile. You can go now—the light's green."

"What?"

"You have any heat in this car?"

"Sorry. It takes awhile. Do you like it?"

"Your car or your smile?"

Was the guy nuts? "Your apartment. Do you like your apartment?"

"It's okay. What the hell were you doing walking up the ramp? You don't like stairs?"

She felt her cheeks flush. "I couldn't remember where I parked. I was wandering around furious at myself for being an airhead. I'm surprised you didn't hear me swearing."

"I thought you were drunk. Wait a minute. Who were you talking to?"

"Nobody. I pretended there was a whole crowd of us to scare off those ruffians. Shoot! I almost went through the stoplight." She braked and the car lurched.

"Ruffians?" He turned to look at her, and his crooked smile showed off his full lips and his white teeth. "It worked," he said as the smile spread. "I never would have thought of it."

"When I was a kid I used to imagine I could save someone. I can't believe I actually did it. It was

9

horrible watching them beat you up. God, my hands are still shaking."

He touched her shoulder. "You should have run. You risked getting beaten up too, or worse."

His kind words distracted her, and she nearly missed his street.

"Whoa, turn here! This is my building. You can let me off at the corner."

She stopped the car in front of a fire hydrant.

"Thanks," he said as his huge hand engulfed hers. His thick fingers were surprisingly warm. "I'm extremely glad you showed up." His eyes sparkled in the glow from the streetlights.

"You're welcome."

"I hope to find a way to show my appreciation," he said, still cradling her hand.

The smile was intimate, as if he had been saving it just for her. Before she could react, he touched his lips to hers. Astonished, she didn't think to push him away, and the kiss went on, sweet and soft like summertime on the beach. No pressure, simply a waft of pleasure radiating from her lips all the way through her body. Stopping her breath. Stopping time.

"Merry Christmas, Lauren," he whispered to her cheek. "Thanks for scaring off the bad guys."

Chapter Two

Lauren pulled into her garage, turned off the car and forced herself to breathe in and out, in and out. Her hands were sweating and freezing at the same time. Though she only had to cross the alley to reach the back stairs to her apartment, she was afraid to get out of the car to close the overhead garage door behind her, because men in knit hats might jump out of the dark and beat her up.

She wasn't thinking straight. Of course she was safe in her own garage. Nevertheless, she crept out of the car, slammed down the garage door, dashed across the alley, and bolted up the fire escape stairs to her kitchen entrance.

Inside she'd be fine.

She wasn't fine. She couldn't get warm, even after a hot shower and hot tea. She must be in shock. Who wouldn't be after doing what she had done? Her impulse to rescue the professor had turned her into a whimpering wuss.

The bad guys. Lauren repeated the professor's words in her head. She'd scared off two bad guys. She clutched the cold rim of her bathroom sink and flashed a fake smile into the mirror. A very brave thing.

When she couldn't hold her toothbrush still enough to put toothpaste on it, she gave up, climbed into bed, and pulled a sheet, two blankets, a quilt, and her electric heating pad over her trembling body.

Sleep would help, of course, but the second she

closed her eyes, she pictured the vicious men slugging the professor into a mangled mess and her trembling began again. To banish the thugs from her mind, she focused on the professor sitting in her car, alive and safe, kissing her.

As Lauren watched the digital clock blip over to 10:00 pm, her cell phone rang. She picked it up and recognized the number. "Sorry, Rocky," she croaked. "I just had to get out of there."

"And leave me, your best friend, with a crowd of professors? If you'd told me you were leaving, I'd have ditched too. The chancellor took about an hour to introduce Enid, going on and on about what a distinguished poet she is. Jeez, that guy can talk. Then I had to sit through Enid's boring speech about writing poetry. Oh, sorry, it wasn't really boring, Laur'. It's just that I couldn't figure out where you were."

"Enid was at her worst. I had to get out of there."

"I heard. A couple of martinis and she went after you about your parents."

"Yes."

"She's jealous of you; that's it, you know? She doesn't treat you right. Tell her you quit."

"Tell my biggest, oldest client to take a hike? How would I pay my mortgage?"

"You're good at what you do. You'll find new clients who respect you."

"Maybe someday I will, but not until I've paid the remodeling bills. So how bad was she when she gave the speech?"

"Not quite drunk, but obviously loose, you know, like she was lounging on a couch at some cocktail party. The crowd loved her. She should have her own TV show. How about I come get you and we go somewhere for a bite and a beer?"

Lauren had intended to tell Rocky about the

mugging, and that was her opportunity, but something held her back. "I feel awful, Rocky, like I'm getting a cold. I'm already in bed."

"Hey, I'd be glad to come over to rub your back and help you sleep through the night."

"No, thanks, Rocky."

"Okay, but let's go out tomorrow night. Dad promised I could get off work early again. I'll call you. And, Lauren, I got a question for you, an advice question."

Lauren hoped her brain would work well enough to answer Rocky's question. "What is it?"

"What should a guy do if he falls in love with his best friend?"

"Oh, Rocky, please, don't say that."

Rocky's laugh sounded sad. "Too late for that, isn't it? Anyhow, you answered the question. Good night, Lauren."

****

Lauren woke up the next morning wondering why Luis Hernandez had refused to call the police or go to a hospital. At first, she thought she'd stumbled upon a drug deal gone bad, as they would say on the news, but Luis had mocked that idea. Still, his behavior was odd. If he had a connection to those men, that would explain why he wouldn't want to go to the police, but why would a distinguished professor be mixed up with thugs?

The kiss was another worry. She slid farther under the warm covers and analyzed her reaction. She hadn't felt an instant attraction like that since college. She'd ached for that kiss, and more, which stunned her. She pictured Luis studying her as if he could see through her clothes and liked what he saw—and then forced herself to block the image.

Lauren was glad she hadn't told him her last name. With luck she'd never run into him again.

The scent of coffee alerted her that Julie had

arrived at the office below, and Lauren dragged her stiff body out of bed. The best part of her decision to convert the building she inherited from her grandfather into first floor offices and upstairs condos was the convenience of throwing on jeans and a sweatshirt and zipping down the stairs to her public relations office each morning.

At the bottom of the stairs, Lauren swung open the oversized office door with its stained glass window and closed it behind her.

Julie looked up from her paper-laden desk. "Morning, boss." Her sleek black eyebrows shot up above her glasses. "Sleep late?" Julie asked in her melodious voice. "Coffee's on your desk. How was the speech? Did the crowd clap long enough to please Dr. Godwin?"

"I assume it went well." On her way into her corner office, Lauren registered Julie's purple gypsy-style shirt and the matching tinge of purple in her thick braid. She was dying to tell Julie what happened in the parking garage, but held off until she could understand—and manage—her own reactions.

Julie glided in behind her. "Assume? Didn't you stay for it?"

Lauren shook her head and took a careful sip from the mug. "No. Mmm. You are good at making coffee."

"Even better at picking it up at Starbucks. Did Enid have very many additions?"

Lauren rolled her eyes and inhaled the steam. "You wouldn't have believed it. Took me hours, but I got the edits done in time. That woman makes me nuts."

"Don't tell me she was spinning more romantic tales about your father."

"It's her favorite topic. Is this the final copy of the insurance company newsletter?" Lauren started to read and hoped Julie would leave her alone to think about the kiss.

"It is. Now tell. Details."

Lauren looked up. "I met Enid's newest." That was the perfect topic to distract Julie from sniffing out the other story.

"And?"

"An archeologist. Geeky. Under forty, I'd say."

"What is she, fifty-plus? Jeez! How does she do it?" Julie perched on the edge of the visitor's chair. "Did Enid say anything about giving you a year-end bonus like last year?"

"She was too busy with her entourage."

"It's strange how Enid can be so nice to you sometimes, like when she helped you find buyers for the condos."

"Yeah, well, she sure likes to maul me in front of her friends."

"What else happened last night?"

"Later. I need to get something done here."

Once Julie left her alone, Lauren bowed her head over her computer, hooked her hair behind her ears, and read the entire report. "Julie!" she yelled. "What's the name of the guy who wrote this idiotic annual report? It's full of jargon and big fat words that don't mean anything!"

Julie appeared in the doorway and frowned. "Wintergard. You liked his stuff last quarter." She wiggled her eyebrows and pointed toward her desk. "You want a blueberry muffin? Mom made them."

"No thanks. I couldn't eat anything this morning."

"You sure you're okay?"

Lauren nodded. "It's this annual report. The guy uses the word *arguably* three times. Every other word ends in the syllable 'ize.' In one paragraph he used a colon and a semi-colon, and he performed the number one sin according to the Lauren Richmond bible of writing."

Julie laughed. "He used the possessive '*its*' with an apostrophe?"

"Close."

"He used an apostrophe in a simple plural?"

"Told you he was impossible."

"Okay, I've been watching you play with your hair until I think that clump is going to fall out. No fair keeping secrets. You met someone, admit it."

Lauren decided she'd feel better if she blabbed the whole story and got it out of her head. "I didn't meet someone—I saved his life." She felt proud saying those words.

Julie's mascara-smudged eyes grew round, and her chandelier earrings swung as Lauren told the story. "You could have been killed, Lauren. You should have run back to the reception and called the cops."

"I had to help, Julie. They were beating him bloody."

"Oh, God; I'd never have had the nerve."

"I've never been so scared."

"You should have called me when you got home."

"I was afraid of opening my door to anyone, even you."

Julie's eyes softened and she smiled. "But jeez, Dr. Gorgeous actually kissed you! My sister says he's famous around campus. All his students are in love with him, but no one ever sees him out with anyone, not even women from outside the campus."

Lauren nodded and sipped her coffee. "That's interesting."

"Even when women throw themselves at him, he pays no attention. Some people say he's staying faithful to his Latina lover in Mexico. Of course other people say he's gay." Julie bunched her lips to the side and nodded. "That would explain it."

"How do you explain the kiss he gave me?"

"Hey, maybe you're the first gringa he's taken a liking to."

"Me, the seductress in a sexy down coat. Did your sister mention his research work?"

"She showed me the campus paper that had a big spread about it. I guess he found some long-lost document from the time before Columbus."

"He hasn't found one yet, but you should have heard him last night. When he described how he searched archives in Spain for letters from Conquistadors, he drew a huge crowd. He was mesmerizing."

"What I think is interesting is that you haven't mentioned your reaction."

"To what?"

"The kiss. Who knows what might have happened if he'd invited you up to his apartment after that?" Julie sighed and looked up at the ceiling. "Here you have an exciting evening with a sexy professor, and what happens to me? I get my car towed for parking on the wrong side of the street during a snowstorm."

"I warned you to move it yesterday, Julie, but you said the weather man was always wrong." She imagined the kiss again and sighed.

"You'll hear from him, I'm sure. He had to notice how you liked the kiss."

"I didn't like it. It was rude and repulsive." More like sweet and seductive, but Lauren refused to let herself say the words.

Julie squinted at her. "Yeah, so repulsive you're in some other world."

"I hardly slept and I have a lot of work to do."

"He'll ask you out to thank you. Wait a minute, what will Rocky think?"

"Rocky doesn't need to know anything about this. Besides, Luis doesn't even know my last name, thank God." She shook off the image of his eyes glistening like jet crystals as he kissed her.

"Luis, she calls him with sugar on her tongue. Too bad." Julie hugged herself and closed her eyes. "Now the professor will keep thinking of you and searching for you, like *Sleepless in Seattle*. He'll put ads in the paper."

Lauren dug in her desk drawer for her lip balm. "If I ever run into that creep Luis Hernandez again, I'll die of embarrassment." Luis was a sexy name, Lauren thought as she swabbed her lips, recapped the tube, dropped it back into the drawer, and slammed it shut.

"Embarrassment, because you liked what he was doing."

"End of discussion, Julie." Lauren glared at Julie so she would return to her desk.

"That confirms my mother's theory."

"What theory? Never mind. I don't want to hear it." Lauren reached across her grandfather's solid, antique desk and began to restack papers.

"Mom says you have a completely negative attitude about romance."

"It's a sensible attitude."

"She thinks you're afraid of love. Otherwise you'd give Rocky half a chance."

"I simply know the down side of 'romance' is not worth it."

"The down side. You make it sound like a financial investment. Falling in love is fun."

Lauren groaned. "Yeah? Well, that lasts for about ten minutes."

Julie folded her hands against her heart. "Some people fall in love forever."

"Not in my family."

Julie cocked her head. "Come on, your parents were artists. Their emotions got in the way of their true feelings. You're too intelligent to let superstition rule your life."

"It's genetic, Julie. Just look at your friends. Some of them have parents who can't agree on what time it is, who insult each other every chance they get, who grunt instead of talk to each other."

"Enough!" Julie spread her hands in front of her face. "What's your point?"

"Their parents never should have married. Yet, in spite of the disasters right under their noses, those friends march down the aisle, toss the idiotic garter and the ridiculous bouquet, and make the same mistakes. It's preventable."

"By never falling in love?"

Lauren nodded. Never falling in love sounded very sad all of a sudden. "Or thinking they're in love. That's the genetic flaw, the delusion they're in love." She had to steel herself from those feelings. "If they like having sex with someone for more than, say, six months, presto! They gamble their entire life and their fortune, I must add, on the theory that they can love someone forever, when the whole episode lasts about as long as it takes to melt snow."

"My parents stayed together."

It was true. Julie's parents were different. "And how do they show their boundless love today?"

"Okay, Lauren the snot-nosed know-it-all, so they like to duke it out now and then, verbally of course. It clears the air so they can go back to watching their TV shows together."

"Falling in love takes the right genes. Some day scientists will prove that. People like me should do without it." Without kissing. Without touching. Without looking into dark, dangerous eyes.

"People like you are crying out for love."

Lauren chewed on her cheek. "Julie?" She clicked a key on her computer and exhaled. "I have to deliver the first proof of the Startech Annual Report over lunch today." She looked down at her battered jeans. "Shoot! I'll have to get dressed up."

Julie's skirt swirled as she scuffed her clogs
across the creaky wood floors toward the outer room.
"In that case, I'll take phone duty," she called over
her shoulder. Before she closed the door behind her
she ducked back in. "Are you taking any calls?"

"No. Not even from Rocky. And I don't want to
hear any theories about me and Rocky either."

At two-thirty Lauren returned from lunch and
kicked off her Eskimo-style boots in the entry hall.
Coming home to her great old building always made
her feel good. She wasn't sure whether it was the
smell of the old wood, the creak of the stairs, or the
swirls of memories of her grandfather that welcomed
her.

As all her friends told her, she was crazy to
restore her grandfather's legacy, an edifice that had
been empty for a decade. She'd probably owe the
bank until she died, but none of that mattered. After
years of bouncing around with her parents from
rented house to rented house, she finally had a
home.

Julie jerked open the office door, and Lauren's
thoughts scattered. "You missed him," Julie blurted,
her eyes round with excitement.

"Missed who?"

"While you were at lunch... Professor
Hernandez... He was here!"

"No." She bit her lips so she couldn't ask her to
describe him in every detail.

"He looked so hot in his jeans with a beat-up
leather jacket over his shoulder. He definitely pumps
iron."

"Pumps iron. Oh, brother. How did he find me?"

"Enid."

"Enid told him who I was? How did he happen to
get to her?"

"I told you he'd hunt you down."

Lauren hung her coat on the coat tree and tried

to keep her voice calm. "What'd he want?"

"To see you, of course. He'll be back tonight."

"You told him to come back tonight?"

Julie's hand covered her grin. "Not exactly. I let him talk me into telling him when you'd be back."

"I spoke to Rocky on my way to lunch. He's taking me to dinner tonight."

Julie's grin faded as she folded her hands in front of her. "He called to cancel. Sorry."

"Why this time?" Relief swept over Lauren. Being with Rocky was sure to make her feel even guiltier about her reaction to Luis. Luis. Boy, she wished she could banish his name from her head.

"Dinner with his parents. There's some sort of decision he has to make about finishing college. Poor guy. He said he'd come over later."

Lauren slumped into her desk chair and picked up her pen. Should she ask Julie to repeat every word Luis said?

"Don't you want to know what time he's coming?"

"No, I want his number so I can tell him I'm busy."

Julie leaned against the doorjamb and bit her lip.

"Okay, Julie, give me the rest."

"I told him you'd probably do that."

"You're sleeping with the enemy."

"I wish! He's coming at six-thirty. He said it's not a date."

"Damn right it's not a date. So, go on. What else did he say?"

Julie grinned. "He said he was not going to give me his phone number so there would be no way you could cancel. Even if you call him at the office or find his home number, he won't be around to get the message. He was so cute and funny, you should have been here."

"Cute and funny, huh? I won't be here."

Julie's fake laugh sounded like a toy machine gun. "You'll be here. You'll shower and do your hair and all that, and you'll put on a pair of jeans that fits your butt perfectly, but looks really old, so he'll think you didn't care what you look like. You'll do that, Lauren just to see what's next."

Julie started to back out of the room, but slapped her hand over her mouth and popped back in. "I almost forgot to tell you. Ken's on his way over."

The outer office door slammed, and Lauren and Julie jumped.

"Anybody here?" Ken's raspy growl echoed. "There you are," he said as he poked his wrinkled face around the doorway. "We got problems."

Julie waved her fingers at Ken. "Speak of the devil. Hi, Ken."

Ken pulled off his giant leather mittens, pointed his crooked, bony finger, and glared at her through his fogged-up lenses. "Lauren? Julie there forgot to tell you I'd stop by, didn't she?"

"She told me as soon as I got here. What's wrong, Ken?"

Ken unzipped his Army jacket and slid his bottom onto the corner of Lauren's desk. "She have to hang around and listen to this?" He nodded at Julie. "Or you got some actual work for her to do?"

Julie glided through the door and grabbed the knob. "Don't worry, you old asshole. Even if I didn't have anything to do, I wouldn't spend another second here with your foul tobacco breath." The door slammed behind her.

"Well, wasn't that fun?" Lauren shook her head. "I suppose you and Julie will never get along."

"Spoiled brat. You pay her too much."

"I'd go under without her."

Ken reached into his chest pocket for his

cigarette pack and shook out a cigarette.

"No smoking in my building, Ken. You know that."

Ken looked up and nodded. "Sorry. Forgot. I been worrying all night."

"About what?"

Ken slid the cigarettes back into his pocket and buttoned the flap over it. "Julie tells you I'm too old and crippled to keep your dang alley clear and everything in its proper order."

"Not true. We both know you do a great job, Ken."

Ken scratched his stubbly chin with his shaky hand. "That woman thinks I been drinking again."

"You wouldn't do that."

"Damn right. Then why's she treating me like crap?"

"Good question. I expect you to respect each other."

"Your grampa woulda fired her, if he saw how she treats me."

Lauren took a deep breath. Perhaps she could build a sliver of a bridge between her two employees. "She worries about you, Ken." Lauren hoped the little white lie might smooth the way toward peace.

Ken's head popped up, and his blue eyes grew large behind his lenses. "Julie worries about me?"

Lauren nodded. "She thinks you don't take care of yourself."

Ken stood up and hiked his baggy pants above his skinny waist. "Gimme a break. That's what my stepdaughter says."

"She thinks you should eat more."

"What, she gonna bring casseroles to my house?"

"She thinks you should quit smoking."

"Okay, like I haven't heard that ever since the diagnosis."

"Emphysema is serious."

Ken stuck his knuckles on Lauren's desk and leaned into her face. "I deserve to pick my own death, after all I been through. Now, you want to hear about the intruders last night or not?"

"What intruders?" Lauren held her breath and pictured the men who beat up Luis trying to break into her building.

"Here's the deal." Ken stretched to his full six-foot height and squared his shoulders. "'Bout midnight I see the snow had stopped, so I get out of bed to come plow the alley one more time. I get the garage door open and turn to start the walk-behind snow blower, see, because the tractor needs gas, and I hear a noise on the fire escape. God damn if there aren't two guys up there next to your kitchen door. They duck, but I see 'em. I yell, flash my light on 'em, and they come clambering down the stairs. I chase after 'em. Think I can't run? Well, I did anyhow, and they run. Turn the corner up there. By the time my game leg gets me there, I see a car pulling away from the next corner."

A chill spread through Lauren's chest, and she had to sit down at her desk. "What were they doing?"

Ken pulled a crumpled handkerchief out of his pocket and wiped the drip from his nose. "Looked to me like they were trying to break in. So I call the police." Ken sniffed and shoved the handkerchief back in his pocket. "Pretty dumb of me to think they'd do anything."

"What did the police say?"

"Said they'd drive by." Ken's nose wrinkled. "Asked if I'd been drinking. Which I hadn't. The footprints are there for anyone to see. Did you notice them this morning?"

"No, I didn't." Her nightmare was true. The men were after her too.

"Well, they were there. So watch yourself when you come and go. Can't be too careful, even in this neighborhood. Plus, you gotta let me install a new security system. The old one hasn't worked worth beans in ages. It'll only cost you a coupl'a thousand."

Lauren gulped her cold coffee. "A couple thousand bucks I don't have right now. What'd they look like?"

Ken shrugged. "It was dark. They wore dark clothes, knit hats, shoes, not boots."

Lauren got up and came around her desk. "I'm glad you chased them off, Ken." She clung to his boney back. "Really glad."

Ken nodded, inched away from her, wiped his eyes with his handkerchief, and looked down at his mittens on her desk. "Ever since your granddad died, you been my charge. I promised him I'd watch out for you." He zipped up his coat and pulled on the mittens. "You look out for yourself. I can't be following you around. Now I gotta go plow that alley again." When he reached the doorknob, he mumbled, "Goddamn snow."

Chapter Three

Lauren's afternoon was a waste. She dug out the quote she received for a new burglar system, glanced at the price, shoved it back in the drawer, and tried to stop thinking about her miser's budget and get to work.

Lauren could barely sit still long enough to work on a draft of a speech for a bank CEO. The image of the muggers breaking into her building made her legs twitch. She moved to her next project, editing a final draft of an annual report, until a stream of grammar mistakes made her scream.

She needed action. Calling the police was action.

The response was more like inaction. The officer Lauren finally reached reported that a squad drove through the alley and walked around the building, but saw no signs of forced entry or suspicious behavior. The officer claimed the squad car made regular trips around her neighborhood and would continue to do that. Lauren began to wonder if Ken had exaggerated.

Lauren didn't feel any better after she hung up, but she managed to complete both projects before she let herself stew about Luis's impending visit. One of her options was to go to the movies or out to dinner by herself and leave Luis knocking at the door. She wondered what he would wear, if he did show up. She also wondered how his hair would look if he ever combed it.

When Julie left at 4:30 to pick up her mother's dry cleaning, Lauren gave up and did exactly what

Julie said she'd do, right down to the jeans. At six o'clock, she paced back and forth in front of the television like a foolish teenager waiting for her first date.

When the phone rang, she jumped at it.

"Hi." The voice was deep, but almost a whisper.

"Who's this?"

"Luis." The name sounded exotic on his tongue.

"Hi." She wasn't going to chatter. She wanted him to know he was an intruder.

"Okay if I come over?"

Lauren waited a beat before answering. "Sorry, but I have a dinner date."

"I went to the doctor today. He said I was lucky those guys didn't break my ribs or puncture a kidney. I just wanted to show you how much I—"

"I said you should have gone to the hospital."

"You were right. Lauren?"

"Yes."

"I'm parked in front of your building. I promise I'll stay only a couple of minutes."

"A couple of minutes? All right." Even as she waited for him at the top of the stairs, part of her wanted to skip out the back way. He climbed the steep front staircase with a bottle of something in a brown bag in one hand and a battered briefcase in the other. "Wow! Your cheek is really bruised," she called to him. "It's almost the same shade as your beard."

He touched his cheek with the back of the hand that held the bottle and shrugged. "Forgot to shave, didn't I?"

Lauren nodded. His hair looked like one of those thick, bristly doormats. He was still wearing the jeans Julie had described. The rumpled jacket was unzipped, revealing his nicely curved Adam's apple. A black T-shirt stretched across his chest. The only sign of his profession was the briefcase.

Unfortunately, Julie was right. Even in his casual-verging-on-sloppy state, he looked good.

"I've messed up your evening," Luis said when she didn't speak. His smile broke and one cheek bunched higher than the other.

Lauren shrugged. "You can come in, if you promise me one thing."

"What's that?"

"No kissing."

"What?" His thick eyebrows flew up, and he even blushed a little. "I guess that's reasonable. I promise," he said and laughed. "No kissing."

His warmth and the scent of fresh soap and toothpaste filled the tiny hallway. "Beautiful building." He sounded shy, perhaps even nervous. "Are these moldings original?"

There wasn't enough room to stand where she wanted to be, far away from him. "Nearly everything's original. They were in terrible shape when I inherited this building. I've been rehabbing it a bit at a time. I did the condos first, to get some income. It's been quite a project."

"Place must date back to gaslight days."

She reminded herself not to talk too much so she could get him out of there as quickly as possible. "It was built in 1874. I've learned the hard way, old buildings are no bargain, but I love it anyway."

"Amazing craftsmanship. Should I hang up my jacket here?" He pointed to the coat tree.

Lauren shrugged again. She imagined they would talk right there and then say goodbye.

He handed her the bag with the bottle in it. "I hope you drink red wine."

"Thanks." She was definitely not going to offer him any and turned to put the bottle on the counter just inside the kitchen. She watched Luis sling his jacket over the coat tree and drop his briefcase beside it. He was slimmer than she'd thought the night before, with wide shoulders, a muscular chest, and thick arms. She tried not to picture him lifting weights and followed him into her living room.

Luis strode over to the fireplace and began to inspect it. "Marble surround. Nice. Original light fixture there, too." His muscles bulged under his shirt when he put his hands on his hips. "Converted to electricity." He leaned toward her wall of photos and pointed. "Is this you?"

"Yes, with my grandfather."

He grinned at her. "At a ball park?"

Lauren nodded. "Milwaukee County Stadium. He took me to a lot of Brewers games."

"You still a fan?"

She nodded again. "Baseball's my favorite sport. I still have a crush on Paul Molitor."

"Interesting. You going to let me sit down?"

Lauren shrugged. "If you like."

The smile flashed again. "I wasn't sure you'd let me in. After all, we're strangers."

She wanted to tell him polite people didn't kiss strangers, but resisted. She was relieved when he started toward the only overstuffed chair in the small room, leaving the couch for her, but the moment she settled with one leg under her, he crossed the room and joined her.

"I was going to introduce myself, since we didn't get to that last night. I'm Luis Hernandez." He didn't offer his hand. "I teach at the University." He swung his arm to the back of the couch, his fingers inches from her neck.

Her laugh sounded forced even to her ears. "I know who you are. I'm Lauren Richmond." She wished she had the guts to get up and go sit in that chair.

"Of Richmond Public Relations. I noticed the sign on the door. You like your work?"

"Sometimes it's rewarding. I wrote the speech

Enid gave last night, or I should say I rewrote it a dozen times after she fiddled with it."

"Did the speech go well? Oh, you were in the garage when I was, so you must have missed it too." He glanced at her sideways again. "I've heard her speak." He sat forward, crossed his leg, and picked at the skin on his thumb. "I think it was a couple of months ago, just after I came to the University. She had everyone in the meeting laughing and crying at the stories of her crazy childhood."

"She's a pro." Lauren turned sideways against the arm of the couch, farther away from the reach of his hand and the heat of his body. "You said your ribs were sore. What did the doctor say?"

He tipped his head and the hand climbed up again, inching toward her along the back of the couch. Small cuts crisscrossed his fingers. "Banged up, but it'll heal." He lowered his lashes. "How are you?" His hot hand touched her shoulder and then inched away. "I was worried about you. You looked pretty shaken last night."

Lauren nodded. "I had trouble sleeping. I thought they were going to kill you."

"Thanks to you they failed." The smile disappeared. "As I said last night, I was lucky someone like you showed up, someone with guts." He lifted one eyebrow and glanced at her sideways. "You're a nice surprise."

"Why?"

"I didn't, uh, expect you to look so, um—" His knee began to bounce, and he glanced over at the fireplace.

"You have to finish that sentence. You didn't expect me to look so what?"

He faced her and stroked the bristles on his chin. "Last night you were a mystery of contrasts. All I could see was a gorgeous pair of legs beneath a giant coat and a pair of big eyes peeking through a huge wooly thing wrapped around your head." His eyelashes lowered as he grinned. "Brave and beautiful—that's the surprise."

Lauren had to look away from his admiring eyes. The jolt of power she'd felt in the parking garage filled her chest once more. "Thank you," she said, as if men always showered her with such compliments.

She wished she could touch his wrist right where the hairs began on his arm. She also wished she could feel the muscle of his forearm and wondered whether his eyebrows were stiff or soft. If he didn't start talking again soon, she'd have to fill the vacuum. "Um, I um, last night?" She looked up as Luis resettled himself closer to her. "Last night I heard you talk about your search for a mysterious codex. It sounded pretty exciting."

Luis nodded and jiggled his foot. "It is."

Lauren noticed his bootlaces had been broken and knotted in several places as she waited for him to say more, while he watched her with a hint of a smile.

"I think you said a codex is a primitive sort of book?"

The smile faded as he nodded. "Actually codex is the term for any ancient manuscript. The Mayans, my ancestors by the way, made paper from fig bark or deer hide and then they coated it with stucco. Instead of binding sheets together like our books, they folded the long pieces of bark like an accordion." He demonstrated by opening his palm to the ceiling and then to the floor. "They used the paper to record their history and their scientific discoveries, particularly astronomy." His voice took on the tone of the teacher. "Unfortunately for us, the Spanish burned most of them."

"You mean the Conquistadors?"

Luis's dark eyes came alive. "They're the ones."

31

A. Y. Stratton

"We never studied that in school. What did the writing look like?"

Luis ran his fingers back and forth through his hair, making some clumps stand up and matting the rest. "They used symbols, glyphs, drawings of animals, both real and imaginary, in bright colors." He waved his hand toward the fireplace where Lauren had hung her mother's painting of an orange and red sunset. "Colors even brighter than those. To the Sixteenth Century Conquistadores it looked like the work of the devil." His eyebrows slid up, and he shot a sideways grin at her. "I have to admit the first time I saw markings like them they gave me the creeps."

"But the Spaniards tried to burn them all?"

He nodded. "And nearly succeeded." The words shot out like bullets, and Lauren jumped. A muscle flexed in his jaw. "King Philip the Second ordered the extermination of the so-called 'heresy' in his realm. In the mid-sixteenth century the Bishop of Yucatan ordered his men to burn all Mayan records." Luis's voice faded away like the first rumble of a thunderstorm as he touched her elbow. "Imagine how you'd feel watching invaders burn all the books from the Library of Congress."

"But some were saved?"

"In the eighteenth century three Mayan codices turned up in the collections of European royalty, probably souvenirs Cortez gave out to whichever power would support him in his exploration. Except for a fragment of debatable authenticity, everything they've found since has been a forgery or an indecipherable mess."

"Yet you think there's another one?"

"I do." Luis licked his lips as his eyes drifted away from Lauren's face to her neck, then to her hands and back again. "You really want to hear this lecture?"

Lauren watched his lips. "I do," she echoed him and wondered if the man himself was the devil who made her want to feel those lips again.

"Are you sure there's no kissing here?"

Lauren giggled in shock. "I'm sure. Keep talking or leave."

He feigned fear by raising his eyebrows and biting his lip. "Right. Okay, then. My grandmother still lives in the Mexican village where my father grew up, so every summer we'd visit her, and we'd hear the old people tell stories about a priest, El Católico, who saved an ancient book from the flames of the Inquisition." He flicked a glance at her as if he was deciding how much more to tell. "Last year I received a grant to go to Madrid to do some research in a collection of papers dating back to that period. I found a reference to a letter from a priest who worked with the Mayans in that region during the time of the book burnings." His eyes glinted as if he saw something faraway.

Lauren imagined a friar in his long robes running from soldiers. "You found the letter?"

Luis raised his eyebrows and nodded. "I was allowed to read many of the priest's letters and copy them."

"Did the priest describe where he hid it?"

"The codex?" He brushed a lock of his hair off his forehead and stretched his arms behind his head. "The priest was a teacher and wrote many letters to his family. In one he tells his sister how sad he felt as he watched the books burn. He said he hoped his courage, "the bold spirit of righteousness," is the way he phrased it, in Spanish, of course, would guide him to save some of the books for future students. He must have died soon after he wrote that letter, because it turned out to be the last one she received. Apparently, the family kept all his letters, along with the papers informing his sister of her brother's accidental death. Because the family took pride in their ancestor's connection to the Conquistadores, the letters have been cared for and handed down in the family through the generations. Eventually they were sent to the historical society."

"It's a detective story." Lauren felt a chill down her back.

Luis nodded. "You like mysteries?"

"I've read lots of them, but nothing as exciting as this one. So what now? Where do you go for more information to track down this codex?"

Luis slid his hand down her arm, squeezed her hand, and held onto it. "I like your enthusiasm. What now? I'll continue to reread all of the letters carefully, looking for hints of where the priest might have hidden something. The village isn't far from the University's research site, where I'm going to spend Christmas and semester break. Every time I have a spare day, I'll be back in my grandparents' village interviewing the oldest people I can find to tell me the legend again, again, and again, until I pick up a new clue or until something else leads me in another direction."

"Where is the research site?" She squeezed his hand, hoping he'd release her, and he did.

"Near the border of Belize, deep in the rain forest, surrounded by caves."

"Did you know about the ruins when you were a child?"

"We knew there were crumbling temples and steles, old stone tablets, scattered around the forest, but no one had ever come around to excavate until about ten years ago when I was in grad school at the University of Chicago. As soon as I heard about it, I volunteered to work. I've been digging there every year since. After I had taught at the University of Indiana for a few years, the University here offered me a professorship, along with the chance to oversee the dig site. This year twenty of my students and students from other schools will come down and do our dirty work over semester break."

Luis leaned his elbows on his knees and turned to watch her. "You're nice to act interested in all this stuff. I didn't mean to go on and on." His glance moved from her face to her hair, then down to her shirt, her legs, and her ankles, his face unreadable.

Lauren wanted to stand up and usher him to the door, to get him out of her apartment before she let her fingers touch him again, but her body wouldn't move.

Still watching her, he rubbed his fingers across his upper lip. "You make me nervous, you know?" He frowned at her, waiting for her response.

"Because I might beat you up?"

He shook his head and frowned. "Not sure why, but I felt it even before the no-kiss rule."

Why would he be nervous, when she was the one who was overwhelmed by his surprise move the night before? What did he expect her to say—or do?

She forced her thoughts back to the subject of the codex. There had to be more information for him to go on, something besides a letter describing the priest's emotions. Maybe he knew more than he could, or wanted to say. "If you find a codex, would it be valuable?"

"If I find the real thing, a codex in good enough condition to read? Hell, yes."

"You'd sell it?"

He threw his head back and laughed. "It wouldn't be mine to sell, but absolutely not. I'd study it, copy it, and share it with every scientist in the world."

"You'd be famous."

"Possibly." He sounded surprised. "That's not what motivates me." His nostrils flared as he sat up straight and gazed down at Lauren. "Each discovery has the potential to prove the intelligence, the power, and the brilliance of the Mayan heritage. That's what I'm after."

"An impressive goal."

"It's fun to show up the gringos once in a while." He cocked his head at her. "Your turn. What does a public relations person do?"

Lauren was relieved to have a subject that might keep her from thinking how smooth and soft his lips looked when he smiled. "There's no way for me to make my job sound as exciting as yours, that's for sure. Most of our clients own small businesses and need someone to write speeches, annual reports, and press releases. We design public relations plans which might include special events for their customers, which we plan. We also arrange speaking engagements for them."

"Your job is quite varied."

Lauren shrugged. "My quest has nothing to do with rescuing a heritage, unless you count correcting horrible grammar and forcing people to make their thoughts precise."

"How did you get interested in that?"

"All my parents' friends were writers, so I thought that's what everyone did. While my parents entertained their literary friends every night, I wrote stories in my notebooks. I thought they would read them aloud and be impressed."

She should stop talking right then. She'd told him enough. He was acting too interested in what she was saying. It was time to get up and say good night to this man whose fingers were too close to her neck, whose lips were too wet, whose eyes were too dark, and whose body made the room so warm she was perspiring.

"And were they?"

"What? Oh, were my parents impressed?" She shook her head and crossed her arms. "They were

36

too consumed with their own work to bother with mine."

"Did you share your stories with your friends?"

Lauren rolled her eyes. "Didn't dare show any of them how weird I was." She was showing off for this man and was annoyed at her inability to stop.

"I heard you write fiction as well."

"Who told you that?"

He lifted one shoulder. "I had to call all over town to track you down." He raised his eyebrows. "Did you know, if you write down the license number of someone's car and then call the police, they won't just hand out the name and address?"

Lauren felt her cheeks flush. The man was either crazy about her or insane. "That's reassuring," she said as she thought of one more reason. Maybe he wasn't interested in her at all. Maybe he was checking on her to see if she suspected him of being involved in something illegal with those men the other night. "You've worked very hard to find me simply to thank me."

Luis nodded with his eyes half-closed. "Tell me about your novels."

"They're all unpublished—so far. End of story." Why would Enid mention her novels?

"Semi-autobiographical? Sci-fi? History? What genres?"

Lauren shook her head. "None of the above. Are you thirsty?" She was desperate to get off that couch and away from him.

He shook his head. "Suspense? Mysteries?"

"I'd rather not talk about what I'm writing until the manuscript is complete. I was wondering, do the people around your dig site steal artifacts and smuggle them out of the country the way the Italians do?"

"Sure. Happens all the time. My ancestors thrived on the stuff they'd stumble across after a pounding rain."

"So you must be very careful about the clues you have to find this codex. Couldn't someone else find it first?"

"Here's how I look at it: assuming the priest managed to rescue one of the codices from the fire, and assuming he hid it where the temperature and humidity were just right for it to survive more than four hundred years, and again assuming no one else has ever stumbled across it or destroyed it, and assuming we can still get at this hiding place, it's pretty unlikely that someone else is going to beat us to it."

He rubbed his hands on his knees and his eyes sparkled. "The whole caper is an adventure I've dreamt of since my grandfather first told me there were temples hidden in the caves." He grinned and touched her shoulder sending a jolt of heat down her arm. His smile was sweet. "Break your date and have dinner with me. Let me pay you back for having the guts and the brains to do what you did."

Guts and brains. God, the man was a schmoozer. Lauren felt her nipples stirring and hoped he couldn't tell. "Sorry," she said, and rose to her feet.

His eyes followed her and the crooked grin reappeared. "I'd like to see you again." He stood and reached for her elbow.

She looked into his pleading eyes with those long lashes. "My boyfriend wouldn't like that." She had to stay away from those eyes.

"Boyfriend wouldn't like it? Hmm. I'm wondering whether you'd like it." His hand slid down her arm to her hand. "There's some sort of connection here, wouldn't you say?"

That was her opening. Right then and there, she should tell him she had no interest in him at all. She shook off his grasp and escaped to the hall. "Of course we're connected. We shared a frightening experience, but that's over now." She reached for his jacket and held it out to him. "I'm just glad you're okay."

In the tiny space, it wasn't hard for him to crowd her until they were chest to chest. She took a step back. He moved forward. "I believe in building friendships slowly like the craftsmen who built this place."

The words sent her into a panic, not because she had a clue what he meant, but because he so obviously was not about to leave. Anxious to jump to another subject, she said, "Did you figure out what those men were after last night?"

Luis took his jacket from her and slipped it on. "No." His eyes narrowed and his lips parted in a slow smile.

"Did you call the police when you got home?"

He shook his head, his eyes steady on her lips. "My guess is the goons mistook me for someone else." He said the words too quickly, as if he'd rehearsed them.

"What if they were trying to steal information about the codex? Have you thought of that?"

"They were just a couple of muggers." He inched even closer. His breath touched her forehead.

"But you said they weren't after money."

"I said that?" He whispered. "Maybe they couldn't wait until I got out my wallet." He laughed softly and reached for her hand. "They'd have been really ticked off if they'd gotten my wallet."

Lauren tried to wiggle out of his grip, but he held on. "This is serious, Luis." She spoke loudly to break the crackle of sex in the air. "If the police knew how dangerous the parking garage was, don't you think they'd put a patrol there?"

Luis grinned and shuffled closer until the toes of their shoes touched. "You are a dreamer." His thigh touched hers. "You live here with the boyfriend?"

"No." She should have lied and said yes.

Luis frowned at her in a quizzical way, as if he were digesting something. "Well, thanks again for chasing off the ruffians, and for letting me see you." He spoke slowly in his hushed voice. "I really needed to." His eyes glinted through his heavy lashes.

Hoping he'd finally let go of her hand, Lauren squeezed his fingers, but instead he put his other hand on top of hers. Lauren caught her breath as his hot fingers tickled her wrist. She wondered how those fingers would feel on her breasts.

"I'd like to read one of your novels," he said softly. "I'll bet you have quite an imagination. "

Her ears were buzzing so loudly, Lauren could barely hear him. "Thanks," she whispered back, mesmerized by his eyes, by the scent of him. With her hand still trapped in his, she retreated until her back was against the closet door. Luis moved in quickly.

She meant to push him away, but his lips were so soft Lauren kissed him back, without thought, certainly without logic.

His kiss flashed from sweet to hot. She matched his burst of passion, every nerve alert for his next move. As if she'd thrown a match on gasoline, Luis's body burned against hers. Fire spread wherever he touched her. His chest crushed the air from her lungs. His hands slid up to her neck. His fingers locked in her hair.

Lauren wanted those lips everywhere, Luis's wonderful, fluid lips. His tongue teased and begged, and Lauren breathed him in, urgently, needing more of him, her body alive, her knees melting beneath her, the ache for him growing, overpowering her. She wanted all of him. Right then. Right there.

Luis tore his mouth away still cupping her head between his hands. The tiny hallway seemed to lift off the earth.

Luis whispered to her burning lips. "I want you."

She wrapped her leg around his and pulled him against her. "Oh, God, I want you too." She couldn't believe the words had come from her mouth.

Somehow, they found the couch. His lips and tongue were everywhere. Her tingling hands flew to his waist. She frantically pulled off his shirt and unbuttoned his fly. The smell of him was intoxicating. She couldn't stop and didn't want to.

Luis struggled with her buttons until she pushed him away and stripped off her shirt. He had no trouble with her bra. His touch spread bliss and agony everywhere.

Luis's body was spectacular in every way possible, but her exploration was interrupted by his mouth and his hands. He ended up on top of her, crooning into her ear as their bodies exploded together.

Later he whispered, "What's the punishment for breaking that no-kissing rule?"

Chapter Four

Lauren woke up from her haze of warmth and tried to roll over, but something even warmer was in her way. She opened her eyes, saw Luis's cheek, and sat upright. "Oh, shit!" she said and covered her bare chest.

Luis watched her through the slits of his eyes. "That wasn't the word I was thinking."

"How did we get on the floor and how long have we been here?" she asked.

"You rolled off and pulled me with you, and I have no idea—an hour, maybe two?"

Lauren flopped back down and covered her face. "And you dragged my bedspread in here?"

"Hope that's okay." Luis slid his arm farther around her and snuggled against her side.

"Okay? Nothing's okay. I screwed up."

Luis's stomach jiggled with laughter. "Screwed, but not screwed up."

Lauren stared at the ceiling and tried to find a graceful way to usher Luis to the door and tell him never to visit her again.

He leaned on his elbow and gazed down at her. "This wasn't in my plan either. It just happened, but if I could've planned it, I wouldn't change a thing."

Lauren blinked up at Luis. "You'd probably like to get out of here."

"Nope. I like it here. I have plenty to occupy me." His eyes reflected the sparkle of the streetlights as his fingers swept across her thigh.

"Oh, dear." She wanted to inhale the scent of his

cheek once more and to hear him talk about her breasts again. At one point she'd been quite eloquent. "Oh, dear."

"We're making progress from oh, shit to oh, dear."

Lauren tried to think how she could get out of this embarrassing position. Should she say something like, 'It's been nice having sex with you—time to go?' However, that was impossible as long as Luis was kissing her thigh.

He smoothed her hair off her face and smiled. "I have something to tell you."

"I'll bet you do—something about how we don't need to see each other ever again, and it's been real nice knowing me."

Luis shook his head slowly. "It's about your hair."

"What about my hair?"

"It's not blonde."

"It is too!"

He twirled a lock of her hair and shook his head. "It's five shades of gold. Each one ought to have its own color name." Luis guided his hot fingers along her throat, around her breast and then up to her shoulder. "I have something else to tell you."

Lauren had trouble remembering to breathe. "Oh, dear."

"I like your left shoulder better than your right one."

"Mmm," she murmured into his cheek. "Why?"

"Because it fits perfectly into my arm." His lips hovered just above hers. "Maybe I told you this before."

"Told me what?"

"That your breast, this one here?"

"Yes, oh, yes?" Why did his hands make her talk gibberish in single syllables?

"Fits my hand as if it was made for it."

It was happening again. She needed to touch him everywhere, to have all of him. "Mmm. What about the other one?"

"My other hand?"

"My other breast."

"What was that?"

"What was what?"

"Your jeans are ringing."

"It's probably Rocky." She licked Luis's ear.

"Who's Rocky?"

"He thinks he's my boyfriend. Don't stop what you're doing."

Leaving his hand where it was, Luis leaned up on one elbow. "You have a boyfriend named Rocky?"

"He's more of a friend than a 'boyfriend.' It's complicated."

"Rocky is a name for a big guy. Is he a big guy?"

"Maybe I should get that call."

"I was afraid you'd say that. Want me to crawl over there and grab your jeans?"

"Yes. Hey, Luis, you can move faster than that."

After Luis handed her pants to her, he scrambled back under the bedspread and frowned, which made his eyelashes appear even longer. "How big is this guy?"

Lauren snatched the cell phone from the pocket. "He was a football star at Wisconsin but don't worry—he fights fair, unlike those guys in the garage. You might be able to take him." Lauren flipped open the phone. "Hello?" She listened for a moment, punched in a number and listened again. "I missed the call. He left a message." Lauren tossed the pants aside and turned so her nose was nearly touching Luis's chest and tried to concentrate on what she should do next.

Luis massaged her neck and sighed into her ear. "Did the big boyfriend give up tonight's plan?"

"He's on his way over." She marveled at the

brevity of her thoughts and the way words seemed to float from her lips. In an hour, two hours? In whatever time they'd been making love, she'd become another person.

"Over here?" Luis bolted upright, dumping Lauren's head to the floor. "I have to get out of here."

Lauren sat up and tugged on his hand. "Let's pretend I'm not home."

Luis grinned and bent down to kiss her. "Good idea."

"He'll come in anyhow, though."

"Even if you don't answer the door?"

Lauren didn't respond right away, because she had decided to lick Luis's other ear. "He has a key."

"I'm leaving." Luis stood up again and pulled on his briefs and his jeans.

"Good point. I wouldn't want to hurt his feelings."

"Makes two of us. How soon will he get here?"

"He might be out in front right now parking his car behind yours." Lauren pulled the tangled covers around her and rose.

"I'm going." He stood with his hands on his hips.

Lauren snagged her shirt from the arm of the couch and turned on the light. "Good luck."

Luis grabbed her shoulders and kissed her quickly. "You seem so calm, Lauren, as if you do this all the time."

Lauren hunted around scooping up the rest of her clothes. "Me? Hardly. I figure you're the one who does this all the time, and no one has killed you yet."

"I'll call you." He strode to the hall, grabbed his jacket, and then bounded back into the room as Lauren picked up the cushion and replaced it on the couch. "You are beautiful, brave, and sexy." He kissed her again and fled.

Lauren stumbled to the bedroom to get dressed and remake her bed. Back in the living room, she straightened the pillows on the couch. When Rocky still hadn't arrived, she brushed her hair for a minute and then threw the brush in her bureau drawer. Maybe she shouldn't try to look good for Rocky.

She intended to block out everything that had happened after the kiss. That way she'd be able to talk to Rocky in her normal way. But she wasn't normal any more. Every inch of her skin crackled. Her fingers hummed, her head was light. She was alive. More than alive. Electrified. The effect Luis had on her body and her mind made her wish for contact on a daily basis.

"Wish for contact on a daily basis?" She couldn't believe those words had entered her mind. Her clients would love a bogus line like that, one that sounded intelligent, masked emotions and distanced the reader. Say what you mean, she always advised them, so she edited herself: she yearned to feel that passion every day, every month, every year.

"Damn!" she said aloud, imagining her books, her grandfather's bookcase and her limp, dusty bedspread were all in on the joke, the joke that she was falling fast for a man she hardly knew. If she halted things right then, his power would fade. Had to fade, for lots of reasons.

Rocky adored her. He hoped someday she'd feel the same about him. Rocky trusted her honesty. If he ever heard about this night, he'd be terribly hurt. He'd think she was a cheater and a liar. She didn't want to lose her loyal buddy over a stupid, brief affair.

Once she had tidied the room to her satisfaction, she crossed her arms, leaned against the windowsill, gazed down at the street, and was surprised to see Luis's old Jeep was still there.

Behind it was Rocky's pick-up truck. Her stomach lurched. The two men stood at the foot of the steps to her building. She recognized Rocky's Green Bay Packers cap and Luis's thick hair. By the swirls of condensation billowing above them, she could tell they'd been talking. A lot. What could they possibly be talking about? Did Rocky want to know what the hell Luis was doing at her apartment? Was Luis lying about it? Either way, she was fried.

They were crazy to stand outside in the cold this late at night, but still the men talked. She looked at the clock and was surprised it was only eight-thirty. She'd lost track of the time while they were making love. Love? Okay, not love, but sex, when they were making all kinds of really good whatever.

At last, she saw Rocky lope up the front steps, as Luis clambered into his salt-coated Jeep. Before she answered the door, Rocky was in her hall, his face scrunched with concern.

"Hey! Lauren, you look weird. Are you mad at me about dinner?" Rocky closed the door behind him and turned on the hall light. Tall, blond, blue-eyed, with the perfect V-shaped body—even beneath his down parka, Rocky looked like Hollywood's version of the collegiate male athlete. As he engulfed her in his arms, she wondered why he had to fall in love with her instead of one of the girls who followed him around at bars.

"I'm fine, Rock. Just exhausted."

"I broke our date. I owe you, Babe, big time."

"That's okay. Your family dinner takes precedence."

He shook his head as he unzipped his jacket and tossed it over the coat tree. "It was more like an inquisition."

Lauren tagged along as Rocky marched toward the living room. "Your dad wants you to finish your degree, right?"

Rocky swung around to face her with his lips curled into a pout. "It's like he can't think of anything else to talk to me about." He rested his thick fingers on his wide Harley Davidson belt buckle and shook his head. "I've been working really hard at the dealership. I even sold three cars today, but does he care about that?" He snatched up Lauren's hand. "Come on, I'll rub your back, and you can tell me what to do."

Lauren didn't want to sit back down on that couch. The cushions were probably still hot. "I have to go to bed, Rock. Let's talk tomorrow."

"That's right. You're going running with me. Seven a.m.?"

"Seven a.m.?" Lauren had forgotten what day it was. "Of course. Tomorrow's Saturday. You think the weather will be clear?"

"Sure. Didn't you get out today? The snow melted and all the roads are clean. We'll finally get in a good run." Rocky folded himself onto the couch and patted the cushion next to him. "Dad gave me the ultimatum."

Lauren resisted sitting next to him, until she spotted one of Luis's socks jutting out from under a cushion and plunked down on top of it.

Rocky brushed his hand through her hair and smoothed her cheek. "Do you know you're the most beautiful woman I've ever known?"

Lauren pulled his hand away and held onto it. "You think your dad will really fire you if you don't go back to school?"

He nodded and continued to stare at her as if she were a goddess. She felt like an evil witch. Rocky nodded and rubbed his thumb across her knuckle. "This time he means it. He said he's ready to announce that my brother will be the new general manager of all three Milwaukee dealerships—Waukesha too." Rocky's lips bunched as he shook his head. "My little brother."

"You're supposed to get one of the dealerships."

"Only if I sign up for second semester classes at U.W.M."

"So why don't you?"

He leaned his elbows on his knees and ducked his head between his hands. "I never liked school the way you did. I just can't get up the enthusiasm for going to class. What if I flunk out?"

"Does it matter what courses you take?"

"Not as long as it gets me enough credits." He collapsed back against the couch. "Listen to this." He slid his arm around her shoulder. "I ran into a guy outside your apartment who teaches at U.W.M." He twisted a lock of her hair.

"Really?"

He nodded. "I was just pulling up, and this guy came along and was getting into his cool old Jeep. I had to ask him what year it was. It was a '76 . I told him about the one Dad bought in '80, and we got to talking cars. You should have heard the rumble when that thing started up. Anyhow, he said I looked familiar, like a football player he knew. I said I was, and he says he's been driving that car to Mexico and back for ten years. Get this: he goes down there to dig up antiquities, and he teaches archeology at U.W.M."

Lauren let her breath escape. "What a coincidence."

"I told him I was thinking of taking a class there, and one thing led to another, and the guy tells me I should sign up for his class."

"You want to take archeology?"

"Sure, if it's worth three credits. Besides it meets two nights a week, so I could still work a full schedule and get to Bucks games too."

"Come on, you'd hate that subject." This was crazy. She couldn't let this happen to her.

"Maybe, but get this, the class goes on a trip to Mexico over semester break."

"It's probably too late to sign up for that."

"He says it's not full. And think of this—I'd get a vacation with Dad paying for it."

"I don't know, Rocky."

"Don't you want me to work for Dad?"

"I didn't say that."

"This is why I had to see you, Lauren, so you'll tell me—do you want me to manage a car dealership? If so, I'm going back to school." He smiled, as if he was certain Lauren would want what he wanted.

"You have to decide your own future, Rocky. I can't tell you what to do."

"Let me put it this way: would a woman like you want to marry a car dealer?" He stood up with his chin up and his arms at his sides like a soldier. "A really great car dealer?"

"A woman like me would want her husband to have a job that made him happy."

Rocky bent over and hugged her. "Thanks. Come on, walk me to the door." He grabbed her hand, tugged her off the couch, and led her to the hall.

She crossed her arms and leaned against the doorframe so he couldn't hold her the way Luis had. "Drive carefully, Rock," she said as he shrugged on his jacket.

"Where'd you get that old briefcase there?"

Lauren's heart blipped when she spotted Luis's battered case beneath the coat tree. "One of my clients left it in the office today. I suppose he'll be back for it tomorrow."

While she stood staring at Luis's briefcase, Rocky moved in for a kiss and nailed it.

Chapter Five

The next morning Lauren and Rocky followed their usual circuit, east to the park overlooking Lake Michigan, south along the lake past the Summerfest grounds to Chicago Street, in a zigzag through the Third Ward and its quaint old warehouse apartments, but this time Lauren turned west on Wisconsin Avenue across the river and past the public library toward Marquette University so they would skirt Luis's apartment building. Was she hoping they would run into Luis? Of course not. She'd die if they did. The man had turned her life into chaos.

The only action near the apartment complex was a pick-up truck idling in front of the fireplug near the entrance where she'd dropped off Luis after the mugging. As she and Rocky jogged by, Lauren made eye contact with the driver, and a chill chased down her spine. Everywhere she went she noticed strangers who reminded her of the men who attacked Luis. Ken's news certainly didn't help. The night before, she not only locked the doors after Rocky departed, but she also dragged a small chest to block the back door.

"Rocky," she began. "I've been thinking about what you said last night.

"Good. Let's hear it."

"You love cars, don't you?"

"Sure." He started running again.

"You're a good salesman. Meeting people is easy for you. How do you picture your future?"

"My future? With you in my bed every morning and every night and a great car in the garage. I want to play golf and go fishing every weekend. That, I'd say, would be heaven."

Lauren darted ahead of him. She was about to lose her best buddy, and no one would replace him.

"That's not what you want, is it, Lauren?"

Once they turned east the icy wind pierced their faces, and it was too cold to talk. Lauren pulled her knit cap down over her ears and forehead and pushed herself faster than she had before. The world around her vanished as her feet pounded the pavement and her breath synchronized with her feet, until Rocky sped ahead to open the front door of her building and yelled at her to hurry, he needed a drink of water.

Before Lauren got to the entry, a man bounded down the stairs, bumped her aside, and kept on moving. She'd have fallen if she hadn't grabbed the stair railing.

"Hey!" she screamed at the guy's back. "What the hell are you doing here?"

"Sorry, lady," the man yelled without turning around. "Wrong address."

Rocky took the stairs two at a time and unlocked her apartment. Inside he took his cool-down by trotting.

"You should have tackled him, Rocky. He was breaking into the building. That door was locked when we left."

"The guy was a jerk, but, come on, you know the door sticks sometimes, and the old geezer tenant who lives upstairs always forgets to pull it shut. Besides, why would a guy try a break-in in daylight?"

"Because he's a burglar, and he waited until I wasn't here. He must have picked the lock. Besides the geezer is in Florida."

"Is anything missing?"

"I can't tell. I should call the police."

With a spray of sweat, Rocky whipped off his hat and whirled it onto the hook of the coat tree. "Three points! What're you going to tell the police? Can you even describe the guy?"

"Maybe not, but it gives me the creeps that someone was in my hall."

"You need a roommate like me to protect you." Rocky stood still with his hands on his hips. "That was a joke, Lauren. You didn't laugh."

Lauren pretended she hadn't heard him and trotted off to the bathroom. She wasn't sure what she was going to say to him, and she wasn't ready to watch him when she said it.

When she finally came out, Rocky's face looked pinched and his eyes glossy as he touched her gently on the elbow. "Lauren, it's okay if you don't love me that way yet."

"I don't want to hurt you."

Rocky looked down at his running shoes for a moment. "Someday you'll see how perfect we are together, Lauren. We make each other laugh. All those movies you pretend you don't like, the romance ones? They always have friends fall in love."

Lauren reached for his hand. His grip tightened around her fingers until it nearly stopped the circulation. He pulled her against his chest, forcing her to look up into his eyes. "Before you and I became friends, I was a role model for every kind of wrong behavior. Isn't that what you called me in the newspaper?"

Lauren nodded. "That's what I said, but it wasn't true, Rocky. I was the new reporter showing off to get the editor's attention by insulting the Big Ten's golden boy."

"Listening to you has been great for me."

"We're just good friends, Rocky. If you dated

other women, you'd see the difference."

He let go of her and began to strip off his sweatshirt. "I could say the same thing."

"What?"

His mouth twisted into a grimace. "You should date other guys and maybe you'd see how great you and I are together."

Lauren immediately thought of Luis. "I never meet anyone I want to date."

"Good, because I'd kill 'em if you did. God, Lauren, right this minute, even after you told me you don't love me, I still really want to make love to you."

Lauren noted the sadness in his gray eyes and a patch of his reddish beard that he missed when he shaved. This man was handsome, sweet, and kind. She wished she could see him as a lover instead of as a brother. "I'm sorry, Rocky. I want you as my friend. I need you as my friend, but—"

"I got to get home and shower." His eyes looked colder than the ice chunks in the gutters. "I'll call you tonight if I get a chance."

Lauren felt her life had become a twelve-car pile-up, starting the moment Luis kissed her.

****

When she got out of the shower, Lauren expected Rocky to be long gone, but as she watched the condensation ebb across the bathroom mirror, there was a knock on the door.

"Lauren? That was Dr. Godwin on the phone. She said to tell you she has a business proposition for you. She's taking you to lunch at her club today."

Lauren wrapped herself in a towel and opened the door. "Today? On a Saturday?"

Rocky squinted and his lips spread into a leer. "Yeah." He nodded. "You look nice that way."

"Why today?"

Rocky tried to barge into the bathroom, but

54

Lauren held the door firm. "Something about a new plan with that Frank guy she was with last night."

"What else did she say?"

"She's picking you up at noon. You sure you don't need me to dry your back? Even good friends like to dry each other's backs."

"Goodbye, Rocky. Thanks for the message."

"I'm telling Dad I have to leave work at eight. We could get a pizza or something."

"Okay." Lauren closed the door on his angelic smile.

"One more thing," Rocky yelled through the door. "The FedEx guy delivered a fat envelope from a company with a funny name. Chubb. Hey, it's a chubby letter from Chubb. You couldn't get me to work for a company with a name like that. I had to sign for it, so it must be important. It's on the kitchen counter."

Lauren knew the 'Chubby' letter wasn't going to be good news. After the insurance inspector had visited her two years before with his odious brown leather notebook that matched his clothes, he'd said the rear fire escape stairs must be rebuilt. Rebuilding the stairs wiped out her savings account. She feared they'd come up with another reason to raise her rates or cancel her policy.

Still in her towel, she stood at the kitchen counter and ripped open the envelope. The news was almost as disastrous as a cancellation. The company claimed her "aging structure" was historically valuable and therefore more expensive to cover. The next, much larger quarterly payment was due in March.

Lauren stalked into the bedroom and flung the letter on her dresser, grabbed her hairbrush, bent over and brushed her hair until her scalp hummed. Due in March. Where was she going to get enough money to cover that bill when most of the funds in her account had to go for taxes and mortgage?

Lauren suspected Enid's sudden invitation to lunch wasn't about a business proposition at all. The old broad probably wanted to get the scoop on Luis Hernandez. That would make sense, since Enid must have been the one who gave Luis Lauren's name and phone number. For once in her life, Lauren was not going to tell Enid anything.

As soon as Lauren climbed into Enid's black boat-like Chrysler, Enid flashed her most sugary smile. "I have something to ask you, Lauren," Enid cooed in the higher tones she usually reserved for men she'd just met. She pulled away from the curb and nearly collided with a bicyclist bundled up to his eyeballs against the cold. "Heavens, where did that fellow come from?" Her voice dropped an octave. "Shouldn't he be riding the bus?"

Lauren hastened to buckle her seat belt and tried to hold her breath so she wouldn't have to inhale the poisonous cloud of Enid's latest perfume. "What's that smell?"

"Frank's favorite. Chanel, of course. Lovely, isn't it?" Enid flashed her contact-induced violet eyes and skidded around the corner through a red light.

Lauren opened the window and stuck her head out for a breath. "What'd you do, pour it on?"

Enid chuckled as she accelerated up the hill toward the University Club. "He poured it on." She sighed. "Such a good lover! Speaking of good lovers, Lauren—"

"Red light, Enid!" Lauren braced herself for the jerk of the brakes and hoped Enid wouldn't mention Luis just yet.

"Oh, dear, yes." Enid shifted into neutral and revved the engine like a teenager.

"What are you doing?" Lauren asked.

"Frank said this would keep my car from stalling in the cold weather. It works," she added as she shifted into drive, sped through the intersection and turned into the parking lot. "We're dining on the roof. I've already ordered for us."

Inside the elegant Georgian lobby, Lauren helped Enid remove her jumbo fox coat and lost the argument to deposit it in the cloakroom. She followed Enid onto the elevator and punched six.

"I've ordered tomato soup and a tiny crab salad," Enid said. "We're dieting today."

"I think crab is pretty high-calorie stuff," Lauren countered as she shifted the ten-pound coat to her other arm.

"Portion control is the key." Enid glanced at her image in the elevator's mirror and sucked her tongue against her teeth. "I feel thinner already."

Enid's well-preserved beauty always impressed Lauren. The woman swore a good diet, regular exercise (including sex, of course) and the right products, kept her young. She neglected to credit the scalpel of a brilliant plastic surgeon.

The elevator doors opened to a blast of dazzling sunshine reflecting off the snow-covered roofs as they stepped into the glassed-in bar area.

"We're sitting around the corner where we won't be disturbed. Isn't the view glorious, Lauren? I love how the windows wrap around the entire floor. And look, the Art Museum's elegant wings are open."

"They open every day," Lauren observed like a grump.

A short, gray-faced man in a dark suit with a paunch that looked like he was hiding a basketball greeted them with a bow. "Good afternoon, Mrs. Godwin. Your table is ready. Follow me."

"David, dear, it's Doctor Godwin." Enid raised her nose high as she spoke and nearly bumped into a large palm tree.

The man didn't seem to hear her. "Here we are," he said and he pulled out a chair at a table for two against the window.

"We'd prefer to sit over there." Enid strode past the man to a table for four and waited while he scurried over to pull out another chair.

Lauren followed like a puppy on a leash and slung the coat over one of the empty chairs. Enid eased into her seat and placed her voluminous leather satchel on the carpet next to her feet. "Is our lunch ready yet, David?"

"Nearly so, Mrs. Godwin. May I take your drink order?"

Lauren noticed the tag on the waiter's jacket clearly read 'George,' but Enid continued to call him David as she ordered red wine for both of them. Perhaps in retribution, Lauren thought with pleasure, he continued to call her 'Mrs.' Godwin.

Enid patted Lauren's hand. "I do enjoy the winter's many variations, crystal-clear days like today, where the sun glints off the snow and blinds you. Gray, overcast, sad days are lovely, too, days that chill you to the bone and chase you home to a warm fire. Then there are the snowy days, where the world is topsy-turvy, and you can't tell the lake from sky. However, now and then I like an escape. Don't you, dear?"

Lauren slipped her napkin into her lap, took a sip of her water, and leaned toward Enid. "Julie mentioned you had a business proposal for me?"

Enid's bony fingers felt like ice cubes against Lauren's wrist. "You're going to love this idea."

"Just give it to me without embellishment."

"I think I told you about my young professor, Dr. Jerome?"

Lauren hoped her face didn't show her dislike for the arrogant man. "Frank? Yes. I met him at the reception."

"Indeed. Well, last night he asked me to come along on an archeological dig down in the jungles of

Guatemala, to serve as one of the chaperones and as artist in residence. I'll be giving a class where students create as they work on the dig."

"In Guatemala? What in the world would the students create?"

"Stories, poetry, memoirs, if they like. It fits perfectly into the new interdepartmental studies theme the chancellor has endorsed for the university."

"Fully-funded by a big donor."

Enid acknowledged the delivery of her wine, took a sip, and left a purple lip print on the rim of the glass. "I'll be compensated for my time. I believe the professor's project will garner some of the grant money as well."

"No offense, but he must really need the dough."

Enid stopped chewing her cracker and frowned. "Why do you say that?"

"Wouldn't you think an archeology professor would rather have his students doing the grunt work instead of writing poetry?"

"Ah, our soup is here. That should warm us up."

Enid and Lauren sipped silently while Lauren tried to imagine Enid in grungy jeans digging through the tangled rain forest. "Are you sure you can handle this assignment, Enid? It's going to be tough on your manicure."

"You think so?" Enid's thoughts seemed to be as far away as Lauren's were.

Lauren dug a wheat roll out of the bread basket. "I can't picture you living without your usual necessities. I doubt they have four-star accommodations."

Enid dabbed her lips with her napkin, and left another blotch of purple. "I'll have to sleep in the hot dorm on a bunk." Enid said bunk as if was spelled with four k's.

"What are they paying you?"

"Enough to allow me to accept my dear old friend Marvin's invitation to spend six weeks at his villa in the Mediterranean this summer."

"Ah, the motive."

"As you know, I never spend more than I make, nor do I touch any of my investment income."

"You save your salary, live wisely and invest long-term."

"And earn what I need as I need it."

"And get others to pay for the rest. So what's my part of this venture?"

Enid closed her eyes and shook her head before answering. "You speak Spanish, don't you?"

"I do, or at least I used to."

"And you majored in English literature."

"Yes, but what's—"

"I need an assistant at the dig."

"An assistant? Would I have to carry your luggage, make up your bunk bed, and put toothpaste on your toothbrush?"

Enid smiled as she lifted a spoonful of tomato soup to her lips and watched the steam rise. "All representatives of the university are supposed to be fluent in Spanish."

"And you speak only Italian."

"They're making an exception for me, but only if I bring along a translator." Enid sipped the soup and dipped the spoon in again. "I told him you speak excellent Spanish." She reached for a cracker and crumbled it into the bowl. "I thought you could use both the vacation and the money, dear."

Lauren recognized the look of apology on Enid's face. "You're feeling bad about last night."

Enid continued sipping her soup. She put down her soupspoon, nudged the bowl aside and frowned with her whole face. "Last night after Rocky heard you'd left in such a hurry, he said an odd thing to me."

"What?"

"He said I'd probably been telling people about your parents again."

"Rocky said that to you?"

"Surprisingly perceptive of him to recognize your hypersensitivity on that subject, don't you think?" She dabbed her lips with her napkin, smudging lipstick onto her teeth. "I do get overdramatic when I'm nervous. You should know that by now. The mention of your dear parents sets me off."

Lauren watched Enid reapply a slab of color to her lips. "I accept your apology, Enid."

"And the trip?"

"We'll see."

Enid frowned again. "I must know soon. To be accurate, Frank must know soon. The trip is in three weeks. Is your passport up to date?"

Lauren took a sip of soup and nodded. "It should be." She took her time swallowing her wine. "Let's get serious. How much would you pay me?"

Enid's nostrils flared in triumph. "The staff members receive a month's pay, plus airfare." She waited a beat. When Lauren shook her head, she gripped Lauren's hand. "Of course, I'll pay you a stipend as well."

"I have a business to run."

"It would be like a paid vacation. You never take a vacation."

"I can't afford to."

"What if the stipend is another five hundred dollars?"

"Not enough." Lauren was impressed at the figure, especially since Enid never spent a dollar she hadn't budgeted months in advance.

Enid played with her gold bracelets while the waiter refilled her wine glass and replenished the bread basket. "I'll make it a thousand," she said when the man was out of earshot.

"You really need me to do this?"

"Frank's quite excited about the work there."

Lauren thought of the insurance company letter. "Make it twenty-five hundred and it's a deal." She'd earn nearly enough to cover the insurance.

The reflection of the Art Museum's delicate wings glinted on Enid's glasses. "That's a third what they're paying me."

"They're paying you seventy-five hundred dollars to lead a few poetry classes?"

"The university will receive excellent publicity if I'm there. They already have an agreement for a piece in National Geographic."

"In that case, make it three thousand."

"You're a thief."

"There must be others who would do it for less."

"I'm used to you."

"And you think you can control me."

"Julie said she'd be delighted to cover for you, so you'll have no worries on that score."

"You've already spoken to Julie about this?"

"David" arrived to remove the soup cups and to deliver the so-called tiny crab salad that filled a dinner plate. Enid stabbed a hunk of crab with her fork and paused. "Twenty-five hundred dollars is a lot of money. All your expenses will be covered. You'll enjoy a lovely vacation during the worst part of Milwaukee's depressing weather." Enid fondled her pearl necklace and grinned as if she was about to win a bet.

"Three thousand and you have a deal." The money would not only take care of Lauren's insurance payment, but there would be some left over.

Enid sighed. "Twenty-five hundred from me, and I'll get another five hundred from the University. Shake on it."

62

Lauren was elated. She'd followed Enid's advice. She'd figured out a way to raise money, as she needed it. So far, Enid hadn't mentioned Luis.

While Enid prattled on about her latest issue with her publisher, Lauren ate her salad and worried whether Julie could keep up with the work while she was gone.

"I received the strangest call a few days ago," Enid said as she swept a roll through the remaining olive oil on her plate. "Dr. Hernandez, you know, the very attractive new professor in Frank's department? He called when Frank and I were, well, you know, busy." Enid's eyebrows wiggled beneath the frames of her glasses. "He said he'd met you in the strangest way."

"Hernandez?" Lauren quickly filled her mouth with the last of her lettuce, chewed and nodded, as if she was trying to recall the name. "Oh, right. Wasn't he the man who was talking about his research on some missing document? You pointed him out at the awards event. I think you mentioned his complexion and his hair."

"Indeed I did. And that pronounced jaw line. They say he has affairs, but is very discreet about them." Enid's eyes sparkled. "Half Mayan, half something else. Reminds me a bit of a Greek athlete, dark, sharp-featured, and muscular." She closed her eyes as if she'd tasted something deliciously sweet. "And seductive as hell."

"Sounds like you have the hots for him."

"Please. The hots? Such a degrading phrase. Oh, did I mention he'd be on the dig too?"

"Who? Hernandez?"

"Mmm."

"But I thought his dig was in Mexico, not Guatemala."

"Mexico? Guatemala? What difference does it make? It should be quite fascinating."

63

"You said that Frank was in charge of the dig."

"He is—he and Dr. Hernandez. What's your problem? Frank, Dr. Hernandez, and I are the ones going from here—and now you! And here's what I've been meaning to tell you: Hernandez said the strangest thing, Lauren: he told me you'd rescued him from muggers."

Lauren slugged back her wine and felt her heart speed up. "Me? Can you imagine me saving anyone from muggers?"

To Lauren's annoyance, Enid laughed so hard she began to choke on her roll and then coughed until "David" came over to pat her on the back.

Chapter Six

Enid guided her monstrous car through slushy streets babbling about how Lauren should attend more university events in order to meet "truly interesting men." Lauren nodded, pretending to listen, while she tried to adjust to the news that she'd agreed to go on a trip with Enid, Frank, and Luis, and maybe even Rocky. When Lauren noticed Enid had failed to turn onto her street, she braced her hands against the dashboard.

"Oh, dear, I missed it!" Enid shouted, jolted to a stop, shoved the car into reverse, and collided with the truck behind them. Enid swore as the car lurched on the impact. Lauren's seat belt dug into her neck. Another jolt sent Lauren's head bobbing forward and backward like a yoyo, as the driver of the truck wheeled around them and sped down the street.

Enid pointed her red-gloved finger. "Hit and run!" she screamed. "The bastard hit us! Call the police, Lauren. Did you get the license plate?"

Lauren couldn't get her eyes to focus. "You backed into him! What were you thinking? No, I didn't get the license plate. It was covered with snow. Shoot, Enid, my neck hurts!"

"The idiot was following too closely. He fled the scene of an accident. I'll bet he doesn't have a driver's license." Enid shifted into forward and spun her wheels until the car skidded back into traffic.

"Enid, why didn't you get out and check the damage to your car?"

"And step into that gigantic snow bank? I'll just do a U-turn here."

Lauren rested her head on the back of the seat and closed her eyes until she felt the car stop. With Enid still blathering on about auto insurance and police reports, Lauren stumbled out, mouthed her thanks, and made a new personal rule to avoid riding anywhere with that woman.

"Wait!" Enid called, as she struggled out of the car and ambled around the ruts to the sidewalk. "You're right. I should call the police about that truck. My cell's dead. I'll use your office phone."

Lauren let Enid into the office, told her to lock the door behind her when she left, and then remembered to thank her again for the lunch.

While she counted out each of the thirty stairs up to her apartment, worries flooded Lauren's mind. How would she juggle her duties with Enid, her friendship with Rocky and her irrational reaction to Luis's smile and touch? The trip to the Mayan ruin had all the makings of a French farce. She'd have to find another way to earn the money for the insurance.

Before she took off her coat, she checked her voice mail. Luis hadn't called. Even if they were a one-night stand, the possession of his briefcase assured her that she'd hear from him at least once more.

She wanted him at least once more. He'd gotten what he wanted. She had too, she admitted with a sigh. She took two pain pills, stripped to her underwear, and fell into bed. An hour later, she sat up and could barely move her neck. She lay back down and moaned at how screwed up her life had become.

Even with the stiff neck, she had to attend to her Saturday cleaning ritual, so she pulled herself out of bed, got into her lived-in jeans and a

sweatshirt and went to work on floors, sinks, toilet—
the lot. Once she had collected the garbage and the
recycling, she lugged the bags down the alley stairs
and dumped them in the garbage can.

There at her feet in a ring around the fenced-in
garbage cans, was a pile of soggy cigarette butts. She
trudged back up the steps wondering why Ken would
smoke outside in such cold weather.

As the kitchen door slammed behind her, a sick
ache grew in her stomach. Maybe the men Ken had
chased away the night before were the ones who left
the butts. Inside her apartment, the phone rang.

"Did he come?" Julie's voice grew too loud when
she was excited.

"Yep."

"In more ways than one?"

"Julie, what am I going to do?"

Julie chuckled. "So it was great?"

"No. Yes. I don't even know the man, Julie."

"The sex was amazing."

"This is crazy. This is not me."

Julie hummed as if she had tasted something
delicious. "This could be the real you. He stayed the
night?"

"No. Rocky came over."

"Damn. So how did it evolve? First, he thanked
you for saving his life. Then you asked him about his
work, and he asked you about what you do and
touched your arm and then your shoulder, and then
what?"

"Hold it, Julie. Do you write the scripts for this
stuff?"

"Come on, then what?"

"When he was about to leave, he kissed me and
that was it."

"He made love to you."

"Oh, yes."

Julie sighed into the phone. "More than once?"

"If he hadn't left his briefcase here, I'd never see him again."

"You lucky dog."

"And now I'm screwed. I told Enid I would go on the dig with her as her translator."

"Yeah. She mentioned that project to me. She said it would be like a paid vacation for you, and made me promise I'd take over your clients."

"The insurance company raised my rate on the building. Of course, I can't afford it. I'll probably go bankrupt like my father did."

"As your father did. You always think you're going broke. You manage your money very well. You hardly buy any clothes. You don't go anywhere—not even to the movies. Besides, it's time to raise the rent on those apartments."

"The money from the trip would really help right now, just when I need it."

"When and where are you going?"

"Over winter break, Frank Jerome, Enid's new man, is taking his students to an archeological research site in Mexico. Enid's going along to teach poetry. I'd be her Spanish-speaking assistant."

"Pretty good deal to get paid to go to some exotic place."

"Luis will be there."

"Sounds even better to me. Get paid and get laid."

"Where do you get that trash talk? I have to get out of this. No way I can be there if Rocky goes too."

"On the dig? You're kidding. He's going on the same trip you are?"

"He doesn't even know I'm going. Luis doesn't either. This just happened today."

Julie's evil laugh made Lauren shake her head. "If you want to see him again, Lauren, you have to go."

"With Rocky and Enid there? I can't face that."

Julie laughed even louder. "This could be the best thing that ever happened to your over-controlled sterile life."

"Julie, as my friend and my associate, your job is to help me figure out how I'm going to get out of this."

"Right this minute my job is to drive my parents to my cousin's wedding. I'll call you tomorrow, unless I happen to rescue a hunk in a parking lot who drags me off to make love."

After Julie hung up, Lauren stood at the kitchen sink wondering what she should do next. Call the police about the cigarette butts and hope they would take her seriously? Go to a doctor about her whiplash? Or call Rocky to try to talk him out of going on the dig?

The police came first. With her neck still aching, she stretched out on the couch and made the call. Lauren dozed off while she was being passed from person to person and put on hold. An impatient woman's voice roused her. Lauren reviewed her first phone call to the police and explained how she'd found the man in her hall that morning and the pile of cigarette butts that afternoon, evidence that someone was staking out her building and planning to break in.

The woman sounded as groggy as Lauren felt, but promised to send another squad to check it out and make more passes through the neighborhood. Before they hung up, Lauren heard the blip of an incoming call. Still a blob on the couch, Lauren listened to a message from Rocky telling her a customer had given him four tickets to the Milwaukee Wave indoor soccer game, and he would pick her up at six so they could get a burger with Eddie and Rich beforehand.

Lauren enjoyed going to any kind of game with Rocky, even though his buddies treated her like a boring wife or an ungrateful chick who had wounded their hero by not worshipping his every word. She didn't blame them. They were jealous because he referred to her as his best friend. She stripped off her clothes and was about to step into the shower, when the doorbell rang. Assuming it was Rocky, off work early, she pulled on her clothes and went down the front stairs.

"Luis!" When she opened the door, his fist was still poised in the knock position.

"Hi, Lauren." Luis's lips were set in a straight line. "Thank God you're here." He looked beyond her into the hallway. He was obviously there on a mission, but this time it had nothing to do with sex.

As a test, she waited before getting out of the way. "Is something wrong?"

When his eyes finally met hers, his smile flashed on. "I'm really glad to see you." He leaned close and kissed her ear, sending chills down her neck. "Mmm. You smell like soap."

"More like detergent. I've been cleaning the apartment." She stepped back to let him in.

"I left my briefcase here last night."

"Yep, it's where you left it." Lauren felt her face flush. He was near her again. They would be alone in her apartment again, and already her body was alive to his presence.

"I just needed to know where the damn thing was. It has some important stuff in it. There it is," he said as the door swung open and he glanced behind it. He reached for the briefcase and unlatched it. "Thank God!" He bent down to sort through the jumbled papers.

"I didn't notice it until, uh, until Rocky arrived after your evacuation last night." When he didn't smile at her lame joke, she watched him stand up and noticed his eyes were rimmed in red and his hair stuck out in patches. "Are you okay? You look, I don't know, all white." She touched his forehead to see if he had a fever.

Luis closed his eyes at her touch. "That feels good." The color was returning to his cheeks. He edged closer."Lauren, about last night."

"You want to forget what happened?" Why had she said that?

"Forget about it?" He dropped the briefcase and reached for her hand. "Hell, no. I want, uh, I've missed you all day."

"Missed me?" She wanted to say more, but Luis covered her lips with his. There was that amazing kiss again, soft, magnetic, mesmerizing. His grip around her waist was firm. She relished the feeling of being trapped in his arms, and opened her eyes to watch him. His eyes were closed with his lush lashes brushing his cheek, as if he had yearned for the kiss as much as she had.

When she stretched her arms around him to feel the strength in his shoulders, he opened his eyes and laughed.

Lauren pushed him away. "What's so funny?"

"You're fantastic."

Joy flooded up through her chest. "Your fingers are freezing." She moved his fingers to her mouth and blew on them.

He kissed her forehead and then her ear. "I'm never wearing gloves again."

She pulled his head down so she could kiss his eyelids and feel the tickle of the lashes against her lips, but got distracted when he pulled up her sweatshirt and cupped her breast.

"No bra. I like that. Are my fingers still too cold?"

"I can take it. Ooo, I can take it." She started to slip his jacket off, but Luis grabbed her hands and stepped back.

"I can't stay. I'm supposed to be somewhere."

Though he looked and sounded sad, Lauren wondered for a moment if it was an act to cover a date with someone else. "Are you sure?"

Luis pushed his sleeve away from his watch. "Maybe a few more minutes won't hurt."

Lauren kissed his neck just once, but that's all it took to spread the fire. Luis pressed her against the door with his hips, and certain parts of his body grew hot against hers. His lips and tongue radiated sparks through her fingertips and down her legs.

"Off with your shirt." When he pulled her shirt over her head, she lost her balance, fell into his arms and together they both toppled to the floor.

Luis rolled on top of her and exhaled onto her neck. "Hmmm. I want to kiss your ears, but they're too far away, and I don't have the energy to get there."

"Hectic day?"

"Nightmare day." He pushed himself up and reached down to help her stand. "I hate to leave you."

"Where are you going?"

Luis backed up, stumbled over his briefcase and scattered file folders and papers across the rug. "Look what you made me do."

"Do you have to carry all those papers everywhere you go?"

"I like to read the grad students' theses at home. Crap, I'll never get them back in order."

Lauren reached for her shirt and pulled it on. In the scattered papers, she noticed a stained piece of parchment, picked it up and opened it. "This research paper's been around awhile."

"Hey." Luis frowned and carefully took it from her. "That's fragile. I don't let anyone touch that." His tone was sharp.

"Is it a treasure map?"

Lauren thought her comment would make Luis

laugh, but he looked annoyed as he refolded the parchment and quickly inserted it in his briefcase. "Not exactly."

Lauren watched Luis pack away the rest of the folders and click the lock. "No kidding. It's really an old map?"

His eyebrows lifted. "An old drawing, as far as I can tell." His eyes remained on the briefcase.

"Is it from Mexico?"

When he looked up and squinted at her, she observed how he covered his annoyance with a smile. "You're nosy, did you know that?"

The way he dodged her questions made her more curious. "I told you I like mysteries. Is it a clue to the missing codex?"

His smile stiffened, and he nodded the way guys did when they wanted women to think they were listening and agreeing. "I like mysteries too." He stood up and pushed the briefcase into the corner of the hall. "That's why I intend to keep coming to see you." He slipped his arm around Lauren's waist and held her close. "You are a mystery to me."

"Are all your women mysteries?"

"All my women?" He laughed into her ear. "There's only you."

"That's not what I heard." Lauren gave him an easy shove. "Besides, you revealed yourself as a rat." Lauren strode to the kitchen and started putting her cleaning materials away under the sink.

Luis leaned against the doorjamb. "A rat? How did I do that?"

"You talked Rocky into taking your archeology class." She tucked her hair behind her ears.

"Sorry about that. It just seemed like a—"

"Bad idea! Thanks to you, my friend Rocky, who thinks he's my boyfriend, intends to take a class with you, the man who seduced me, made unbelievable love to me, the man who—"

"Wait! I like this part. Repeat it, please."

"Don't interrupt. The man whose life I saved, who kissed me rudely, who tore my clothes off, who would not stop making my body do wild things."

"Yes! Let's hear it for wild things." He took her hand, kissed her neck, and made her giggle. "I can't leave, if you keep giggling." Luis let her hand drop and looked at his watch again.

"Another woman's apartment? Another briefcase pickup?"

Luis tucked his shirt into his ragged corduroys.

"To the police department. Someone broke into my office last night."

Lauren backed away. "You're kidding."

Luis threw his hands up in the air. "I got to the office this afternoon and found the glass door panel smashed in."

"That's terrible." She hoped she would never be the cause of those angry eyes. "Why would anyone do that?"

"You got me. For a second I thought they'd stolen my briefcase. Then I remembered I left it here, thank God."

"This time you called the police."

He nodded. "The campus cops are hot on the trail. Might even catch up to the culprits before we die." His eyes twinkled, lively again. "Luckily, they alerted the real cops."

"Do you think it was the same men as the other night?"

He put his hands on his hips, looked down at his boots, and shook his head. "Probably some students, maybe some kids who got bad grades last semester. You can't believe what a mess they made of the office."

Lauren followed him as he turned and strode into the hall. "What were they after?"

Luis stopped and leaned his hand against the

doorframe and brushed a hand through his hair. "Beats me. Couldn't be my exams. I give students the topics before the exam."

"I wondered, because some men have been hanging around here too."

Luis grabbed her wrist so hard it hurt. "What do you mean?"

"Late that night after you and I met, my handyman Ken chased a couple of men off the fire escape, and this morning Rocky and I caught a man in the front hall who claimed to have the wrong address."

Luis frowned and dropped her wrist. "You called the police?"

She nodded. "They said they'd drive through the alley more often, for what that's worth."

"Be careful. Lock the doors. Don't go out alone at night. Luis pulled on his coat and paused with his hand on the door. "Was Rocky here all night?"

"No." What kind of woman did he think she was?

"Maybe you shouldn't be alone at night." He leaned down and touched her cheek. "Stay right here, and I'll be back to take you to dinner as soon as I'm through at the police station."

Lauren shook her head. "I can't tonight." She straightened his frayed collar and thought how sweet his voice sounded. "I'm busy."

He dropped his hand. "Oh. The non-boyfriend is taking you out?"

"Yes." Lauren patted him on the shoulder. "Sorry."

With a shrug, Luis strode out the door and paused at the top of the stairs to glance back at Lauren. "You know I'll be back, don't you?" He zipped up his jacket and galloped down the stairs.

Lauren closed the apartment door on his retreat feeling confused and scared. This amazing and very exciting man seemed to be pursuing her, and she obviously liked it. However, Luis's reaction to her story about the strange men made her wonder, yet again, if he was telling her everything he knew about the men who jumped him.

Being near Luis put her at risk in more than one way. She should have told him she couldn't see him again. At the sound of the Jeep starting up on the street below, she turned and stumbled over the briefcase. The fool had left it again.

Chapter Seven

Every Saturday Lauren liked to spend time working on her latest project, a collection of short stories with a common theme or character. Each time she had finished another one, she'd sent the batch to one of the many literary agencies her father had respected, and each time she'd received a curt rejection. She kept the final copies in a file folder on her desk where she could proof them and make corrections whenever her computer stalled or someone put her on hold. The file wasn't there. It wasn't in the file drawer, where Julie might have put it, or on the console behind her desk.

Lauren made a note to ask Julie to track it down, and printed out new copies before she got to work on the latest story. This one featured a sexy archeologist, an adventure in a South American country and some subtle sex scenes.

After a shower, while she was drying her hair, her home phone rang. Lauren picked it up, said hello, but no one spoke. She repeated her greeting. After a moment, she heard a click and the dial tone.

She reentered the bathroom, and her cell phone rang. This time there was a voice on the other end.

"Hi, girl buddy." Rocky's voice was low. "I'm still here at the dealership. Dad can't spare me tonight. He let the other salesmen head home to be with their families. Dad likes to give them time off on the weekends during the holidays, so I get to fill in for all of them."

"I understand, Rocky." Just hearing Rocky's sad

voice made her feel guilty all over again for the way he looked as he left her apartment that morning. It was selfish of her to try to keep Rocky as a buddy. She should confess and let him go. "We can go another night."

"Yeah, sure. I still plan to meet the guys after the game at McCabe's. You want to come too?"

"Thanks, but I can't stay out that late with my work schedule, even on the weekends. I'll just go get a bite somewhere and go to bed early."

As soon as she hung up, her landline rang again, giving her a jolt that set her heart pounding. Again, there seemed to be no one there.

At six p.m. Lauran put on several layers to combat the cold and headed out of her apartment. Streetlights cast eerie shadows beyond the trees and onto the snow banks. Ice glistened along Ken's freshly shoveled sidewalk. No men in knit hats lingered on the corner. A car pulled into the garage in the alley behind the building next door, and a woman got out and retrieved her grocery bags.

Lauren had considered Luis's advice not to go out alone and decided she wouldn't let anyone change the way she lived. Besides, peanut butter on stale bread was a lousy choice for dinner, when she could brave the cold (and her fear of two evil men in knit caps) and use some of Enid's promised money to treat herself. Down the street was the quaint German restaurant where her grandfather used to take her, the perfect place to eat alone and read.

A car turned the corner off Prospect and accelerated in her direction. For a second the lights blinded her. She sucked in her breath, started down the steps to the sidewalk, and turned west toward the restaurant. City lights glimmered in their holiday colors. Every window on the top floor of the tallest apartment building flickered red and green.

Remembering her mother's cure for unwanted

fear, Lauren began to sing. "She Loves You Yea, Yea, Yea," trickled out of her lips and grew stronger by the time she reached the first of two stoplights. Lauren dutifully waited for the walk sign as a man strode toward her from the other direction. Instead of stopping on the sidewalk for the light, he paused, let the car go through, and kept walking in her direction. The collar of the man's overcoat covered his face, and in the shadows, she couldn't tell if he was wearing a knit hat. "With a love like that you know you should be glad," she sang into her scarf. The man looked over at her when the light changed, and Lauren bolted across the street.

Just ahead was the dimly lit entrance to the restaurant. Through yellow stained-glass windows, she saw shadows of heads and the safe, welcoming glimmer of candles. The sound of footsteps behind her caused her to speed her steps along the icy sidewalk. She caught the light at the next corner, trotted across the street, and pushed open the heavy, rustic door of the restaurant. It clanged against the doorstop so loudly all six diners stopped their forks in mid-air and stared.

For decades, the Bavarian Garden Café had served knockwurst and schnitzel at the same address. The neighborhood had been residential for a hundred years, but in the last twenty years, buildings were torn down or rebuilt, while condos, coffee shops and even an upscale grocery store were added to the mix. Within the café nothing had changed, not even the waiters' uniforms, good old German lederhosen worn with knee-high stockings.

The maitre d' clomped over to Lauren. With a nod of his long, wrinkled face and a flash of his yellow-toothed smile, he ushered her to a tiny table against a back window and asked if someone would be joining her. She shook her head. In his tobacco-charred voice, the man spoke about the terrible early winter they were having. He asked if she would like a cocktail as he handed her a large, ragged-edged menu. Lauren shook her head again and read the menu.

Immediately she spotted a punctuation gaffe, "Chefs' specialty." If the restaurant boasted more than one chef, the apostrophe was in the right place, but Lauren doubted that was the case.

The waiter returned and hunched above her, his blotchy pate glistening in the candlelight. "The special, my dear, is our venison. No one but our Schultz does it so tender."

"Thank you, but I'll have wiener schnitzel and your house salad."

When the waiter tried to expand her order to include liver dumpling soup, she shook her head, and refused his wine suggestions as well. Lauren opened her folder containing the chapters she'd just written and dug a pencil from her purse. A chilly breeze on her ankles made her glance toward the entrance.

"Lauren? Is that you in that dark corner?"

Lauren recognized the voice before she noticed the leather jacket. "Luis? What are you doing here?"

He strode over to her table and removed his cap. "The same thing you are, I guess, getting something to eat." He waved a hand across the room where the old maitre d' stood watching expectantly. "Where's Rocky?"

Lauren made a face. "He had to work again tonight."

Luis's dark eyes studied her. "Poor guy." He looked up at the shelf of giant beer steins hanging above Lauren's table and whistled. "I haven't eaten here before. How's the food?"

"It's usually good." She noticed with surprise that he had a tie on, a very wide one with ugly swirls of beige and brown.

The waiter loomed behind Luis with Lauren's salad. "Pardon me, sir," he said.

Luis sprang back out of the way. Assuming Luis was with someone else, Lauren expected him to duck away to another table, but he didn't, and the situation grew awkward. Luis, whose body was seldom still, was obviously waiting for her to invite him to join her, but she hesitated.

"There, miss," the maitre d' said, and shifted the other chair slightly. "It's no problem to have the gentleman join you, if you wish. I would be delighted to make adjustments."

Lauren watched Luis shuffle his feet. "I don't want to intrude on your reading," he said quickly.

"Please, join me. I thought, uh, I guess I assumed you were with someone else." What she wanted to say was, hey, Prof, buzz off so I can figure out why I find you irresistible.

"You've already ordered."

"I'll bring you a menu right away," the maitre d' said, as Luis tossed his jacket over the back of the chair and sat down.

"Never mind. Do you have calves' liver?"

The waiter stood taller and smiled. "Yes."

"Good. I'll have that and whatever salad she ordered, if that's okay."

"Perhaps some wine, sir, or something else to drink?"

"Are you having something, Lauren?"

"Red wine, I guess, thanks."

Luis looked pale in the candlelight as he spread the napkin in his lap. "You can bring us a bottle of your best red."

Looking smug, the maitre d' nodded, his eyes huge behind his thick lenses. "I'll choose something simple, yet appropriate for two friends meeting by accident," he said and drifted away before they could respond.

"The old guy thinks we make a nice-looking couple." Luis settled back in his chair, looking for a moment like a young boy who had gotten away with something.

"What did the police say?"

Luis frowned and straightened his silverware. "They're looking into it. No one noticed any strangers in the classrooms or anywhere else in the building."

"No other offices were broken into?"

Luis shook his head. "I left my briefcase at your place again." He grinned.

"It's almost as if you did it on purpose."

He smiled. "Almost. Maybe I should just store it there."

Lauren tried to ignore the constriction in her chest. "It may be the safest place for your mystery map."

Luis laughed as he tried to find a space on the tiny table for his elbows and finally gave up. "Those look like important papers you have there, Lauren."

Lauren nodded. "Proofing my work."

"Are you okay with us being here together in public? "

Lauren shrugged. "It's safe enough tonight. Rocky's still at work, but I have to be careful not to hurt him. He's had some challenges with his family."

Luis nodded. "He told me. So you're not going to say anything about us?"

"I may have to."

Luis reached for his water glass. "Are you sorry we, uh, got together?"

"Should I be?"

Luis raised his eyebrows. "Hope not. I don't want you to be sad, and you looked sad when I walked in here."

"I'm cold. My nose is an icicle from the walk over here." She wasn't going to confess her fear of the men in knit hats.

He reached across the table to touch her nose. "You exaggerate. It's a warm, healthy nose you have."

"Like a poodle?"

"No, like a lovely, healthy woman I could make love to right here, right now."

Lauren glanced over at the elderly couple eyeing them over their schaum tortes as a blush warmed her cheeks. She held her tongue until after the waiter delivered the wine along with Luis's salad. "The couple across from us is very interested in the way you touched my nose."

"Really? Wait till they see what else I intend to touch."

"Not going to happen." Lauren spoke through gritted-teeth.

"I've never seen you dressed up before, Lauren. I like it." He rested his hand on hers and interlaced their fingers.

"Better than my old sweats?" His touch felt gentle and possessive. "Your tie is a surprise, I can tell you that."

Luis looked down, flipped his tie over his shoulder with his other hand, and chuckled. "You like it with this plaid shirt? Here's my idea of style: I wear the same thing every day, and when I go out, all I do is add the piece of silk."

Luis shifted his knee so it pressed against hers and then began to butter a roll.

Lauren reached for her water. "Goes well with the corduroy pants with the ripped pockets."

"Hey!" He looked down at his pants and frowned. "You're mocking a poor bachelor for his helpless state. Should I find some young coed to stitch them up?"

The man had the astonishing power to turn her on any time he wanted. All he had to do was touch any part of her body, like her knee, for example. "A young beauty might pop you in the teeth for assuming she exists to serve your helplessness."

The roll he was chewing muffled his laughter. "Well said. The truth is my sisters showed me how to sew on buttons. I even learned to patch my clothes, but I don't seem to get around to it."

He took a sip of his wine, watching her so intensely she felt a strange urge to blab her deepest thoughts.

"Tell me, Luis. Did you follow me or was it just chance that you happened to come here tonight?" She rested her free hand on the table and hoped he'd touch her again. At that moment, she wanted to make love to him.

"I passed this place after I left you, after you pretended you were busy for dinner, and I thought someday you and I should eat here."

"I wasn't pretending. We really did have plans."

Luis reached for her hand and played with her fingers. His eyes grew cloudy and he moved a little in his chair.

"You okay?" She whispered the words and then licked her lips.

He shook his head. "I got distracted thinking about last night and forgot what I was saying."

"How you happened to be here tonight." She managed to pull off one of her boots and slide her foot between his thighs.

"Yes, well! Oh, yes, okay," he said and grinned. "So, uh, the police asked me the same silly questions over and over, and then I left and realized I'd left my briefcase in its favorite place, so I stopped by to get it, but you were not at home." He smiled and reached under the table, grabbed her foot and began to massage it. "Next I sat in my car at the stoplight on the corner, felt hungry, and decided to come on in."

His hand was hot against her cold foot. "And it was truly a coincidence?"

Luis's face softened into a smile that showed off his laugh lines. "Milwaukee's a small town. You like sauerkraut? My grandmother loved that stuff, but we all hated the smell. That foot's all warmed up now. Do you want me to heat up the other one?"

"No. I mean yes. Luis, you make me do crazy things."

He nodded. "Nice, crazy things. Other foot?"

Lauren slid out of her other boot and switched feet. "We have to stop this."

His grin widened. "Turning you on, huh? Want to see how far we can get, before the old couple notices?"

Lauren shook her head and glanced over at the couple again. "They just stare at each other and sip their coffee." She tried to pull her foot away, but Luis held on.

"I'm simply warming your toes to keep you from getting frost bite. Think of something else." His teasing squint was back.

"Okay. There are two mistakes on the menu."

"Really? Do you come here now and then to edit the menu?"

"'Soups of the day' has an apostrophe, and, uh, I can't remember what the other one was."

"What are you having?"

"What am I having? Oh, for dinner? My grandfather's favorite, wiener schnitzel. Here it comes." She sat up and put both her feet on the floor just before the waiter slid their dinners onto the table.

Lauren carefully sliced two bites of her wiener schnitzel and took a taste. It was as good as she remembered. She chewed for a while, waiting for her body to cool down and wondering what it would be like to watch Luis at work instead of at play. She considered telling him about Enid's invitation, but dismissed the idea as premature. First, she must find another way to pay her bills. "Luis, tell me about your dig, or whatever you call it."

Louis wielded his knife and fork efficiently like a European: he cut with his left, stabbed with his right, and never let either one rest. "Oh, thanks," Luis said, when the waiter offered more wine. "We call it a research site, when we're with other professionals. The students work hard, doing the grunt work, you know, but they get a pretty accurate idea of what it's like to be part of an archeological team. This year's promising. Last summer one of the teams dug a trench that intersected what we think is a royal crypt."

"How old?"

"Because of its location, it must be pre-Columbian."

"Mayan?"

He nodded. She could feel the vibration under the table as his knee, no longer touching hers, started to bounce. "One of our projects is to prove our site was a way station for travelers to Tikal." His eyes sparkled in the candlelight as he sipped his wine. "If so, we might be able to locate another village a day's distance away."

"Royal crypts must be good for your project."

"You bet. Donors, museums, universities compete to support research that has anything to do with a pre-Columbian ruler." He smiled and raised an eyebrow. "It helps when the grant-writing team hints about gold and jewels." He buttered a roll with his large, square hands, took a bite, and chewed as he spoke. "So far we've uncovered a nice hunk of turquoise."

"Does the whole archeological team help your effort to find the missing codex?"

His knee began to bounce again. "I'm on my own

with that one."

The candle on their table flickered as the last of the other diners left at the same time and the front door banged shut. They both turned toward the sound. A man in a ragged coat and baggy pants with his face wrapped up in a large striped scarf hesitated at the door and glanced around the room. Just as he eyed Lauren and Luis, the waiter blocked his view and murmured to him. In seconds, the man was outside again.

Lauren turned back to Luis, feeling sorry that a cold, hungry man couldn't find a warm place on such a night.

Luis pushed back his plate and leaned toward her. "What were we talking about?"

"Your dig. So the quest to find the missing codex has no connection to your work there?"

Luis leaned so close to Lauren that his hair nearly touched the flame of the candle. His eyes sparkled the same way they did when he was about to kiss her. "Finding another one could change our knowledge of Mayan history."

Lauren felt his eyes penetrating her thoughts, forcing her to receive the weight of his words. "I don't understand how a codex made of wood or paper could survive five or six hundred years."

Luis grinned, crossed his arms, and leaned away from her. Lauren noticed the frayed cuffs on his shirtsleeves. "It's impossible. I admit it. The few we have preserved in archives in Europe are in such bad shape they can't be handled. If any others survived the burning, it's extremely likely they disintegrated long ago."

Lauren felt herself sigh with Luis. "A waste."

"Even if I never track it down, even if the last codex doesn't exist, we'll always be able to find clues about how people lived, about their religious practices, or their government. You might like to go on a dig yourself some day."

Lauren watched Luis scrape up one last bite while she reconsidered telling him about her bargain with Enid.

"I'm curious," Luis said and paused to wipe his mouth.

"About what?"

"What's the deal with you and Rocky? That isn't his real name, is it?"

"His name is Robert, but his little brother always called him Rocky."

"He's built like a Rock. So answer my question."

"What question?"

"You're a beautiful woman who has some sort of friendship with an athlete everyone but me has heard of, and the guy stands you up all the time."

"He has to work long hours. We went running together this morning."

"Running?" He nodded as a frown flitted across his forehead. "Sometimes you call him your boyfriend and other times just a friend. From personal experience I know you have no sexual hang-ups, so what's the deal?"

"Sexual hang-ups?" Lauren faked a laugh.

"I repeat my question: the deal is?"

"Why do you want to know?"

He leaned back in his chair and chewed on his cheek. "Research."

"We're friends. The other night I called him my boyfriend to make you think it wouldn't matter to me if I never saw you again."

Luis's mouth dropped open. "Whoa! That is too convoluted for me. What are you afraid of?"

She smiled and stretched out her toe until it touched his ankle. "You."

He reached for her hand and nodded. "If that's true, you're responding very well to my immersion treatments."

"Am I an experiment? Do you think your sexual powers can change a poor frigid bitch into a smoldering sex machine?"

"Nice description, but who are you kidding? You were the hot one that night after you drove me home, not me."

"That's not true! I was scared to death."

"You were on fire."

"On fire?"

"I'm watching the fire burn in front of me right now."

His laugh irritated and thrilled her too.

"Tell me why you'd want to waste your amazing vibrant spirit."

"I don't want to talk about this anymore."

"Let's let out all our secrets."

"You first, Doctor Luis."

He looked down at his hands and picked at a fingernail. "I get claustrophobia in caves. Scared shitless." He looked up at her through his eyelashes and bit his lip. "Your turn."

Lauren reached for his fingers. "If that's true, that has to be a serious problem for you."

Luis nodded and refilled his wine glass. "Indeed. So far, I've managed to deal with it. "What's your deep secret?"

"I intend to live down the family jinx."

Luis's shoulders bounced with his laughter. "The family jinx?"

"I wouldn't be telling you if I hadn't had this wine, but I'm serious." She took another gulp of wine to emphasize her point.

He reached across the white tablecloth and grasped both her hands. "Explain the jinx. I promise I won't laugh."

"It goes like this: the Richmonds are unlucky in love. Their lovers, husbands and wives all desert them, destroying homes, their children's lives, businesses. My parents were the latest example."

"This is sad." Luis's face turned somber as he squeezed her fingers.

"My great-grandmother ran off with the gardener." Lauren began to count with her other hand. "My great-great-grandfather was a bigamist who kept his other wife in a house down the street from his office. My grandmother ran off with the horse trainer. In every case, the result was the dissolution of the family's livelihood, never mind the broken hearts and dreams. I won't let that happen to me."

"Is there any reason for the curse?"

Lauren yanked her hand away. "It's a jinx, not a curse."

"There's a difference?"

"A jinx is an unbroken trend of bad luck. A curse is caused by a malevolent spirit."

"Curses and jinxes have power only if people believe in them." He took a sip of his wine. "I've seen what a curse can do on a research site."

The waiter stood between them with two small menus in his hand. "Excuse me, would the gentleman and the lady care for dessert?"

"Why not? Lauren, what's your favorite dessert in the world?"

"Anything chocolate."

"Excellent. We'll have your best chocolate dessert and some cappuccino with plenty of sugar and cream."

Lauren watched Luis finish his wine, dab the corners of his lips, and squint at her. "This campaign is more complicated than I anticipated."

"Am I the target of the campaign?"

Luis nodded, still studying her.

"Is this a war?"

Luis nodded again.

"You against me?"

He shook his head as the waiter placed a circle of shimmering chocolate in front of each of them. When he returned with their coffee, she pointed at the dessert. "What's this called?"

"Chocolate Voodoo," the man answered with a nod. "Enjoy."

Lauren dipped her spoon into the molten goo and licked it off slowly. "I repeat, you against me?"

Luis lifted a large dollop and held it in front of his lips for a moment. "Nope. Us against the jinx."

"Don't tell me you like happy endings."

"Oh, I'm a happy guy."

"All your girlfriends make you that way."

Luis hefted his spoon and frowned. "Someone is spreading lies about me."

Lauren kept her frozen grin and raised one eyebrow. "Aren't you going to taste your dessert?"

Luis looked down at the molten mass on his spoon and nodded. "This dessert is like a special moment in life. It looks unbelievably good." He inhaled with his eyes closed. "It smells like a gift from your god of jinxes." He watched her again, his eyes glistening in the candlelight. "I'm eager to taste it. Perhaps I'll eat every moist spoonful. I wonder if the sweetness can possibly match the anticipation."

Lauren thought of the taste of Luis's lips on hers, and her heart thudded crazily. Sometimes chocolate had that effect on her. "One bite is already too much for me. It's like two cups of strong coffee."

"That happens in life too."

"What?"

"People quit just before they accomplish their goals."

"You are the philosopher tonight. Are you saying that I can't commit myself to a truly sweet experience?"

Luis raised his eyebrows and shook his head. "Is that what you think I said?"

A. Y. Stratton

"You answered a question with a question. Well, Socrates, I've had too much wine and too much chocolate. I'll be up all night."

Luis drained his coffee, set the cup down, slid his chair back, and uncrossed his legs. "Help is nearby."

Lauren looked down at her plate. Did she want him? Yes. Was she ready to be with him again? How could she protect herself from the feeling of joy that settled in her chest each time she was with him?

Luis glanced around. "Look, the place is deserted. The staff must be dying for us to get out of here."

He nodded and the waiter brought the check. Lauren tried to pay her half, but lost her battle. Luis claimed dinner was his gift to her for saving his life. As soon as Luis signed the credit card bill, they bundled into their coats and headed out into the cold. Just outside the door, Luis paused and looked up and down the street.

"Are you looking for someone?" Lauren asked.

Luis shivered and shook his head. "No."

"Did you lose your car?"

He snickered. "Who in the world would ever misplace her car? Note the pronoun." He frowned into the snowflakes that flickered in the streetlights and took her hand. "Mine's in the lot across the street." As they waited for the walk sign, he added, "Did you remember your folder?"

"It's in my bag. You know where your briefcase is?"

"I do." He glanced up as a man strode around the corner and waited with them for the light. When the light changed, Luis let the man cross the street ahead of them.

"You didn't like the look of that guy?"

"Nope." Luis kept his eyes on the man.

Lauren hugged his arm closer to her body. "Your

parking garage experience has made you more cautious." When his grimace remained, Lauren watched the man too as he continued down the sidewalk without looking back. "When do you leave for Mexico?"

"Day after tomorrow."

She stopped walking and turned to him. "So soon?" Why had she said that?

"Are you sorry, or relieved to get me off your doorstep?" He gave her a one-armed hug as the wind kicked up a swirl of old snow and they continued walking. "I was supposed to leave just before Christmas to visit my grandmother first, but I had to change my plans after I got a call this afternoon. This season we've had a batch of problems. Rain washed out the walls of the Castillo, and the rubble covered the staircase we've been working on for the last six months." He groaned. "Rain always wins the battle."

At the next intersection he stopped, tugged her sleeve, and looked down at her. "I'm going to miss you, Lauren."

This was the moment she should confess she'd be traveling to the dig with Enid. Then, if the streetlights were bright enough, perhaps she'd be able to tell whether he'd be glad of her company or whether he had a lover waiting for him down there.

Either way, once she had told him, her course would be set.

While all that whizzed through her brain, her mouth had not responded, and the traffic light had changed. With their bodies touching and their steps echoing in the chill, they crossed the street under the green glow.

She glanced over at him as they hurried along the sidewalk. Icy gusts off the lake made her eyes water. His head was down, and he'd pulled his knit cap over his eyebrows. He slowed near her doorstep and tugged on her hand.

"I'd like to see you before I go, that is if it doesn't mess up your life."

Lauren unlocked the entry to her building as a honking car drew Luis's attention. She was trying to think of the perfect poetic farewell that might make Luis forget his obligations in Mexico and stay with her, when he gripped her collar and leaned close to kiss her.

"I'm glad we had dinner together tonight," he said, and his eyebrows took on a devilish angle.

She inhaled, expecting his kiss to interrupt her. "I'd like to see you too, to say goodbye." A snowplow clanked down the street toward them, its yellow light flashing on the snow banks. His lips touched hers and she felt herself melt in the warmth of his mouth.

"I have another secret to confess," Luis whispered into her ear.

Lauren pulled away and searched his face. Was he going to tell her he was married with three kids?

"What?"

"I followed you tonight. That's how I ended up going to the restaurant."

"You followed me?"

"I decided to drive by your building, and saw you walking down the street, alone, doing just what I told you not to do, and I was worried. I pulled over and watched until you entered the restaurant safely. I waited, thinking Rocky might join you, but then I got to thinking he'd have picked you up and walked with you."

"So you knew I'd be alone."

He nodded. "I wish you'd be more careful."

Luis was worried about her, protective, even possessive. Lauren smiled and pulled his face to hers and kissed him. "Thank you, Luis, my body guard." Lauren felt and heard his cell phone buzz in his pants pocket and pulled away.

"Whoa! Excuse me Lauren, I have to get that. It could be the research station." Luis unzipped his jacket and snatched up his cell. "Yes?" He pulled Lauren to his chest to block the wind. "What the hell? I'll be right there." He turned back to Lauren, his eyes wide and his voice tight. "That was the guy who lives above me. Someone tried to break into my apartment. I've got to go."

"What about your briefcase?"

"Tomorrow. I'll be back tomorrow." Luis pulled her close again. "I want you, Lauren with a jinx."

He stepped back down the stairs and took off jogging. Lauren watched him until he got to the next intersection and crossed against the light.

Chapter Eight

Later that night, Rocky called from the sports bar to invite her to watch the Packer game on his brother's new television the following afternoon. Lauren begged off, saying she had too much work to do. For the next two hours, she reworked the same scene of her manuscript, getting nowhere. Three hours after Luis left her he still hadn't called to tell her what had happened.

The excuses she concocted for Luis were lame. Even if he were preoccupied with the police, he should be able to call her. No matter what had happened, even if his apartment were a gigantic mess, he still ought to be able to call her to let her know he was okay.

The later it got, the more her imagination raged. Perhaps the call he received wasn't really from his neighbor, but from another woman. Once she had shoved that thought into the deepest corner of her pocket of insecurity, there was only one possibility: Luis had had an accident on the way to his apartment.

She reached for the phone book, found the number for the hospital closest to him, and punched it in.

Then she chickened out, gave up, and went to bed, acknowledging the man was unpredictable. He'd call when he felt like it and drop in when she didn't expect him. As she had predicted, because of the wine, the chocolate, and the worry, she barely slept.

The phone rang at noon on Sunday, while Lauren hunched over the computer hoping to resurrect something from the disaster of the night before. It wasn't Luis.

"Ken here," came the raspy growl. "We got more problems. Hate to say it, but it's time you replace that snow blower."

"That is a problem."

"I got a guy who can get us one for half off, a like-new tractor, mower deck, and blower attachments. Less than five hundred."

Lauren had never understood the meaning of "like-new." Either it was new or it was used. "Not this year, Ken. The bank owns me." Ken would understand those words. Once the bank had owned him too—and foreclosed.

"Hmm. 'Fraid of that. Okay, then we'll have to make it work. About that stalker who's been hanging out in the alley?"

"You saw him again?"

"Nope. Have you?"

"I noticed more cigarette butts."

Like an advertisement for a nicotine patch, Ken wheezed and coughed for a minute before he continued. "Oh, yeah, well it wasn't me for a change. Might be a dumpster diver."

"You mean a guy who goes through garbage?"

"Doesn't make sense in this weather, does it? Well, you keep an eye out. You see anything—you call the police and me ASAP. I got a couple of weapons stashed over the garage, and I'm not afraid to use 'em."

"What? You have guns?"

"You never know who's listening, Lauren. I didn't mention what kind of weapons. Could be baseball bats. Just call me. Now, where's my list? Oh, yeah. You're out of salt for the walks, and that sidewalk in front is slick again. Somebody's gonna break a neck and sue you, 'less I get to the hardware store right now while it's open and get you some more. Hate to say it, but I'll need to be repaid for the expenses as soon as you can manage." After such a long sentence, Ken wheezed into the phone and then choked out a cough. "I'll skip out early from dinner with my ex-son-in-law and his wife so I can get back here and spread that stuff. Anything else you need me to do, Little Lauren?"

Lauren smiled when Ken used her grandfather's pet name for her. "When Rocky and I came home yesterday, a man was in the front hallway."

"You're kiddin'? A stranger?"

"He said he had the wrong address."

"One of your other tenants let him in?"

"They're both down south until March. You think that door latch could be broken?"

"I'll check it out. Why the hell you didn't call me yesterday, I can't figure. Prob'ly too busy wrestling with both your boyfriends. Gotta go."

Lauren rested her fingers on the keyboard and tried to twist away the kink in her neck. She reminded herself that Ken overreacted to anything remotely threatening and hoped this time was no different. On a daily basis, he was prepared to combat suspected toxins in the drinking water, convicted child molesters in the neighborhood, illegal aliens making bombs in the apartment down the street, police on the take, and neighbors siphoning gas from his truck.

Just as Lauren returned to her computer, she heard someone pounding on the door at the front entrance. Before she could get there, the office buzzer sounded. When she finally unbolted the door, it burst open, and Luis toppled against her.

"Whoa!" He righted himself by gripping Lauren's shoulders. "I must have been leaning pretty hard on that door there."

"You surprised me." Her worry spilled into anger. There he was staring at her with a sleepy look, when she was mad and hurt enough to tell him to buzz off. "I suppose you were too busy to call me last night and tell me what happened when you got home."

"They pretty much messed up the place."

He sounded drunk. Lauren checked his eyes. They fluttered, and he began to sway. "Are you okay?" Lauren grabbed his elbow.

"Don't feel too good."

"Can you make it up the stairs?"

He inhaled. "Not sure."

He didn't smell drunk. They began their ascent, with Luis gripping the railing and Lauren hugging him around the waist. About half way up, she noticed bloody sutures in the back of his head. "You're hurt!"

"Been to the, uh, you know—"

"The hospital?"

"That's it."

"Keep going, Luis. What happened?"

"Sandbagged."

They were nearly at the top. "Don't let go of that railing." She felt his weight shift to her arm and thought he was about to fold.

"Sandbagged. You know, like a guy tosses a bag of sand, hell, I don't know what that means."

"Somebody got the drop on you."

"Good one." Luis smiled one step from the top.

"Don't stop. You need to lie down."

"Doctor said."

"The doctor said what?"

"Lie down. Like a dog."

Lauren propped him against the wall while she unlocked her apartment door. Once she guided him into her living room and helped him to the couch, Luis smiled faintly. "I feel rotten."

"I'll get you some water."

He sipped the water eagerly before he spoke. "I felt okay until I got out of the car just now. Mind if I rest here a few minutes?" He lifted his head, took another sip, handed the glass back to Lauren, slumped against the cushion, and closed his eyes. Lauren struggled to get his jacket and boots off, and then went to grab a blanket from her bed. Once he was covered, she sat on the floor, stroked his forehead, and watched his eyebrows relax.

"That feels good." Luis touched her cheek. "Thanks."

"Sorry I overreacted. I was worried about you." Terrified and crazy with jealousy, to be accurate, but she didn't tell him that.

Luis opened his eyes and smiled. "You were? That's nice."

"It didn't feel nice. What happened?"

Luis winced and closed his eyes. "Guys were in the apartment. Slugged me. That's all I know."

"And the police?"

He rolled his head back and forth. "Not there."

"Didn't the neighbor call them?"

Luis's eyes stayed shut. "Apparently not."

"You walked into a trap."

He gripped her hand. "Hit me from behind with something hard, like a gun." He settled his arms under the blanket and closed his eyes again.

"But why? What were they after?"

"Don't know. Place is a mess."

"You said that. Like your office?"

He sighed. "Mild concussion."

Lauren kissed his cheek and continued to smooth his forehead. "What do you have that they want, Luis? You can trust me."

"Feels better with your cool hand there."

"What did the doctor say you should do?"

"Ice and rest."

"I'll get some ice." In the kitchen, Lauren spooned ice cubes into a baggie and hurried back. With Luis's help, she rested the pack against the swelling in the back of his head.

"Would you do something for me, Lauren?"

"Of course."

"Wake me up every hour or so. Doctor's orders."

"I will."

"And one more thing."

"What?"

"Food. I haven't eaten since last night. Anything, toast, whatever."

"I can whip over to the deli. What should I get you?"

"Deli?" He opened his eyes. "Roast beef on rye would be great. Thanks."

"Do you feel well enough for me to do that now?"

"Yeah." He struggled to dig in his pocket. "Here, let me get some cash."

"Later. You must be starving. I'll be right back."

"Sorry to be such a pain in the ass."

Lauren watched his thick lashes at rest, and studied the curve of his lips. She remembered their softness and kissed them gently.

"Okay, Luis. I'm going now."

He opened his eyes and pulled her closer. "Thanks." He flashed a smile that might give Lauren a concussion too.

As she reached the doorway, a bus screeched to a halt on the corner outside as a blast of wind rattled the old windowpane, and Lauren jumped. "Luis," she said as she turned to look at him. "What do you have that someone wants?"

Lauren waited for an answer, but Luis's chest began to rise and fall. Soon a snore buzzed at the back of his throat.

Lauren zipped on her down coat, pulled her wool hat over her ears, and rested her hand on the doorknob. There sitting on the chair in the hall was Luis's briefcase. Inside the brown scuffed leather, she suspected, was the secret to Luis's mysterious events. She peeked into the living room once more. Luis was motionless and breathing steadily. She hunched over the case and tested the lock. The clasp flipped up easily. For a vanishing second she reviewed the pros and cons of invading Luis's privacy and gave in to her urge.

She unfolded the thick, rough paper about the size of a newspaper page and noticed ragged edges on two sides, as if the ends of the original document were missing.

It appeared to be a diagram with markings of rocks, paths, building shapes, surrounding a shaded oval colored light blue, possibly indicating a body of water. There were no letters at all, no glyphs or symbols. No "X marks the spot."

In the center of the paper, a wild-eyed head of a serpent-like beast stuck out its jagged red tongues through horrible bloody fangs. The monster gave Lauren the shivers.

Might it be a map of a Mayan ruin or an archeological site, she wondered? Again, she itched to know why Luis was so secretive about it. She had to know more, but she also had to get Luis something to eat and be back in an hour to wake him up. She slid the map back into the case with care and clicked the lock. Once more, she paused at the door.

Kinko's was three blocks away, right next door to the deli. Both were open Sunday afternoons—and deserted during Packer games. She slipped the map out of the briefcase and fitted it gently into her handbag. If he found out, well, she'd deal with it.

When Lauren opened the outside door to the alley, a gust of wind almost blew it out of her grip. Frigid air stung her eyes as she descended, and she pulled her scarf up over her nose.

At half past two, the sun made a limited appearance as a smudge of pink behind a steel-gray cloud. To the east, Lauren couldn't tell where the lake stopped and the sky began. Along Prospect Avenue, the cross street next to her building, naked maples shivered in the wind. The only one on the jogging trail was an elderly man walking his dog. On Packer Sundays, everyone stayed home in front of the TV. She thought of sweet, safe Rocky watching the game with his brother and their football buddies.

Lauren clutched her bag to her chest and crossed the alley toward her garage. Except for the section behind her building where Ken had done his job, the sea of slush had frozen into ankle-turning ridges. She had to concentrate so hard on her footing as she clambered over the ice that she didn't notice the dirty-white truck until she heard it rumble toward the other end of the alley and turn out of sight.

Walking carefully over the ridges, Lauren headed toward the spot where the truck had been parked. There in the tire tracks lay a scattering of cigarette butts. Her heart thudded. The truck was a different color than the last one, but she supposed someone could steal a different vehicle every day. Maybe she was paranoid, but she was determined to find out why anyone would work so hard to spy on her, or on Luis.

Lauren couldn't think of any honest reasons a guy who drove a delivery truck might idle his car, smoke cigarettes and drop the butts in the alley behind her building. She climbed into her car and locked the doors. She had to hurry. She didn't have much time to accomplish both her missions.

On the corner, the neighborhood looked peaceful and empty. Traffic lights flicked red or green without an audience. On the eaves and steps of the row houses opposite her building, multi-colored Christmas bulbs glowed next to a Santa and his reindeer in mid-leap. The dirty white truck was not tailing her to the strip mall.

She ordered a chicken salad sandwich for herself and the roast beef on rye for Luis. The kid behind the counter said they were filling a large order so hers wouldn't be ready for about ten minutes. Instead of waiting, she hurried to Kinko's. At the largest color copy machine, she gently opened the document, taking care not to crack any of its folds. In order to capture every detail, she copied the map in three sections.

At the checkout desk Lauren's heart pounded so loudly she could barely understand as the clerk offered her a large bag for the copy and the original.

"Oh, look!" the woman said as Lauren slid the old map into her bag. "Someone scribbled there on the back."

Lauren noticed the words were in Spanish. "Hey, you're right. You have good eyes." She flashed her fake smile at the woman, left the store, and trotted back to the deli. She paid for the sandwiches, hurried to the car, got in, locked the doors, and sat for a moment. She'd done it. She had both the lunches and her copy of the map. She had to examine the scrawl on the back once more before she got home, in case Luis was awake when she got there. Again, she pulled the original out of her purse.

The faint script read, "Salmos 32: 7." Because of the configuration and the colon, she guessed it was a Bible passage: Spanish for the Psalms, book thirty-two, verse seven. She copied it precisely into her notebook and drove home at barely twenty-five miles an hour. No one would be able to follow her discretely at that pace.

Lauren pulled into her garage, looked up and

down the alley as she hurried across, and climbed the back stairs to her kitchen door. If Luis had decided to get up and open his briefcase and had discovered the map was missing, how would she explain her actions?

When she entered through the kitchen door, Lauren heard the blare of a football game. Still in her boots, she strode to the hall. The briefcase stood exactly where she'd left it, and she sighed with relief. She glanced into the living room. The couch was empty, and the blanket was on the floor.

"Luis, where are you?" Fear tickled the back of her neck as she strode to her bedroom and flipped open her cell phone to call the police. Then she heard the toilet flush.

Quickly Lauren returned to the hall and put the map back into the briefcase. By the time the bathroom door swung open, she had hung her parka on the coat tree, removed her boots, and was combing her hair in front of the tiny hall mirror.

"Lauren? I'm glad you're back." Luis's voice was stronger.

"I have our lunch. How do you feel?" She turned in time to watch him look at her.

"Wow." His eyes glistened in the dim light as he leaned his shoulder against the kitchen doorjamb. He raised his eyebrows and grinned.

She put the bag of sandwiches down on the chair. "Here, let me help you back to the couch."

"Okay." He draped his arm so his hand fell on her breast. "I've been thinking, public relations expert, that a person could make a giant dictionary out of the words that describe your beautiful body."

Lauren laughed and drank in his warmth. "Where did you learn to say such things?" She settled him on the couch, and he reached for her face.

"Your cheek is hot."

"I turned the heat way up in the car. You're better."

He whispered into her ear. "All better."

She fetched the lunches and set them on the coffee table next to the napkins. "Want something to drink?"

"Water's fine." He sat up and took a huge bite. He grinned at Lauren with leaf of lettuce clinging to his lower lip. "Thanks. I needed this." He waved his hand around her living room. "All of this, you included."

Again, the man surprised her. He had told her in many different ways that he enjoyed her company and her body, which both delighted and scared her. There was always something he held back, something about the map or the men who attacked him, that made her suspicion grow along with her desire.

When he finished both halves of his sandwich and his cup of soup, he pulled her onto the couch next to him. "What were you doing all that time? I missed you."

"The deli was short-handed. Does your head feel better?"

His fingers found her bra clasp and unhitched it. "It's better when I'm touching you."

"Even with a concussion, you have the fastest hands in the city."

"But I can be slow when I need to...wait. Let's get rid of all this."

"My clothes? I don't think so. You should rest."

Luis smiled with his eyes half closed. "The doctor recommends sex as therapy."

"For you or for me?"

"Good question."

"You should lie down, Luis. I'll rub your, um, your forehead again." She watched him pretend to close his eyes. "You're faking."

"Keep rubbing. Your hand is nice, but don't think I'm giving up."

"On what?"

"On making love to you before I go."

She laughed. "I'm not giving up either. Sleep now and answer questions later."

When he seemed to fall asleep, Lauren searched her bookcases for the Bible her grandfather had given her and finally found it in the stack of unshelved books in her closet.

The passage in Psalms read, "You are my hiding place; you will protect me from trouble and surround me with songs of deliverance."

If the passage was the key to the map, it sure didn't unlock anything in her mind. She still needed to find out more about the map itself. As long as Luis claimed ignorance, the job wasn't going to be easy.

Lauren turned down the volume on the Packer game and settled into the easy chair with the Bible in her lap. Questions swirled through her head. Luis's voice penetrated her dreams.

"Lauren, come sleep next to me."

His droopy eyes drew her to him. She slid under the blanket and snuggled against him spoon style.

"Can you tell I'm better?" His voice was a low growl.

"I'm trying not to."

He pressed against her. "That only makes me work harder, you know?"

"I need some answers, Luis."

"Uh-oh. True confessions?"

"You could call it that."

"I admit I've had other women."

Lauren tried not to laugh. "That's self-evident."

"Your turn."

"This is not about sexual histories. This is about your situation."

107

"I'm not married. Never have been."

"Probably never will be either, but you know what I'm talking about."

"I thought I did."

He pressed his mouth to her ear and set a bomb off in her head with his tongue. He began to move in a tantalizing rhythm while Lauren kissed his neck, his chin, and then his mouth. When he knelt over her to remove her shirt, she slid off the couch.

"What's wrong now?"

Lauren pulled her shirt back down and crossed her arms in front of her as she recovered her breath. "First I need some answers."

Luis flopped on his back and frowned. "That's blackmail." He sat up and reached for her, but she shook off his hand. "Okay, what do you want to know?"

"I told you someone's been watching me. When I went to the car today, I saw a truck in the alley, but it drove off."

Luis covered his face with his hands. "You think it has something to do with me."

Lauren turned away from him, walked to the armchair, and sat down. "I do."

"Did you get a look at them?"

"No. Tell me more about last night."

Luis hung his hands between his legs. "The guy who called me said he was my upstairs neighbor. He said he heard someone in my apartment and called the police."

"Do you know this neighbor?"

Luis closed his eyes. "No."

"And it turned out it wasn't him anyway?"

Luis shook his head. "The guy must be out of town. No one answered his door or phone, and his mail box is bulging."

"Okay. Keep going."

"I was an idiot, okay? I fell for it. I went home,

expected the cops to be there, and they weren't. I thought that maybe the intruders had already left. That was stupid too. They jumped me as soon as I opened the door."

"Two men again?"

"I think so. I heard them talking after they hit me, but before I blacked out."

"They were speaking Spanish?" He was hiding something, but why?

Luis leaned on his knees and shook his head. "Maybe."

"They must have been the same men who attacked you in the garage. Tell me, Luis, what's going on?"

"Lauren, it was dark and they were busy beating me up. It was hard to pay attention to small details." He bent his head toward his lap. "I don't want to think about it anymore."

"What do you have that these people want so much?"

He threw his hands up and let them fall. "I'm a poor college professor. All I own are books, an ancient television set, and a great set of Cuban CDs." He tipped sideways, stretched out on the couch, and adjusted the pillow under his head. "I could use more ice in this ice pack."

"In the parking garage you told them you didn't have what they wanted. You must have known what it was."

"Where'd you hear that?"

"I was there that night, remember? They called you 'primo,' cousin in Spanish, and said they were going to mess up your face."

He rolled his eyes and flopped back against the pillow. "The woman didn't tell me she speaks Spanish."

"So, were they your cousins?"

"I've never seen those men before in my life."

"Yeah, right."

"You don't believe me?"

"You tell me what they were after, Luis, and then I'll believe."

"I feel really weird, Lauren. Maybe I should close my eyes again."

Lauren suspected Luis of exaggerating to escape more questions. While he slept, she tried to watch the rest of the football game, but gave up, turned it off and closed her eyes to consider what she should do.

She woke up with a jolt. The couch was empty. She heard water running and the sound of Luis singing in German.

"What is that awful noise?" she said as she entered the bathroom.

Luis clanked open the shower door, stepped out. A puddle formed on the tile floor. "Like what you see? It's all yours for a simple down payment." He grinned. Lauren handed him a towel. Instead of wrapping it around his waist, he wound it around his head. "It's called 'Drink, Drink, Little Brother Drink.' My college roommate always sang that when he was drunk. By the way, your shower is great."

"You look nice that way."

"Aha. The ice queen thaws."

"Here, let me dry your back."

"I have a better idea. Join me." He turned the shower back on, helped Lauren out of her clothes, and pulled her into the shower with him. "Now that's a perfect outfit," he said as the water streamed over them.

Lauren kissed his mouth, chin, neck, and belly, until he stopped her and did the same to her. Once they finished lathering each other, the water heater gave up.

Luis groaned. "It's getting cold in here."

"And soapy. Hurry and rinse off, and we'll run to

my bed."

"Didn't know you had one."

"It has a mattress and everything."

****

After they made love, Lauren dozed and awoke with Luis staring at her.

"These are amazing, Lauren."

"What's amazing?"

"Your thighs. They're so smooth, they're amazing."

"You say that word a lot, Luis."

"What word? Amazing? Before I met you I never knew the word."

"Sure."

"No kidding. You are, I can't think of the perfect word."

"Amazing?"

"Yep."

"How's your head?"

"Ask me about another body part."

"I already know the answer."

"I like it here in your warm bed."

"Me too, except for one thing."

"What?"

"You got my sheets wet."

"Not my fault. You walked in on me in the shower. Quite rude."

Lauren wished she could save that perfect moment of peace and satisfaction.

"Lauren?"

"Hmm?"

"Why does that sound happen at the exact moment I decide never to move again?"

"Oh, my phone?"

"Yep."

When Lauren got off the phone, Luis was fully dressed and leaning in his usual spot against the doorjamb in the hall. "So, Rocky's on his way?" His voice was flat.

Lauren nodded, feeling glad at how sad Luis looked. "He just got tickets for the Bucks game. I could tell him I'm sick."

"Is that a lie?"

"Well, technically I do feel different."

"You should." Luis combed his fingers through her hair. "I'm sorry I've made trouble for you." He kissed the top of her head. "I don't know who the men are, or what they want, but it will all be over soon, anyhow."

"How do you know that?" When he squeezed her tightly, his arms felt so strong she could almost believe him.

"Even if they're after me, and I can't understand why anyone would be, when I leave town tomorrow, this'll stop. I don't get back until the end of January, after the class trip. Six weeks is a long time to be away from you. At least I'll know you won't be with Rocky all that time."

Lauren kissed the spot on Luis's neck where she could see his pulse and touched the fuzzy edge of his ear. "Are you jealous of Rocky?"

"No." Luis shook his head and twisted his mouth. "Why would I be jealous of a six foot three pile of muscle?"

Lauren chuckled. "Luis, there's something I haven't told you."

He smoothed her lower lip with his thumb. "Whatever it is, forget it. You don't have to tell me."

"It's not what you're thinking."

Luis's finger crossed her lips. "Never mind, Lauren." He brushed her hair off her forehead with his warm fingers. "Every moment with you has been a surprise. I like it that way."

Luis kissed her again, and a wave of warmth rolled over her. She felt safe and far away from thieves and stalkers, bills and annoying clients.

When he squeezed her to his chest, her bargain with Enid faded out of her worry zone.

"Phone service down there stinks, but I'll call you when I get off the plane in Mexico City and every chance I get after that." He touched her hair again for a moment. "Thanks for taking care of me."

For a long time after Luis left, Lauren stood at the top of the stairs in nothing but her bathrobe and wished he would come back to make love to her once more. In case it might be the last time.

Chapter Nine

After Rocky found a space in his favorite parking lot, they merged with the crowd crossing the street to the Bradley Center. "This should be a good game, Lauren. Miami's in first place, and we beat 'em last time we played."

Lauren had to stretch her stride to keep up with Rocky as he zigzagged around the crowd, through the entrance, up the escalator, and straight to the concessions line.

"Talk about a perfect day. Football all afternoon, then I get to watch basketball with you. Want a hot dog with your beer?"

The game began with ten straight points by Miami, and Milwaukee was behind by eighteen after the first quarter. By half time Miami had scored four three-pointers in a row and Rocky had screamed so much he could barely talk. Luckily, he was too cranked up to notice Lauren's distraction. She had to figure out how to deal with Rocky, Enid, and Luis all together at the dig site in Mexico.

Being Luis's lover posed a serious risk to her entire way of life. Given his reputation, Luis might break it off at any time, like brushing away a spider web. He could even simply disappear, never call her, never show up at her door again.

Lauren tried to picture herself calling him on the phone and telling him the affair was over, so she could get on with her old life, her old, stale, joy-free life. She'd have to do that by phone. She would never be able to look into his eyes or even touch his hand without wanting him, all of him.

Safe out? There wasn't one.

Her mind went back and forth as fast as the players traded baskets. If Luis actually called her from Mexico, that would be a sign he cared for her. That would also be the time to tell him she was going on the class trip.

How would Luis feel about her showing up at his dig site, where he worked and studied? Perhaps her arrival would mess up his arrangement with some other woman, a mortifying thought.

During the second half of the Bucks game, as the home team caught up and tied the game, she made a decision. If Luis didn't call before he left for Mexico, she'd know the weekend with him had been nothing more than a fling, despite his sweetness, his teasing, and his tantalizing, yet gentle touch.

If Luis didn't call at all, at least then she might never have to tell Rocky about her relationship with another man and they could remain friends.

During a time-out in the third quarter, she started to ask Rocky if he'd signed up yet for the class trip to Mexico, but caught herself. Rocky presented another challenge. She had postponed telling him she was going along, too, until she'd figured out the Luis situation. After the game ended in a raucous overtime defeat, Lauren realized she hadn't said more than ten words to Rocky the whole game, and he hadn't noticed.

While Rocky grumbled all the way to the car, she nodded sympathetically, thinking her life would be much easier if she could figure out an excuse to get out of her agreement with Enid.

Her next trick was to say goodnight to Rocky without having to wrestle out of another round of kisses. As soon as they pulled up in front of her building, Lauren yawned, patted his hand, and opened the car door. "Thanks, Rocky." She stepped out and stretched. "It was an exciting game."

Rocky clicked off his seat belt and reached for the hem of her coat, but missed. "Wait, I'll come up for a few minutes."

She waved him off. "That's okay. I'm tired, and I've got a ton of work to do tomorrow."

"At least let me walk you to the door."

"I'll be fine." She let the car door slam behind her.

Rocky lowered the passenger window. "I'll wait here until you turn on the living room light."

Lauren hurried to unlock the outer door and took the stairs two at a time. At the top of the stairs, she couldn't comprehend what she saw. Her apartment door stood ajar, and a body was spread-eagled, face down on the floor in a pool of blood.

She screamed. It wasn't a body. It was Ken. She recognized his Army jacket. She bent down and touched him. His chalky-gray face was as cool as her porcelain sink, and she cried out again.

Red-brown blood spread out beneath his unzipped jacket. Despite her repulsion, her fingers moved to touch his wrist. No pulse. His neck was still, his temple too. The outside door banged below as she pulled out her cell phone and punched 911.

"Lauren!" Rocky called up the stairs. "Was that you screaming?" Rocky bounded up to the landing.

"Ken's been beaten or shot or something," she yelled into her phone. "My address?" Lauren looked up at Rocky. "Rocky, what's my address?"

"Holy shit!" Rocky stood next to her. "It's Ken. Is he dead?"

"I don't know. Wait, they're asking me stuff."

"Give it to me." Rocky took the phone from her.

"Yes. Okay, 1063 East Ogden." He touched Ken gently. "No. No pulse. Blood looks dark. Could be. You're right. Okay. We're leaving the building now. Come on, Lauren." He led Lauren down the stairs to the car.

"We should do a tourniquet or something. Where are we going?"

"Get in the car."

"But it's Ken."

"Get in the car, Lauren!"

Once they were back in the Hummer, Rocky locked the doors and hugged her tightly. "We had to get out of there, Lauren, until the police come."

"Because someone could still be in there?" Lauren felt her body go cold, and she began to shiver.

"Right."

"The bloody footprints went into the kitchen."

"Yep."

"And you think Ken is...what?"

He shook his head. "Sorry, Lauren," he whispered as she cried on his shoulder.

The police car and the ambulance pulled up behind Rocky's car. Two patrolmen got out with guns drawn and crept up the front stairs. Another squad drove around to the alley. The paramedics soon followed.

****

It was after midnight when Rocky ushered Lauren into his parents' guest room and brought her some tea. He sat on the bed with her and held her hand until she told him she'd be okay. He waited while she went to the bathroom to put on one of his mother's nightgowns and climbed back into the cold bed.

"I haven't worn a nightgown since I was ten." She tasted the salty tears as they dribbled off her cheek.

Rocky frowned and rubbed the top of her head as if she were one of his dogs and then pulled the blankets up to her chin. He disappeared for a few minutes and returned with a glass of water and one

of his mother's sleeping pills. He sat on the bed
again and held her until she started breathing easily
and her head grew heavy.

After he turned out the light, he stood in the
doorway. "Lauren, want me to sleep on the other
bed?"

"How far away is your room?"

"Next door."

"So you'll hear me if I call?"

"Of course."

"I'm glad I can count on you," she whispered as
tears choked her voice.

Once he had closed the door, she prayed she
hadn't caused Ken's murder. She swallowed the pill.

****

Before Lauren even got out of the car in front of
the apartment building, both Enid and Julie called
to her from the open doorway.

"Lauren," Enid cooed with her hands fluttering
beneath her chin. "Are you all right? We were—"

"Frantic," Julie finished as she pulled Lauren
from Rocky's grasp and guided her into the office.
"Can I get you some coffee? Rocky, how about a cup
for you too?"

"Rocky has to go to work," Lauren said as she
unzipped her coat and kicked off her boots.

"I do, but if you need me, Lauren—"

"We'll take care of her, Rocky." Enid waved her
hand toward the door. "You can go now."

Julie grimaced, her eyes glinting with anger. "I
thought you had a hair appointment, Enid."

Enid rolled Julie's desk chair over to where
Lauren was standing. "Sit down, dear, and tell us
about our poor Ken. Why do you suppose he had the
courage to challenge those villains?"

Lauren wanted to cover her ears and make it all
go away. "I have to take off my coat, Enid."

"Right." Enid bustled over to the coat stand

where her giant fur hung and fetched Lauren a hanger. "What happened?"

Julie stood in front of Lauren with her arms crossed. "Maybe Lauren would like some time to herself."

In the end, Rocky was the one who described the night before, giving the facts like a reporter, and then rushed away to deliver Lauren's groceries to her apartment.

Julie's eyes grew so wide, Lauren felt she could see her soul. "So the paper had it wrong? They didn't catch the perps?"

Lauren didn't answer. She concentrated on not thinking about the perps and what they did to Ken.

"Are you sure they didn't steal anything?" Julie looked around the office. "Maybe they came in the office first. If so, they weren't after the computers."

Lauren glanced around too. "Last night I couldn't tell if anything was missing. There was too much blood." Rocky's mother's pancakes churned in her stomach.

Rocky poked his head into the office. "You need anything, Lauren, before I leave?"

Lauren got up and hugged Rocky so long he was the one to break free. "Thanks for taking care of me, Rock."

Enid strolled over and patted both of them. "Lauren, you need plenty of water after such a frightening experience."

"Right. I'll get it," Rocky said and headed back up the stairs.

Lauren stood in the doorway and watched him for a moment and then turned to Julie. "Don't let me forget this: the police said they'd be back today to talk to me. I'm supposed to check if anything's disturbed."

Enid played with the pearls around her neck. "Did the police conclude that Ken interrupted a

119

robbery?" Her eyes lit up, as if she were seeing a scene from a movie, and Lauren wondered if she was already crafting phrases for a ghoulish poem on death.

"I guess so." Lauren choked up.

"I see, dear, and what was Ken doing here at that hour?"

"Enid, lay off. Lauren doesn't want to talk about this anymore."

Lauren reached for Julie's hand. "It's okay, Julie. I need to figure it out too." She settled into her desk chair and sighed. "Ken called me yesterday about noon, I guess. Oh, gosh, I can't even remember what he said he needed to buy. He wanted me to reimburse him for whatever it was. Then he said he'd be back to salt the walks and do some plowing." She stopped and covered her face. "It's because of me this happened."

Rocky reentered the office and stared at the floor as he handed her the glass of water. "Dad says to let him know if he can do anything for you, Lauren. He meant it too."

"Thanks, Rocky." Lauren stood up and hugged him. "Your family has been great."

Enid grabbed Lauren's elbow and edged her body between Lauren and Rocky. "After all this, think how good it will be for you to get away on the archeological dig with me."

Rocky took two steps toward the door before he spun around. "What a minute, Lauren. You're going on a dig too?"

"Didn't you know?" Enid said and lifted one eyebrow. "I've been invited as a special guest on Professor Jerome's research project in Mexico. Lauren has agreed to sign on as my assistant. At quite a good salary, I must add."

Rocky frowned at Lauren and shook his head.

Julie's eyes flitted between Rocky, Enid, and

Lauren, and finally settled on Lauren. "Weren't you going to tell Enid you couldn't go?"

"Of course she's going." Enid's lips shriveled into a crinkled line. "It's all settled. What you may not know, Rocky dear, is that Dr. Jerome, a distinguished professor, leads a group of students each year on a research trip to the Yucatan Peninsula. It should be quite an experience for both of us."

"I do know about it, Dr. Godwin, because I signed up for that trip too. Dad gave me the check to drop off this morning." Rocky's eager eyes softened as he turned to Lauren. "How come you didn't tell me you were going?"

Lauren looked up at Enid's towering figure and shook her head. "I can't go on the dig, Enid. Especially now, with all this to deal with." Lauren waved her hand toward the stairs.

Enid pressed her shoulders back and glared. "Lauren, I'm counting on your help, and it's too late to change any of those plans. Besides, I've already paid for the arrangements."

"I'm sorry, Enid. We can straighten all this out later. It's gotten pretty complicated."

Julie coughed. "I'll say."

Lauren reached for the doorknob to her office and held up her other hand. "Thanks for everything, everybody. I need to be alone for awhile."

After Lauren closed the door behind her and clicked on her computer, she heard the threesome interrupting each other like squabbling children. Before her email appeared on her screen, she heard Julie usher the other two out of the office.

Lauren stared at the screen, seeing nothing. Then she reached for the phone book and flipped through the pages.

"Can I help?" Julie's face appeared in the crack of the door.

Lauren nodded. "I need Ken's daughter's phone number. I have to call her."

"Isn't she in the book?"

"I just can't seem to find it. Her name is Cindy Hughes. She lives in Whitefish Bay."

Julie took up the book and paged through it. "Here it is."

"Thanks, Julie."

"Anything else?"

"Are they gone?"

Julie sighed. "Yes."

"Any phone calls?"

Julie shrugged. "Reporters called. I told them you weren't going to talk to them. Oh, and there was a wrong number, someone speaking a foreign language. The guy sounded like he was in an echo chamber."

"Come back in after I talk to Cindy, okay?"

Lauren punched in the numbers. When the line clicked over to voice mail, she left a message to call her back.

Julie reappeared. "She didn't answer?"

"Just think how Ken's daughter must feel."

Julie reached into her voluminous skirt for a tissue and dabbed her eyes. "How long has it been since she and Ken spoke to each other?"

"A couple of years, maybe. Such a waste."

Lauren tried three times to read her notes for one of the annual reports due just after New Year's, when the phone rang in the outer office. A minute later Julie tapped on her door.

"A policeman is on his way over here to help you make a list of any missing belongings."

"I didn't think anything was missing."

"You don't look good, Lauren. Want me to stay with you when he comes?"

Lauren nodded. "I saw people hanging around outside. Is it normal to gawk at murder scenes?"

"The story made big headlines this morning."

"If everyone knows about it, why the hell hasn't Luis called?"

Julie looked surprised. "You haven't heard from him?"

"No. He was supposed to leave for Mexico today. He said he'd call to say goodbye. Can you look up his number at the University for me?"

"You don't have it?"

Lauren shook her head and shrugged. "I didn't need it. He just kept showing up here."

"Wait. I have it, remember, from the first time he called?"

"You said he didn't give it to you so I couldn't cancel his visit."

Julie grinned. "I lied." She left and bobbed back quickly to hand Lauren the number. "Here, can I listen in?"

"No!"

After Lauren had spoken to the department secretary, Julie was back. "That was quick."

"He left early this morning. He might have tried to reach me while I was at Rocky's, but I never gave him my cell number." Lauren plunged her face into her hands. "I'm such a fool."

"About Luis?"

"The whole weekend meant nothing to him."

"You were together the whole weekend?" Julie slid her left hip onto the corner of Lauren's desk and sighed.

"Friday night, Saturday night, and then Sunday afternoon."

"Wow. Lauren, are you thinking that the guys who beat up Luis are the ones who killed Ken?"

"Yes."

"But, why?"

"I think they broke in here looking for Luis, or for his mysterious briefcase. Remember, I told you about the old map he had. Oh, no!" Lauren bumped past Julie, ran into the hall, and dashed up the stairs to her apartment. "What do you bet they stole my bag?"

Lauren bounded through the door with Julie right behind her.

"On Sunday I hung the bag right there on the coat tree when I returned from the pharmacy. Luis was in the bathroom, so I took the chance to sneak the original back into his briefcase and left my copy in my black faux Kate Spade bag."

"Your copy of what?"

"Of his map."

"You put it in the bag I gave you for your birthday?"

Lauren frowned. "Yeah, that one, and it's gone." Lauren braced herself with the doorjamb to keep her knees from shaking.

"Was your wallet in there?"

"No, I took that with me to the Bucks game."

"Where was Ken when you got here?"

Lauren pointed to the doorway. "Right there. See the stain?"

The doorbell rang. "It's probably the police, Lauren," Julie said. "I'll let them in."

****

Sergeant Blank's expression matched his name as he stood on the spot where Ken had died and took a pen and a notebook from his pocket. The policeman looked too young to get into a bar, much less to catch a thief, and too sleepy to ask more than one question an hour. While Lauren and Julie checked closets, bookshelves, walls and Lauren's jewelry box, he made notes.

Nothing valuable was missing. As she told the Sergeant, she had nothing a thief would want. No cash, no drugs, and no electronics, except for her two computers and two ancient televisions. Even her

MP3 player still sat on the kitchen counter next to the landline phone.

The only item the perps had stolen was her bag.

"What do you think happened, Sergeant?" Lauren asked.

The policeman put his notebook away before he responded. "Well, it's obvious the thieves were interrupted soon after they broke in. You see here where they broke the lock." He flicked a glance at Julie for confirmation, and she nodded. "We surmise there were two of them, because of the two sets of footprints on the floor there." He pointed with his pen.

"Ken followed them in, and they killed him," Lauren said.

The man nodded. "Shot him in the chest with a .45 semi-automatic. Just one shot, but it did the job. None of the neighbors were home. No one else heard or saw anything unusual."

Lauren shivered with the image of Ken yelling at the intruders, following them up the stairs, and then being murdered right there in her hall.

Julie touched Lauren's shoulder. "Here, Lauren, why don't you lie down for a few minutes?" Julie took Lauren's hand and led her to the couch. "Are you finished, sergeant?"

"Just need a list of what was in the bag that is missing."

"Okay. You promise not to give us any more details about people getting shot, and we can do that, right, Lauren?"

Lauren nodded. "Just the usual stuff: make-up, Kleenex, pens, a paper I copied at Kinko's. That's it."

"No wallet, right?" the sergeant asked. "House keys? Car keys? Jewelry? Check book? Cell phone?"

"Nope, I had my wallet, keys and phone with me," Lauren said and turned her face to the back of the couch.

"And this paper? What was that?"

Lauren closed her eyes and hoped the man would skip to another topic.

"Ms. Richmond, you'd be surprised how a small thing like a piece of paper in a suspect's trash might convict a guy."

Lauren sat up and leaned over her knees for a moment. "Yes, okay, well, I had a copy of an old drawing with colorful designs on it."

"I see," the policeman said as he wrote in his notebook. "So, can you describe it?"

"Sure." Lauren was pleased with herself for concocting a lie very close to the truth. "It had a drawing of a bluish serpent with red tongues, lots of bloody red tongues."

As soon as the door closed behind the policeman, Julie stared at Lauren until she made eye contact. "Lauren, why would someone kill Ken for a picture of a serpent with bloody red tongues?"

That evening back in her own bed with Julie as her roommate, Lauren told her everything she knew and suspected about Luis and his map. Sitting cross-legged on the bed, Julie listened silently, nodding, and looking thrilled one minute and alarmed the next.

"Should I tell the police I think the robbers were after the copy of the map?"

"You don't know anything for sure, and it would just get Luis in even more trouble, so, I think not." Julie patted Lauren's hand. "Boy, I never thought I'd say this, Lauren, but you lead a really exciting life." She flopped onto her stomach and rested her chin on her knuckles. "Wish I could be there when all of you get to that dig site, wherever the heck it is."

An hour later, with Julie snoozing in the other bed, Lauren battled her sleeping pill long enough to draw a rough copy of the map from memory, just in case it might give her a clue to the trouble chasing

Luis.

Around midnight the phone rang. Confused, Lauren let it ring until it stopped. When she remembered the call the next day, she checked the message, but music and static muffled the voice—another prank call.

Chapter Ten

The plane from Chicago landed in Mexico City, and Lauren, Enid, Rocky, and the rest of the students filed out of the airport into the searing afternoon sun and zigzagged through a gigantic parking lot to a dusty, blue mini-bus. After they loaded their checked bags in the undercarriage, the travel rep, Alexa Vonk, handed each of them a bag lunch and their room assignments for their one-night stay in Mexico City, and all fifteen travelers climbed aboard the hot bus. Luis was not at the airport. Nor was he waiting to greet them as they climbed on the bus.

Still groggy after her nap on the plane, Enid insisted Lauren sit next to her in the front seat behind the driver. When Ms. Vonk explained she needed that seat, Enid elbowed Lauren to the back. While Ms. Vonk narrated the city tour, Lauren rested her forehead against the window.

Lauren felt a thump on her seat and turned to find Rocky next to her. "Wish they'd crank the air conditioning," he said. "Aren't you dying from the heat?" He elbowed her. "Hey, you look sad."

"I was thinking about Ken's funeral."

"You sure said nice things about him. He would have liked that."

"He died because of me."

"Come on, Lauren. He died because someone broke into your place. You didn't kill him." He put his arm around her. "You needed this vacation. You barely took Christmas off."

"Dinner with your family was nice."

Rocky let his arm fall to his side and rolled his eyes. "If you can tolerate Gramma Jean asking you why you're not married with five kids."

"Your mom was sweet to me."

"Not Dad, though."

Lauren shrugged. "He thinks I'm after you."

Rocky patted her knee. "Dad doesn't understand what you mean to me." He touched his lips to her hair and inhaled. "I hope someday you will."

Guilt blipped in her chest. "We're good friends, Rocky. Just good friends."

Rocky pulled her hand onto his lap. "I'll settle for that."

Lauren left her hand on his very firm thigh and thought of Luis. Despite her vow to ignore the urges of her body, every day she yearned for Luis's hands on her breasts in her shower, for his kisses on her lips in the hall, and for his face next to hers on her pillow. Even grief couldn't drive away his image, or the absence of phone calls for the last five weeks.

Her hand rode on Rocky's thigh even after the bus veered around a corner and into a blaring mass of gridlock.

"I have to tell you something, Lauren." Rocky squeezed her hand and gave her a slow smile. "Originally, I was doing this for you, you know, signing up for this class. Not just for Dad. I know I'm not smart enough for you."

"That's ridiculous. Are you saying I'm a snob?"

"No, that's not what I meant." He swallowed and looked past her out the window. "You need a man who can talk about something besides cars and football."

"You and I have a perfect friendship. We balance each other."

He gave her a lop-sided grin. "You think so? Well, anyhow, I'm glad I signed up for this trip, and having you come too is like hitting a three-point shot. Think how much we're going to learn about the history of this country. Today we see Teotihuacán, and tomorrow the rain forest."

Beneath her hand, his thigh tightened. Lauren cast a glance at his tight T-shirt and jeans, his biceps bulging below his sleeves, his muscular forearm next to hers, and wondered what Rocky would be like as a lover. Shy and gentle, perhaps. She noted the intensity of his blue eyes, the comb marks in his close-cropped hair. Every woman who met him thought he was sexy and handsome. Every woman except her.

"Too bad we don't have time to go to Chichen-Itza. Lauren, did you know the Mayans knew so much about the movement of the sun, they built a pyramid so that on a certain day every year, the snakes on the stairs move as the sun rises? Cortez and his men couldn't have understood how advanced they were. They even knew how to record their history."

"You've done the class reading."

"Are you impressed?" He dropped his hot hand onto her thigh.

"I am." Lauren closed her eyes.

"Are you going to sleep again?"

"I have a headache. My ears keep popping. I think it's the altitude."

After an hour's ride through Mexico City, they arrived at the ruins of Teotihuacán and divided into small groups to tour the site. Enid immediately linked up with the youngest guide and battered him with questions. Lauren, Rocky and several other students tagged along.

The grand plaza spread out before them, as broad and flat as an airport runway. Along the sides were small pyramids and many low, flat structures with walls shaped like steps. The famous Pyramids of the Moon and the Sun loomed above the rest. Green hills rose beyond the layers of stone and gradually vanished into a haze of pollution and pale sky.

The guide spoke as they walked. "Here, just fifty kilometers northeast of la Ciudad de Mexico stands the remnant of a great culture. At one time, the city covered at least eleven square miles where 150,000 people lived. There's still more to discover, as archeologists debate who founded Teotihuacán.

"For five hundred years this region thrived. Artisans and merchants traded goods with cities throughout Central America. Museums all over the world exhibit the fine pottery unearthed here. As we stroll, I want you notice how the ceremonial center is laid out like a butterfly on either side of the Avenue of the Dead. Follow me now to the Palace of the Jaguar."

Lauren started off again behind Enid, until Rocky grabbed her hand. "Come on. Let's break away and climb a pyramid."

"Later, Rocky. Don't you want to hear more about the history?"

"Sure, but what if we run out of time?"

"I have to stick with Enid. You go ahead, and I'll try to meet you either at the foot of the Pyramid of the Sun or at the bus." While the guide and Enid studied a wall of carvings, Lauren watched Rocky lope across the plaza.

"The earliest building dates to 200 B.C. The Pyramid of the Sun goes back to 100 A.D. Archeologists believe many of these structures were luxurious homes of wealthy residents." The guide pointed toward the walls. "Note the rows of carvings along here. In this culture, the serpent was a god. See how the serpents' crowns are carved into curling feathers? You see there, traces of red and green paint? And those empty eyes? They once held jewels.

Imagine, jewels the size of golf balls."

Enid waited until Lauren and the other stragglers caught up. "Did you look at the teeth on the jaguar?" Enid said. "The carving is exquisite even after all these years."

Though it was nearly four o'clock, the sun had grown hotter. At the foot of the Pyramid of the Moon Lauren took a long drink from her water bottle and squinted up the steps, but didn't spot Rocky.

"As you see, the upper steps are even steeper than this first level, which makes the climb quite a challenge." The guide demonstrated his point by shinnying himself up onto the first platform and encouraged the rest to join him. Lauren scraped her shin when she pulled herself up. Eventually the other students scrambled up there too, all but Enid.

"Señora Enid, you must come too." The guide hopped down next to her.

Enid shook her head.

"No. You must come." The guide bent down and offered his knee for her to use. One of the students jumped down to help, and together they lifted Enid onto the platform.

"I'm going all the way to the top," another student yelled as he crawled up to the next level. "See you at the bus."

At the Feathered Serpent Pyramid, the guide glanced at his watch and warned them if they wanted to climb the Pyramid of the Sun before the bus departed, they should set out for it right away. With Enid in the good hands of the guide, Lauren gazed again at the towering edifice at the end of the plaza and knew she had to reach the top to take in all of Teotihuacán from its highest point.

Near the temple, Lauren began to feel like an ant on a sidewalk. The sky had deepened, and streaks of white clouds faded into wisps. She trod along the ancient stones imagining what a thrill it must be for an archeologist to uncover the secrets of a hidden world.

Dividing the Pyramid del Sol in half, a ribbon of steep narrow steps rose to the top. Since Rocky didn't seem to be around, she began her climb. Up the layers of stone she struggled, sweat stinging her eyes and the sun's rays grilling her back. The depth of each step was half the size of her foot, so small she had to concentrate to keep from tripping. There was no handhold. If she missed a step, the tumble would be painful. Soon her intense concentration made her dizzy, and she had to give up trying to stand as she climbed. Instead, she followed the lead of other climbers ahead of her, and scrambled up on her hands and feet.

The back of her T-shirt was soaked. Her throat felt like gravel. She didn't dare stop to sip from the water bottle in her bag until she reached the top. The view would be her reward.

At the pinnacle, Lauren was transformed. She was a bird, queen of the world and a god peering down on her creation, awed by the patterns of the ancient courtyard, by the precisely shaped constructions and by the miniature humans below. Beyond in all directions the earth spread as vast as the sky, and she owned the sky.

The platform at the top was large enough for a hundred people to stand. Clustered in the corners were a half-dozen tourists clicking their cameras and puffing from the heat. A dry, dusty wind lifted her cap, but her ponytail kept it from sailing off. She took a long drink from her water bottle and sat down on the highest step to catch her breath and check her watch. She had half an hour to get back to the bus.

"Ah, señorita, you like what's left of our temple?"

Lauren jumped at the low voice. "Si, yes. It's beautiful." A man glowered down at her, his shadow spilling across Lauren's face.

"You feel the ghosts?" The stranger's grin revealed yellow teeth beneath his bushy mustache. His tiny stone-black eyes made her shiver.

Below, a hawk screamed.

"Ghosts?"

"The ghosts of those chosen for sacrifice. Think, Señorita, if you had been up here on this temple one thousand five hundred years ago, you would have been one of them." He squatted suddenly, and the sun blinded her.

"And people say they miss the good old days." She tried to laugh, but the man's face loomed uncomfortably near. His breath was hotter than the air and stank of tobacco.

Fear pricked at the back of her neck, and she leaped up to get away.

"The priest would place you in the center there." He crowded her to the edge of the step and pointed his calloused finger. "With your lovely neck exposed, he would have the honor of draining some blood before lifting out your heart."

Lauren pictured her chest slashed open and her heart wildly pumping itself dry.

The man uncoiled, stepped nimbly down two steps, and turned back to her, the sun full on his grimace. "Remember what happened to your American ambassador's wife not long ago? Such a sad story. She stood up there where those people are taking photos, you see? To surprise her, her husband sent a helicopter to pick her up on top of the Tiemplo del Sol."

"I don't want to hear this."

The man's laugh was like a cough. "The pilot miscalculated the wind, eh? The helicopter whirred and tipped, and so, the blade hit its mark. Witnesses said her head took a long time to roll down all these steps." His mouth opened wide in a toothy grin.

"Go away!" Lauren shouted and looked around to see if anyone would help her.

"I'm going." He pulled a sweat-stained cap from his pocket and slid it on his head. "I must warn you: protecting a lover requires sacrifice." His angry eyes were level with hers. "Be very careful on your descent." He saluted.

For a moment, Lauren pictured him giving her a push. "Get away from me!" she yelled. The man glanced around to see if anyone had reacted to her words, and with a shrug started back down the steps.

What did he mean? How could that horrible man know anything about her?

Lauren pretended to dig for something in her backpack until her hands stopped trembling. By the time she dared to look down the steps, the man had nearly reached the bottom, scuttling backwards like a crab.

Lauren had to escape the cloud of evil that engulfed her, away from that voice and that horrible face. She scrambled backwards down the steps on her hands and feet the way the hideous man had. Once she touched the dusty earth, Lauren didn't stop. The image of the bouncing severed head chased her the whole two hundred yards to the bus. She didn't slow down until she saw Rocky standing next to the bus pointing a camera at two giggling girls. She barged between them and into Rocky's arms.

"Whoa! Lauren, you glad to see me or something?" Rocky laughed, slid his arm around Lauren's waist, and handed the camera to one of the girls. He looked at her, and his smile faded. "What the hell's wrong?"

"There was a crazy man up there." Lauren's voice squeaked.

"Where?"

"On the pyramid. He spoke to me. The things he

said, the way he talked, I think he was one of the men who attacked Luis and broke into my apartment."

Rocky put his hands on her shoulders and frowned. "Where the hell is the guy?" Rocky gazed around the street full of buses. "I'll beat the crap out of him."

"I don't know. Oh, my God, Rocky, he could have killed me too. All he had to do was give me a push from up there."

"Here, have some of my water, Lauren. Okay, now, tell me again."

"I climbed up the, uh, big, you know."

"The Pyramid of the Sun?"

"Yes."

"Did you trip or something?"

She shook her head. "There was a man up there, a creepy man, who spoke to me. He told me girls were sacrificed up there."

"You knew that. And who's Luis?"

"The man knew things about me."

"Like what?"

She couldn't tell Rocky that the man knew about her lover, Luis. Rocky didn't even know she'd chased the muggers out of the parking garage. "He looked like the man we saw that day, Rocky, the one who was in the apartment building when we got back from our run. He sounded like him too."

"Come on, that guy had on a heavy coat. A wool hat covered half his face. We couldn't even describe him to the police. How could you recognize him here?"

"It was his voice. What he said."

"Okay, okay, just take it easy. You're fine now." Rocky brushed the hair off her face. "You're dehydrated, Lauren. It happens at this altitude. Here, we've got to get back on the bus. They're waiting for us."

Settled safely next to Rocky, Lauren had the courage to glance out the window as they pulled away. She couldn't see the hideous man anywhere, but she felt him there watching.

Back at the hotel, Rocky and Lauren stood in the lobby with Enid while the travel rep handed out room keys. Enid grabbed Lauren's hand and smiled. "Do me a favor, dear. Get my room key, take my bags up, and then bring me the key. I'll be in the bar over there beyond that check-in desk. See it? I'm meeting a few of the others for a cool drink." Without waiting for an answer, Enid squeezed through the crowd of students and strode up to the bartender.

"Hard to believe a woman her age can do that, isn't it?" Rocky grinned. "She has a harem of guys."

Just then, Ms. Vonk called Rocky's name and handed him his key. Lauren got hers and Enid's next.

"Here's what we're going to do, Lauren," Rocky said in a bossy tone Lauren had never heard before. "You sit down over there in that chair with your bag and mine. I'll take Enid's stuff to her room. Then I'll be back for our stuff."

Like a child, Lauren did as she was told. Amid the noise and busyness, she felt her stomach unclench. She rested her head on the back of the chair and closed her eyes. In what seemed like only seconds, a cold hand touched her shoulder, and she sprang up. "Rocky, you scared me!"

"Sorry, Lauren. I gave Enid her key. Come on, they're holding the elevator for us. I've got our luggage."

At the fourth floor, Lauren followed Rocky off the elevator and down the hall to the room. Rocky put Lauren's bag on a bench at the end of one bed and his on the other bench. "Room's not great, but it's all ours."

"What do you mean ours?"

"I paid extra to get a room to myself." Rocky's eyebrows arched. "I'm too old to room with strangers. I figured you can take a shower and rest here, where I can keep an eye on you, and when it's time for the group dinner, we can go down together."

"What about my roommate?"

"You can stay here until you feel safe. I don't think she'll mind having a room to herself, do you?"

"Guess not. Thanks, Rocky."

After they each took a shower, Lauren stretched out on limp sheets, and Rocky left to take a quick trek around the neighborhood.

Lauren intended to sleep, but every time she closed her eyes, she saw the man on the pyramid and heard his evil words. To distract herself, she dug her notebook out of her bag.

She had hoped the copy of Luis's map she had drawn from memory would match charts of Mayan ruins she had found on the internet, but none of the archeological sites in Mexico had a layout even close.

She flipped through pages of her notes and then back to her drawing. She assumed the blue oval on Luis's map was supposed to be a pool, maybe a sacred well, that the Mayans called a "ceñote." She'd read that there was a ceñote at the famous Chichen-Itza ruins. In the vast muck of that ancient pool, archeologists had unearthed Mayan darts with finely worked points and objects made of gold, copper, and jade. Also hidden in the silty pits were the bones of dozens of young women, proof of sacrifices just like the ones the terrible man had described.

As far as Lauren could recall, the map had no indication of a treasure or anything of value, no arrows, no X marks the spot, and no signs saying, "Dead Men Tell no Tales." For all she knew, a child had drawn the map and colored it just for fun, except for one thing: Ken had been killed for it.

Lauren flipped the pages of her notebook until she found the Bible inscription she had copied from the back of the original map. "Psalm 32: 7: You are my hiding place; you will protect me from trouble and surround me with songs of deliverance."

When she heard the door open, she pulled the covers over her papers. "Hi, Rocky."

"Souvenirs." He held up two very salty and very full Margarita glasses. "I tested one to be sure it's good enough for you."

"No thanks, Rocky. You can have it."

Rocky shook his head. "Enid says you need some fun in your life, and she ought to know." He handed her a glass and clanked his against it. "Here's to wild Mexican adventures."

Lauren took a few sips and felt the heat of the alcohol slip down her throat. "It's good. Thanks. Is Enid missing me?"

"Are you kidding? She's in the bar surrounded by guys."

"What guys?"

Rocky laughed. "Any guy who'll listen to her. Just now it was one of the Mexican guides who will be going on the plane with us tomorrow."

"What are they talking about?"

Rocky finished his drink and wiped his salty lips on his T-shirt sleeve. "She's teaching him poetry, and he's teaching her useful Spanish phrases." He laughed as he spoke.

"What's so funny about that?"

"I heard her tell him the words in English. You want to guess what her topic is?"

"Romance?"

"Sounds to me like she plans to get somebody in bed with her. Jeez, isn't she too old for that stuff?"

Lauren began to giggle and couldn't stop. "It feels good to laugh with you, Rocky."

Rocky kissed her quickly. His lips were cool and

sweet from the Margarita. When Lauren didn't push him away, Rocky kissed her again. His hot hand touched her neck and slipped down the shoulder of her thin shirt.

A buzzing noise jolted them apart. "Damn!" Rocky said. "It's the phone." He reached over and picked it up. "Yeah, okay." He hung up. "We're late to dinner. Drink up."

Chapter Eleven

Rocky carried two more margaritas as he and Lauren hurried to find two places next to each other in the small dining room. From the buffet line, Lauren glanced around the room, afraid, yet hoping to see Luis. He wasn't there. After they sat down, Alexa Vonk rose, clanked her glass, and explained the next day's travel plans. They were going to take a bus to the airport and then fly to Cancun. From there they would take a short flight on two small planes to the dig site, located along the border of Belize.

As Ms. Vonk finished speaking, the door behind her opened and Frank strolled in carrying a beer. He paused at the door and hitched up his ragged jeans. His faded shirt, Lauren noticed, hung limply off his bony shoulders.

"Dr. Jerome!" Ms. Vonk said loudly enough to silence the room. "Students, this is Dr. Frank Jerome, the head researcher at the site and professor of archeology at the University of Wisconsin-Milwaukee. He and Dr. Luis Hernandez, associate professor of archeology at the University, oversee all work on the dig site." She turned to smile at him. "Do you want to eat first, Frank, or talk first?"

"I'd better speak now, before I fall asleep. Due to the cave-in we had a few weeks ago, Dr. Hernandez was still on duty at the site when I left, and I'm not sure if he'll make it tonight." He set down his beer. "The good news is you all got this far, ready to help us uncover the secrets of a brilliant civilization that rose and fell long before the Spanish ever found their way here."

Dr. Jerome's eyes flicked from one side of the room to the other. "Our research station is surrounded by rain forest, which is an education in itself. When we get there a group of students and professors from Indiana University will join us. As you know we're going to put you to work, but first we have to teach you the basics about archeological research." He leaned his hands on the back of Ms. Vonk's chair. "Two things are of the utmost importance to all of us: your safety and the security of the artifacts. You must follow our rules to the letter. You must wear protective boots, long pants and bug repellant at all times. You must keep yourselves hydrated. That's why we asked you to pack water bottles. There will be several water sources at the dig site. Be sure to refill your bottles regularly." He bit his cheek and frowned.

"Please note: as you walk to and from the dig site, stay on the path. Rain forest plants and animals can be dangerous and deserve your respect.

"Inside our building are other dangers." He grinned. "We eat and sleep in the same building, and we hold class there each morning before we go to the dig site. The dormitories are like an Army camp with cots and bunks lined along each wall. Men on one side of the hall, and women on the other."

He scratched his head and rolled his eyes. "At this point Hernandez always says he knows it's going to be tough for some of you, but please respect the privacy of others." He looked around the table again. "Did I forget anything?"

Ms. Vonk stood. "You forgot to get your dinner, Dr. Jerome. We'll have plenty of time for questions later or tomorrow on the bus to the airport. We meet at seven sharp where the tour bus let us off this afternoon."

When Lauren heard Luis hadn't arrived, the exhaustion of the past month swamped her, and she struggled to keep from crying. She'd been hanging on, hoping for her chance to force Luis to tell her the whole truth about the map, a complete story that would also explain Ken's death. Though it might be humiliating to confront him about breaking his promise to call her, she was determined to hit him in the gut with that too.

However, if they ever had the elaborate conversation she'd been acting out in her head, one with apologies and appeals for forgiveness, she'd have to confess her offense as well. She'd have to admit she'd borrowed his map, copied it, and then lost it to the bad guys.

Lauren glanced at Rocky and felt her taco turn sour in the back of her throat. Val, the woman sitting on the other side of Rocky, was raving about her favorite rock concert, and Rocky seemed to be eager for every word. Lauren hoped her buddy would never find out about her and Luis.

Lauren picked at her refried beans and watched Dr. Jerome greet Enid with an air kiss and then head for the buffet line where he loaded his plate with enchiladas. He looked up and nodded at Lauren. Once he'd doused the pile with hot sauce, he ambled to the empty seat next to her.

"Enid's surrounded by a gallery, as usual. Mind if I sit with you?" He peered down at her as if he were counting his change.

"Go ahead." Fearful of Enid's possessive nature, Lauren glanced over to see if she'd noticed where Frank had chosen to sit, and saw her smile benignly.

Frank put his plate down, bent his long frame into the chair, and stuck out his hand. "You're Enid's associate, right? We met at that event."

Lauren nodded. "Lauren Richmond. And you're

Dr. Jerome."

"Frank, please. Aren't you also a friend of Luis?"

"Yes." She realized she'd answered too quickly. "That is, I know who he is, of course—"

Frank smiled. "Of course. All the pretty ones do."

Lauren tried to laugh at his compliment. "I met him in a parking garage."

He leaned too close to Lauren's face. "In a parking garage?" He shook his head. "That guy finds women everywhere. How'd you like Teotihuacan? Powerful architecture, wouldn't you say?"

Lauren tried to blink away the image of the repulsive man and failed. "I climbed to the top. A creepy man up there told me a woman had her head cut off by a helicopter, right there at the top of the Temple of the Sun." Frank's grin gave her stomach a jolt. "It's not true, is it?"

"Oh, yeah. It happened." He shoved his fork into his enchilada, hefted a mound of it to his mouth, and chewed for a moment. "In Mexico, death is always just over your shoulder."

Lauren leaned away from Frank's beer breath, reached for her margarita, and gulped it down. "Well. Well, so, do you think Luis will arrive tonight?"

Frank wrinkled his nose and shrugged. "He'd better. It's his job to do all this introductory stuff, not mine."

Lauren stared at him for a moment as a cheesy glob of chicken disappeared into his mouth. She turned and glanced again at the doorway. She pushed rice around her plate and wondered if Luis had met another woman since he had kissed her goodbye.

Frank slid his empty plate away and leaned back to rest his arm on the back of Lauren's chair. His smile revealed a chip of green pepper on his front tooth. "We're delighted Enid could join us over winter break. It's a true honor." He swiped his lips with his napkin, pushed his chair back, and leaned his elbow on his knee. "Between her reputation and Luis's latest PR stunt, we should get a mention in the science journals."

"PR stunt?" Lauren was shocked the professor would insult Luis. "Why do you say that?"

Frank tipped his head and lifted one eyebrow. "Luis received a grant to support his great search for the missing codex, which helps our dig site, one way, or another." He shook his head. "But I'm realistic. We're all after our own glory, and the guy is really good at scrounging a leg up on the ladder."

Lauren wanted to take her fork and skewer the cocky man's eyeball. "And you?" she said, after she chose not to stick out her tongue at him. "What ladder are you climbing?"

The man's eyes narrowed as he wiped his mouth with his paper napkin and tossed it onto his plate. "I intend to find something so spectacular I'll be famous and rich."

Lauren laughed. "Like a sarcophagus of solid gold?" Lauren waited as the man swirled his finger around his plate and then licked it.

"Indeed, that would do it; along with a golden breast plate decorated with serpents whose eyes are enormous studs of jade." His eyes sparkled.

"How about one of those stelae or steles, however you say it, covered with a Spanish translation of all the Mayan scripts and glyphs?"

"Excellent idea. I can see the headlines: 'With one tap of a shovel, the brilliant and handsome young professor solves Latin America's greatest mysteries.'"

"That could make you famous, but how would it make you rich?"

He sucked the pepper off his tooth and shook his

head. "To be famous and rich, I'd have to find something like Luis's hoax."

"You think the codex is a hoax?"

"Come on. A document that survived the flames of the Inquisition half a millennium ago?" He stood. "It sure makes a great story." He stretched and saluted. "Nice talking with you. I'm off to bed. Big day tomorrow."

Lauren stood up to follow the others out of the dining room and felt a little dizzy until Rocky grabbed her arm. "Hey, Lauren, a bunch of us are going across the street to a bar."

"You go, Rocky. I'm feeling dizzy, so I'm going to bed."

Rocky grinned. "That's the margarita talking. Okay, then I will too."

"No, I'll be fine. You go and have fun."

"Lauren, I told you I'd stay with you after your scare today, and I will."

Still feeling light-headed, Lauren took her turn in the bathroom while Rocky tried to get football scores on the television. He was grumbling about the transmission, when she climbed into one of the two double beds.

"Jeez, how do these people expect us to see anything on this piece of junk?"

"Maybe tomorrow you'll find a copy of USA Today. I'm going to sleep, Rocky, so if you want to go down to the bar, it's fine with me."

Rocky got up from the other bed and clicked off the TV. "I'd rather shower and hit the sack."

Lauren closed her eyes. She felt a little drunk, but didn't want Rocky to notice. To keep away thoughts of the man on the pyramid, she pictured herself discovering an artifact hidden for half a millennium.

She imagined a dusty cavern surrounded by the rubble of centuries. She and the other workers would be sweaty and parched as they dug in the earth. She'd read that they often used scalpels to pick gently into the earth, so she imagined herself slicing around something solid with her scalpel and lifting it out of its hiding place. The solid form revealed itself to be made of gold, and Lauren felt a rush of joy.

The glorious dream evaporated when Rocky began to bellow the University of Wisconsin fight song in the shower. She pulled her pillow over her head and tried to recapture the moment, but the harsh buzz of the phone jolted her awake and set her heart pounding. She snatched up the receiver and said hello. When no one spoke, she said it again. A man cleared his throat and breathed into the phone, in, out, in, out and then clicked off.

She leaped from the bed and ran into the bathroom. "Rocky!"

Rocky threw back the shower curtain. "What's wrong?" He reached over, turned off the water, and grabbed a towel.

"Someone called just now."

Rocky climbed out of the tub and put his arms around her. "Who was it?"

"I don't know."

"You're shaking. What'd they say?"

"Nothing. Just breathing. Rocky, I think it was the man from the pyramid."

"Come on, Lauren; let's get you back to bed."

"He knows where I am."

Rocky pulled on his boxer shorts, led her to bed, and climbed in next to her. "There's no way some weirdo on the pyramid in Mexico City knows where you are, Lauren," he whispered. "Believe me; I won't let anyone hurt you."

Rocky's body was still hot from the shower as he pulled her against his chest. Lauren could count on Rocky to be there when she needed him—she'd always been able to count on him. He began massaging her arms and then her shoulders. He kneaded her neck and her back, his firm hand inching lower, warming her flesh through to her spine. When she turned over and brushed the hair out of his eyes, he kissed her, innocently, the way he had earlier. She let the kiss ride and was surprised when his tongue slid through her teeth and his gentle fingers massaged her buttocks.

Once she closed her eyes, Luis's lips whispered to her. Luis's smile danced on her cheek. Luis's touch spread fire through her. She arched her back and moved her hips to Rocky's rhythm. Her fear turned to mist and sailed over the hills like the clouds above the pyramid. In its place grew her ache to be touched. Rocky rolled her onto her back and flipped back the covers.

"You're beautiful," he murmured as his heart thrummed against hers, their bodies moved together, and she was lost. She wanted to soar faster, higher, longer, when Rocky rose over her, moaned her name, and collapsed on top of her.

Hours later Lauren lay in the dark listening to Rocky's soft breathing. Every time she closed her eyes, she saw her own bloody head bouncing down the steps of the Temple of the Sun.

Chapter Twelve

The honk of a sick goose woke Lauren. With her nose buried in a pillow that stank of mildew, she couldn't remember where she was until she turned over on the creaking bed and found herself face to face with Rocky, the source of the honking.

She had to cover her mouth to keep from moaning. Why had she let him make love to her? Sex changed everything, ruined everything. She crept out of bed. As a sliver of dawn peeped through the flimsy drapes, she stripped off her long T-shirt, methodically repacked her suitcase, and tiptoed to the bathroom to shower and escape before Rocky awoke.

In the tepid dribble, she tried to frame her words of apology to Rocky, when she heard someone thumping on the hotel room door. She climbed out of the shower and grabbed a towel, but Rocky beat her to the door.

"Hey, you woke us up, Dr. Godwin. I guess Lauren's in the shower."

Enid barreled past him and into the bathroom. "You should have informed me you had switched rooms, Lauren. I've been trying to reach you for an hour." She shook her head, and a lock of hair flipped over one eye. "Dry yourself off and get going." She spun around and marched out of the bath. "I'm placing my key here on the desk, and then I'm going to breakfast with Carlos. Make sure my bags are on the curb next to the bus." Enid paused with her hand on the doorknob. "While I admire your spunk,

149

Lauren, remember you're working for me. From here on, you can unleash your closeted libido with a pile of muscle on your own time." She opened the door, turned and shook her head. "When, dear girl, will you learn to take charge of your life?"

After Enid slammed the door behind her, Rocky laughed. "Is she jealous you had sex with me or does she always act like that?"

Lauren pulled her T-shirt over her head and stepped into her jeans.

"And who's Carlos?"

Lauren zipped up her suitcase, grabbed her handbag, and rolled the suitcase to the door.

"Lauren? You're not sorry about last night, are you?"

Lauren turned to him and saw the old sadness in his eyes. "Enid's a bitch, Rocky. That's given. She provides my only steady income, so I button my lip. Last night was my fault. I shouldn't have let that happen." Rocky reached for her and she stepped back. "Please no, Rocky. I wanted to be your friend, not your lover. Now I've messed that up, I'm afraid, and I used you."

"That's crap, Lauren. It wasn't like that. It meant something."

"I don't want to hurt you anymore." She turned away from his sad eyes and glanced at her watch. "We have to get going. Our bags were supposed to be downstairs ten minutes ago."

Lauren was obliged to sit next to Enid in the front seat of the bus to the airport, while the perverted old broad's venomous eruption still echoed in her brain. 'Closeted libido? Pile of muscle?' One day, Lauren vowed, she'd show the woman how her cruel words drew blood.

Luckily, Enid guarded her silence too, while the group divided and boarded two small planes. Carlos the tour guide insisted Señora Enid sit next to him in the front row of the plane, which allowed Lauren to escape to the back. Seconds later Rocky slid into the seat next to her.

The plane sped up and lifted off the runway. Lauren felt Rocky's eyes on her and knew he was waiting for a chance to break into her thoughts. In hopes of dodging that moment, she concentrated on watching the world shrink below her.

"Neat plane, eh, Lauren? I've never been in one this small."

Lauren continued looking out the window.

"Nice view, hey?" Rocky's voice was tight.

Lauren nodded. The countryside grew lush, the roads disappeared, and all she could see were endless miles of trees. Not a vehicle, not even a track, interrupted the greenery. The cramp in her stomach eased. She let the seat hold her and tried to relax.

Rocky elbowed her out of her reverie. "It's a bummer there's no food. No bathroom, either."

Lauren closed her eyes so Rocky would think she was asleep. The power that surged through her body the night she scared off the muggers had astonished her. When she was with Luis, she was decisive and strong, nothing like Enid's gutless gofer. Her weakness had eroded that power. Because she'd used her body to lie to Rocky, surely they would both suffer.

Unlike the mindless moments the night before with Rocky, when Luis touched her, she throbbed with electricity. With Luis, she welcomed the sweep of emotion, the explosive peaks, and waves of her arousal. She sought pleasure and eagerly shared it.

Her breath caught at the memory and she stifled a moan. She might never feel that way again.

Down below she saw signs of civilization, two buildings along a meandering river. The pilot announced they were about to land at Gallon Jug.

Stepping off the plane was like entering a giant steam room. Every part of Lauren's body began to sweat, even her eyelids. After she peeled off her jacket, her shirt and shorts flattened against her body, and her chapped hands wicked up the moisture. Two young Mexicans in nothing but shorts and heavy boots unloaded the luggage directly onto the grass landing strip as the travelers swarmed around them.

Rocky touched her shoulder. "I'll get Enid's bags and yours too."

"No, I'll do it. Thanks anyway." She finally met his eyes.

"Lauren, what happened last night—"

She interrupted him. "We can try to be friends again, Rocky." She couldn't make herself smile. "That's what worked for us before. Just friends."

He shook his head, and she touched his arm. "Please, Rocky, try it, at least during our time here." She would have said more, but someone rammed her calves with a heavy bag, and Enid barked at her to follow with the luggage. She turned back and watched Rocky walk away, his duffle bag slung over his shoulder and his head down. With an ache in her throat, she noticed he was wearing the shirt she'd bought him for Christmas.

The landing strip in Gallon Jug was a grass path through a tangle of hacked-down jungle. A tiny Bermuda-style white clapboard cottage served as the office. Next to it was an open-air thatched-roof structure that turned out to be the waiting and baggage room.

Heat radiated from the dust right through Lauren's running shoes. Soon after she collected the bags, three vans pulled up. In the midst of the jumble of people and baggage, Carlos read off names and assigned each to a van. Lauren barely noticed her assignment or anything else but the

152

overwhelming beauty of the setting and of its history.

On their way to conquer the rest of the Yucatan Peninsula, Cortez and his rabble of gold-seeking adventurers might have set foot in the very spot where she stood. She recalled how one of the books she'd found at the library represented their conquest: "A few adventurers, barely equipped, managed to find their way to the stronghold of a fierce race, without a map, without a word of the language, and bring them down." It occurred to her that modern-day Mayans might feel the same way about the archeologists who overtook their ancient villages.

Lauren heard a shout and saw Enid waving her giant straw hat. "Over here, Lauren! We're in the first van."

As Lauren waved back, she noticed Rocky loading his bag into another vehicle. She dragged her bags over to the van and dashed back for Enid's. When she approached the second time, the man loading bags through the rear doors looked familiar.

Luis's face froze beneath his impenetrable sunglasses. "Well, if it isn't the amazing Lauren Richmond." He took off his dusty cap and swiped a bead of sweat from his forehead with the back of his arm.

He needed a shave. His nose was peeling, and his teeth gleamed against his tanned face. His name on her lips stopped Lauren's breath. "Luis."

Luis settled the cap back on his head and rested his hands on his hips. "What are you doing here?" He sounded hoarse.

"I'm Enid's assistant."

He bent over and flung another bag into the back of the van. "Tell the truth. You just couldn't let your Rocky boy out of your sight."

The man made her sound like a bratty kid.

"What do you care?" She wished she could read his eyes behind those sunglasses.

His jaw clenched. "You might have told me you were going out of town. I left you two messages." He pointed at her. "Or have you been much too busy to call back?"

"You're a liar. You never called."

He spoke through his teeth. "You're telling me you didn't get my messages?" He reached down and pitched another duffle into the van.

Lauren struggled to keep her voice low. "It's impossible to get messages by intuition."

He slammed the double doors and stepped up to her until the toes of his boots touched the toes of her running shoes. "Right now my intuition tells me your body needs something." His laugh rattled in his chest.

"You ass—"

He touched her lips with one finger and flashed a toothy grin. "Enid's holding a spot for you in front. You don't want to upset the boss."

Lauren reached for his arm, but he backed away. "Luis."

"Get in."

After Lauren stalked around to the front of the van, Enid slid out and made her sit in the middle of the front seat. Luis climbed behind the wheel and started the engine.

Lauren still felt the burn of his finger on her lips. "I have to tell you something, Luis," she whispered.

Luis showed no sign that he'd heard her. They bounced along the grass strip and onto a gravel road. Each time he shifted, his hand brushed her knee. She knew he was doing it on purpose and tried to inch away from him, but Enid's hips took up most of the space. With each bump, Luis's knee banged her leg or his elbow brushed hers. She stuffed her hands into her lap to keep herself from touching the tiny blisters on his forearm or brushing back the lock of hair that stuck to his temple.

While Luis concentrated on driving, Lauren noticed his smile lines for the first time. One knifed down the middle of his cheek. Another cupped the edge of his lip. She blocked the thought of kissing each one and glanced at Enid. Too often, the woman could read Lauren's mind, but this time Enid's eyes were on the tunnel of green ahead.

How could Luis claim he had left messages for her, when neither Julie nor she had received them? Why should she even bother to tell the bastard about the stolen copy of the map?

She watched a bead of sweat roll from his eyebrow to his cheek. She'd lick it off, if she could, just to see his reaction. On the other side of her, Enid had fallen asleep. The woman could doze through anything.

They hit a huge bump and Lauren's left hand bounced onto Luis's thigh all by itself. She bit her lips to keep from laughing.

Luis swore. "Sorry, folks. A downpour washed out the road along here this morning. Hang on." He moved the gearshift and then lifted Lauren's hand and dropped it back into her lap. "Mind your manners, Ms. Richmond."

The words Enid had said to her that morning echoed in Lauren's thoughts: take charge of your life. She sure wasn't doing a very good job of that.

Her eyes grew heavy, as her body settled against the seat. When the van hit a pothole and began to fishtail, Lauren sprang upright and braced herself on the dashboard as the front bumper narrowly missed the hulk of a fallen tree.

"Hope everyone's okay back there," Luis called. "We're nearly at the camp. When we arrive, claim your bags, and haul them up to the dormitory. Then

155

head right to the porch for refreshments. Later there'll be time to unpack and rest. At six, we'll all meet in the dining room for information and dinner."

The van turned off the track onto a narrow sand path. "Up there on the hill is the dormitory. I have to get back to the dig site right away, but I'll see you all at dinner."

Lauren spoke low. "Are you running away from me?"

Luis nodded without looking at her. "I'm scared to death of you." He steered the van toward the foot of the hill and braked. Above them, a long narrow building of wood and stone perched on a ridge surrounded by sweeping palm trees.

As soon as Luis slid out of the van and opened the back, two young men jumped up off the dorm steps and jogged down the hill to help unload the luggage. Despite the fading sunlight, the sky still held a hint of blue, and the air smelled of a rich dampness. Lauren hauled their bags through a tumble of rocks and soft dirt amid the underbrush.

Once the first members of the group entered the building, three giant birds stalked crazily out of the jungle and blocked the way of stragglers. Someone squealed and pointed. "Wild turkeys. Look, they're mating!"

Posing and prancing in shimmering iridescent greens, they looked like anorexic Thanksgiving birds dressed for a formal event.

"Take care near them," one of the guides yelled. "You don't want them to mistake you for a female." The women giggled and pulled out their cameras.

Lauren left the bags at the foot of the stairs and followed Enid across the entry to the porch to get a drink from the bar.

Enid wrinkled her nose. "This place makes that hotel in Mexico City look like a palace. Let's get upstairs and choose our beds before everyone else does."

On the second floor on either side of a narrow hall were two large dorm rooms. The bathrooms were at the far end. Enid pointed at a corner bed in a long line of bunks. "Over here, Lauren. You take the top, so I don't have to sleep under some ditz who won't hold still all night. This mattress is thinner than a term paper. God, how do they expect us to get any sleep?"

Other students filed in behind a bony woman in khaki shorts and heavy boots who clomped across the wood floor to shake Enid's hand. "Aren't you Dr. Godwin? I'm Annetta Fiedler from Indiana University. Welcome."

Enid stood up taller and spread her fake smile. "How do you do?"

The two women shook hands as if they were in a grand ballroom, rather than a prefabricated hut in a rain forest. Annetta stepped up onto the lower bunk and helped Lauren spread her bedroll. "All of us on the faculty here are quite excited about your class, you know. By the way, tomorrow night after a day in the tropical heat, you're going to think that mattress is a piece of heaven!" She nimbly spread her bedroll over her own top bunk. "I promise you'll love the gang showers too, though they're barely a dribble."

Annetta whipped off her T-shirt over her gray curls, revealing a flat chest and muscular arms. "The water is the only thing that isn't hot around here. You'll wish you could stay under that trickle for an hour." She pulled on a long-sleeved shirt and bent down to retie her scuffed boots.

Enid clutched her chest and grimaced. "All I want to know is what's poisonous, and how to stay away from it."

"That's easy." Annetta began counting on her fingers. "Stay on the paths even if you're peeing. Snakes don't like to be where there's traffic. Spiders love warm, dark spaces, so don't put on your shoes or boots without checking to see what's sleeping in them. It's important to remember the generator turns off at ten p.m. sharp each night and stays off until six, so get to bed before that, unless you like undressing in the dark. Oh, and don't ever set your bare foot on the floor without using a flashlight."

All the other women had become silent.

Val, the woman who was so chatty with Rocky at dinner the night before, pulled her blonde hair into a ponytail, and her eyes grew wide. "You mean things are going to crawl around here at night?"

Annetta lifted one shoulder. "You never know. Best to get into a safe routine."

Val looked all around her. "A safe routine? You've been here how many times?"

"Just one trip last year, but I stayed all semester."

Enid joined the cross-examination. "And you survived without any incidents?"

Annetta grinned. "I lived to tell the tale."

Enid shook her head so fast her neck skin wobbled. "That's a relief."

"One little old scorpion settled right under my backpack."

Enid barked at the woman. "He bit you?"

"Nasty little sting hurt like hell. Lucky I'm not allergic." She gave her pillow a fluff and marched for the door. "See you all downstairs at dinner."

Lauren trailed Enid to the porch, where they grabbed bottles of beer off the bar. Just as they took a welcome sip, Rocky squeezed through the crowd toward the bar and shot a cold glance at Lauren. Before she had a chance to greet him, he turned his back and leaned over to say something to Val.

Any hope of patching up their rift had evaporated in the steamy heat of the afternoon. That's what falling in love did to people, Lauren thought. Rocky was simply another victim. Lauren was determined to explain everything to Luis, and then banish both of them from her thoughts.

If she could.

Lauren hung around the hall for a few minutes, sipping her beer and hoping Luis might appear, but gave up and climbed the stairs to finish unpacking.

At dinner, the students and faculty sat around two parallel tables that extended the length of the dining room. The same young men who had unloaded the luggage brought out platters of food from the open kitchen at the far end of the room. When Lauren arrived, Rocky was seated between his new friend Val and another young woman from Pennsylvania. Relieved that she didn't have to look at his sad eyes, Lauren obediently sat at the end seat next to Enid and spoke to no one during the entire dinner. She concentrated instead on watching for Luis's arrival.

As the platter of fruit bars made its way around the table, Luis slunk in as if he'd been trampled by the mating turkeys. His hair was matted with sweat, his dirt-streaked shirt un-tucked, and his eyes hooded. He and Frank faced off, each of them with their hands on their hips. Someone brought Luis a plate of food from the kitchen, but he waved it away. At last, he shook his head, spoke to Frank through gritted teeth, and then strode to the end of one of the tables where he clanked a glass to get the group's attention.

Without an amusing greeting or even his charming grin, Luis read quickly through the schedule for the next day, passed out a sheet of dig site regulations and cautions for everyone to review before breakfast, and then introduced the other co-director of the research site, Dr. O'Connor from Indiana University, an older man with a paunch that challenged the button on his pants.

Lauren hadn't ever seen Luis so agitated. His anger was obviously directed at Frank. She suspected more problems at the dig site were the cause. Dr. O'Connor stood, hiked up his tilting pants, and invited all students to gather outside the porch after dinner to join him and a local naturalist on a night walk along the forest paths. He explained they might see owls, bats, the notorious howler monkeys, and perhaps even an elusive kinkajou or a jaguar. He advised anyone wishing to go on the walk should wear pants, a long-sleeved shirt, carry a flashlight.

Lauren lost track of Frank and Luis after they moved with the crowd to the doorway, still glaring at each other. Luis hadn't looked her way once. When Lauren emerged through the slow-moving crowd, he was gone. She ducked into the porch behind Frank and Enid, but there was no sign of him there. Assuming he had left the building, she stepped outside, crossed the scrabble of grass down to the driveway, and stood still.

Muffled bird sounds came from high in the dark sky. The sauna-like air was heavy with pungent scents foreign to her nose. She crossed the sandy drive toward a narrow path. She knew she shouldn't go any further alone, but the towering growth of vegetation enchanted her.

Lauren stood still, adjusting to the isolation of a darker world than she'd ever experienced in the city. The blackness and the damp air closed in on her like a shroud. Monkeys pierced the peace with sad, desperate cries. Trees creaked and rustled, as if animals crouched on every branch.

Not five feet away a pair of tiny eyes glowed at her.

Behind her the screen door squeaked. Lauren jumped and turned to see the shadow of a man loping toward her.

"Luis?"

"Yes." He walked past her.

She had never heard him sound so lifeless. "Where are you going?"

"Away from you."

"Be careful. There's something there in the path. See those eyes?"

Luis flicked on his flashlight. "It's just a spider." He paused long enough for Lauren to catch up with him, and the spider scrambled under a brown palm branch.

"Is he dangerous?" She could feel the heat of Luis's anger.

"Everything around here is dangerous for you, especially me. Go back into the building. Rocky needs you."

"I have to talk to you." Lauren reached for his arm, but he dodged away.

"Your non-boyfriend is on the porch crying in his beer about how he slept with his girlfriend and got her in trouble with Enid. I'm betting that would be you he's talking about."

"Oh, no!"

"Go ahead," Luis said and turned off the flashlight. "Tell me he's not talking about you." He spoke in monotone.

"It was a mistake, a big mistake."

"Damn right, and I'm the one who made it." Luis resumed his stride along the narrowing path.

Lauren jogged after him, tripped on a tangle of roots, landed spread-eagle with her face in the dirt, and cried out in frustration.

"Jeez, Lauren, are you okay?"

Lauren spit dirt out of her mouth as Luis lifted her and held her to his chest. Leaning against him with his breath tickling her ear, she felt safe for the first time since Ken's death. "I've done a lot of stupid things, Luis." Her voice came out in a moan. "I've screwed up my life and Rocky's too."

"I don't want to hear about it." His voice sounded hard, but his hands still held her tightly.

With Luis's heart thumping against her cheek, she reached up to touch his bristly jaw. "You can forget you ever met me, but first I have to tell you something."

"Oh, hell. More confessions." Luis's hands deserted her shoulders. "This day's been a disaster right from the start, so you might as well finish it off. But we can't talk here. Dr. O'Connor's group will be coming this way soon." He took her hand and pulled her along. "Lauren says she's going to tell me everything," Luis spoke into the darkness. "Why would I believe she's going to do that, after all the dodges I've heard for, how long have I known you, Lauren Richmond? Five weeks. Thirty-five days and nights."

Lauren's funk lifted in response to Luis's grumbling. Though she was insulted to be accused of lying, it was good news to hear he'd been counting the days since they'd met. "Don't put all the blame on me, Luis. You, the famous Latin Lover, you're the one who lied about calling me as soon as you got down here." This was not going the way she'd planned.

"Listen, Lauren. Here's the truth. The minute I got here, I tried to call you. Why? The flight was awful. We sat on the ground for two hours in Chicago. Know what a plane looks like after you lock people up like that? Then we bounce around in the air waiting to land in Mexico City for an extra thirty minutes, while half a dozen people puked into their carry-on bags. Carlos is there waiting for me. I try your number, but my cell won't work there. What else is new? I get in Carlos's pickup and we drive all night. I just wanted to hear your voice before I finally climbed into my cot. Pretty crazy, right? The camp phone line was out. It goes out after every storm." His voice was level, controlled.

Luis flashed his light at her feet for a moment. "Careful, Lauren, look out for that root there. With the phone out, I asked Carlos to call you as soon as he gets back to his office and give you my number. He swore he left you two messages, just to be sure you would call me back."

"Oh." Lauren wished she could snatch back all her insults.

Luis stopped so quickly, Lauren ran into him. "What the hell does 'Oh' mean?" He gripped her wrist.

"There were these two messages, both in Spanish. Julie deleted one, and I deleted the other."

He turned away and continued walking. "Why would you do that?"

"The connection was terrible, with a weird echo, loud music, and a babble of words, some in Spanish. We thought they were prank calls, especially after Ken was killed."

Luis halted and Lauren bumped into him. "Who was killed?"

"Ken, my maintenance man."

"Oh, God, Lauren. What happened?"

Tears numbed her lips. "Remember I told you Rocky and I saw a stranger in my front hallway the day after you were mugged? The guy said he had the wrong address and ran off, but I couldn't help thinking he might have been one of the men who jumped you, even though that seemed crazy. I mean, I don't want to assume every Hispanic guy is a mugger, you know? Then I called the police and they said they'd keep an eye on the building, drive by our block more often, but I don't think they did. Poor Ken told me I needed a new security system, but I can't afford it, of course."

"Okay, Lauren, now slow down." Luis touched

her face and kissed her forehead. "Just tell me, what happened to Ken?"

"He must have shown up to shovel the walks and interrupted them as they were trying to break into my apartment."

"Who? Who was trying to break into your apartment?"

"The police said there were two of them." She had to bite her lips and inhale before she could continue. "Remember Ken said he chased two guys off the fire escape the night you were mugged? He was determined to stop them. He would have given them hell."

Luis covered her mouth for a second and whispered in her ear. "Come on." He took her hand and led her toward a path that forked to the left. "This path leads to the ruins."

While Luis pulled her along through the dark, the sight of Ken lying dead in her front hall filled her head, as it had each night when she tried to sleep. "Can you turn on your flash, Luis? I can't see a thing."

"Your night vision will get better without it. Where were you when this happened?"

"At the Bucks game with Rocky. We came home and there he was, lying in his own blood. What were they after, Luis?"

Luis halted. "You think the men who broke into my office and my apartment hit your place too?"

"Don't you?"

"Jeez, I don't know." Luis was quiet as they turned off from the main path. "You and Ken were close," he said. "I could tell by the way he talked to you that day."

"He worked for my grandfather."

"I'm sorry." Luis turned, leaned down, kissed her cheek, and rubbed away her tears with his thumb. "Really sorry. I thought when I left, that would be the end of it."

She found his face with her fingers, and he covered her mouth with his. Her mind went blank in his powerful grip, and she clung to him until he stepped back. "The dig site is just a little farther this way," he said and led her deeper into the black tangle of trees. "Don't let go of my hand."

"Don't worry. I'd never get out of here without you. What were you and Frank arguing about?"

"You name it. He's making me crazy. We've spent three weeks dealing with the cave-in next to the Castillo stairs, which Frank claims is my fault."

"Why does he blame you?"

"Because I wasn't here when it happened, and because he's an asshole. Wait until you meet him. You'll agree."

"I already have. He has a big ego."

"Based on nothing he's ever accomplished." Luis stopped. "Listen, Lauren, you were right. Those men you saw in the parking garage thought I had something that would lead them to a treasure. They were wrong, but they won't stop until they get what they're after."

"Your map."

"You and that map. Yes, that's what they wanted. Because the map meant something to my grandfather, who must have made it, I've always assumed it referred to a place around here. I've studied it and searched every logical place, every bit of ground that makes sense. Nothing here matches the markings on that map."

"Could it have something to do with the legend of the Mayan codex?"

Luis began walking again. "I always hoped so. I got a call last week from one of the researchers in Madrid who's been helping me. He found a letter in their collection from another priest who had been in this region with Bishop de Landa. In the letter he wrote that his friend was executed for disobeying the Bishop's orders to burn the heathen writing."

"What happens now?"

"I keep searching, but look around you. Where do I begin? Now I have the problem of those guys who jumped me. Who are they? Where did they get their information about me and the map?" Luis was still for a moment. "I should take you back. It's getting late."

Lauren cringed at the mention of the men who jumped him. Because of her meddling, they had a copy of Luis's map. "There's something else I have to tell you."

"If this has anything to do with Rocky, I don't want to hear it."

"It has to do with your map."

"Then let's head up to the top of the temple. I think better up there. The entrance to the dig site is right here."

Luis unlocked the padlock and swung open the gate. An eerie howl from the canopy above made Lauren grab Luis by the sleeve.

"The howler monkeys make your ears ring, don't they?" Luis said. "You get used to them." Luis followed Lauren through the gate and closed it behind him. "You can hear their call from three miles away. They've been watching over these ruins longer than any of us. This way."

At a juncture of two paths, Luis pointed his flash at a giant tree. "That's a bullet tree loaded with bromeliads and orchids. They love planting themselves in that scaly bark."

"Like a Christmas tree full of ornaments."

"Over here's a small mahogany tree. See how it reaches the top of the canopy? Bullets and mahogany are wonderful hardwoods. That strangler fig there gets a piece of the sun by winding its way around the trunk. In the rain forest, everything steals or borrows from its neighbor to survive. It's good to remember that. Here's the original path to the village."

"Did the ruins frighten you when you were a kid?"

"No, but we never came in the dark like this. We'd hike over the hills to see the steles. See that one over there? " He flashed his light on a tilting slab eight feet high. "I was probably thirteen when I first saw it. It was covered in moss. Watch out for that root there." He paused and helped Lauren step over it. "In my great-grandparents' time some of the villagers looted the grounds for gold, silver, or precious stones. Old legends of rich grave robbers fed their need for dreams, I think, like winning the lottery does for people today."

"So they've always known there was something here?" The path grew narrow and Lauren gripped his hand more tightly.

"Now and then someone would come back from a cave or a hillside with a bone or a fragment, and that would set everyone off into the woods with their shovels." He laughed, and his echo laughed back. "Now we loot graves in order to understand the past."

Luis began walking again, guiding Lauren along. "Six months after I started working here, a giant tree blew down next to a steep hillside. Just a hillside, we thought." He chuckled. "Underneath those roots were the temple steps. What a great day that was!" Luis paused and spoke into her ear. "We've been working on the temple ever since."

"How near are we to your grandmother's home?"

"Maybe five miles as the crow flies, but the road has to loop around these rocks."

"You said there are caves."

"Dozens of them. The town is built into the side of a small mountain that juts up against the rain forest. Some of those caves could connect with the caves behind you, but they're so convoluted, no one has ever charted them. Straight ahead is the temple. Over to your right is the ball court. We're scheduled to work on that next season."

"Have you found anything in the caves?"

"We can't excavate caves without reinforcing the walls and ceilings. The threat of a cave-in is too great." He shivered. "I don't have much interest in exploring caves."

"Oh, yes. You're claustrophobic."

"I told you my secret, didn't I? I must have been swept away by passion that night."

Lauren's heart grew lighter as she picked her way up a steep hill behind Luis along narrow steps that jutted from the earth. Eventually the stairs made a turn and became steeper.

At the top, Luis turned off the flashlight and stood behind Lauren with his hands on her shoulders. Everywhere she looked stars filled the blackness. Her eyes couldn't keep up with their endlessness. She felt smothered by them and lost.

Luis was silent for so long Lauren felt she should speak. "It's glorious up here." Lauren reached for his strong, safe hands.

"Here is where the Maya wished to be, near the sun, near the stars."

"This is your true home, isn't it, here in this jungle surrounded by the secrets of the past."

He paused with his face so close to hers, she thought he was going to kiss her, but he stepped back and turned away. "Since we met, I've thought about bringing you here, showing you this. I thought, well, never mind."

Lauren touched his shoulder and felt him start to pull away. "Luis, if you're angry about Rocky, I have to tell you that I..."

"Just skip it. It's done. The whole deal's done.

Let's get back."

"This isn't about Rocky. If you hadn't been such a jerk, I would have told you this at the airport."

He stepped back. "What'd you expect? I thought you'd dumped me, which turned out to be right."

"You don't understand anything."

"You said it, Lauren. Time to go back. My stars are crossed tonight."

"The men who killed Ken stole something of yours."

"What do you mean?" His voice dropped.

"Remember when you came to my apartment, and I went to the deli?"

"The day you snuck a look at my map?"

"How'd you know that?" She rested her hand on his arm, but he shook it off.

"You folded it the wrong way when you put it back."

"I was very careful."

"Very careless, as well as nosy."

"I couldn't help it. You were coming out of the bathroom, and I had to hurry. Anyway, I took the map that day and made a copy of it."

"The hell you did." Luis crossed his arms between them. "Where did you copy it?"

"Kinko's."

"Ah, a nice private place. Only about twenty people there who could get a look at it. And then what?"

Lauren ignored his sarcasm and reached for his hand to steady herself. "I kept it in my bag."

Luis pulled away from her again. "And what happened to the bag when the men broke in and killed Ken?"

"They took it. I'm sorry, Luis. It was a sneaky thing to do."

He gripped her elbows. "Did it occur to you I might have a good reason to keep the map to myself?"

"Yes."

"But you didn't care. You just had to meddle."

Her face prickling with embarrassment, Lauren wished she could do or say something to make everything right between them. "Luis, I'm sorry."

His hands dropped away from her. "Being sorry doesn't get the copy back. Jeez, Lauren, sometimes I wonder whose side you're on."

"Whose side I'm on?" She socked him in the chest. "Are you kidding me? You think someone paid me to show up on that frigid night and rescue you from those brutes? You think I seduced you, so I could snatch your goddamn map?"

"Doubtful."

"Why do you think I came on this trip?"

"At first I thought it was to be with me, but obviously it was to be with your lover, Rocky."

Lauren punched him in the shoulder. "I came on the trip because Enid was paying me and I needed the money, but the real reason was you, Luis. I had to discover the truth about you and me, and about all the other things you've told me. You said you didn't know why those men beat you up. Then you said you didn't have a clue why they'd try to steal from you. Now you say you don't know anything more about the map, and you ask me whose side I'm on? At least admit this much, Luis: you have some idea who your enemy is."

When he was silent again, Lauren fought tears of frustration before she could speak again. "Okay, you're right. I don't deserve to know anything more about your map, or your treasure or the men who beat you up and killed Ken. I screwed up, and I can't change that. Take me back to the dorm."

"Good idea. The generator shuts off at ten. I have to conserve the flashlight batteries, so stay close."

Lauren hurried to keep up as they zigzagged through the depths of darkness.

When they finally neared the gate, Luis strode ahead and vanished into the blackness. Then he swore. Luis's flash clicked on. "The padlock wasn't closed all the way, even though I was sure I locked it after we came through."

"Who else has the combination?"

"Frank and Annetta."

"Could one of them be inside?"

"It's possible. It's also possible that I don't think straight when you're around."

Lauren wasn't sure whether to take that as an insult or a compliment.

Once Luis locked the gate behind them, they set off along the rough ground. The monkeys erupted again, sending shivers down her back with their deafening echoes.

Near the driveway to the building, Lauren tugged on Luis's hand. He turned, and slivers of porch light cast stripes across his face. "What is it?" he said, his face calm again, as his eyes sought hers with the eagerness she'd seen in her apartment.

She worried that anything she said would spoil his improved mood, but she couldn't let the thoughts go. "There has to be a secret symbol somewhere on that map, but if you can't figure it out, how could anyone else?"

"Give it up, Lauren. Let's just say the map was a joke my grandfather played on me. A deadly joke."

"Let's study your map again—get a fresh look." She felt Luis turn away. "Wait. Has something happened to your map?"

"It's gone."

Though Lauren couldn't read his face in the dark, she felt his fury. "They stole that too?"

"The whole briefcase."

"No way."

He pulled her close. His clenched biceps felt like stone beneath her fingers as his chest pressed against her breasts. "One morning, right after Christmas, when I was working on the cave-in, somebody tore apart the dorm room and found my hiding place." He let go of her so abruptly, she stumbled, and he whirled toward the entrance. Before she caught up with him, all the lights blinked out. Lauren yelped.

"Shh, Lauren, I told you—the generator shuts down at ten. Come on."

Inside the dark building, they ran into a dozen students mounting the stairs. The wavering beams of their flashlights cast dancing shadows on the walls. Lauren heard Rocky's laughter and spotted him ahead of her with his arm slung over one of the other guys, as if he needed help walking. Lauren held her breath until he disappeared into the men's bunkroom. If Rocky had seen her right then, right there, bumping her hip against Luis's thigh, brushing her shoulder against Luis's arm, inhaling his lovely masculine scent—if Rocky had glimpsed that, he would know immediately how she felt about Luis.

At the top of the stairs, a question popped back into her head, one that had occurred to her during Luis's explanation of his phone problems. She stopped Luis at the door to the men's dorm room. "Hold it. Why would your friend Carlos think he should speak Spanish when he called me for you?"

Luis threw up his hands. "Because he thought you were a Mexicana."

Lauren put her hands on her hips. "Why would he think that?"

Luis grinned. "Because of the way I described you." In the dim beam of her flashlight, his nostrils flared, as if he didn't want her to see him smile, and he closed the door behind him.

The women's bunkroom was lit by a dozen dancing flashlights. Enid was stretched out in her bunk like a mummy, with her sleep shade covering her eyes, a hair net tucked over the curlers in her hair, and a pair of yellow earplugs stuffed in her ears.

Even if Luis had given up learning anything more about the map, Lauren refused to. She dug out her notebook with her version of the map in it, grabbed her bath kit, and hurried to the bathroom. She decided there was no point in telling Luis that she'd tried to draw another map from memory. After all the years he had possessed his grandfather's map, he ought to be able to make one himself.

In the glimmer of her tiny flashlight, she washed her face, brushed her teeth, and then opened her notebook to get one more look at the copy. Luis was surely the toughest man she'd ever tried to figure out, even more secretive than her father. He was always holding something back, like the fact his briefcase had been stolen.

She wished she could remember details about the frightening monster depicted in the center of the page, because it seemed to be the only possible hint of where to find the treasure, or even what the treasure might be. When the door to the bathroom swung open, she slapped the notebook closed. "Dr. Hernandez!" She watched his eyes light up like a disobedient boy's. "I don't think men are supposed to be in this bathroom."

Straight-faced, Luis slid the bolt into its slot, turned back to her, and brushed her neck. Her pulse jumped.

"I forgot to say a proper good night." He took her face in his hands and kissed her the way he had in the car the first time, like a boy on his first date, sweet but urgent, fearful the girl's father might interrupt. Her body melted against his.

Luis pulled away and brushed her hair off her face. "That feels much better. I thought, I don't know, I wondered if I could trust you." He took her hands in his, stretched them over her head, and pressed her against the back of the door. "I thought we had a temporary thing going, just a flash of heat, but now—"

He moaned when he kissed her again. "I'm sorry I put you in danger, Lauren," he whispered. "To keep you safe, I'd take back that night in the parking garage if I could, even if it meant I'd never meet you, never get to kiss you, never get to hold you like this."

Lauren touched his lips as he spoke and combed his eyebrows with her fingers. When her hand moved to his chin, he gripped it tightly and pressed his body to hers.

"I went crazy standing there at the airstrip watching you, seeing you looking beautiful and innocent with your hair blowing in the wind. I wanted to make love to you right there on the tarmac." He lifted her shirt and fingered her breast. "In the car, when I thought of you being with Rocky, I nearly drove off the road."

His mention of Rocky sucked the air from Lauren's chest. A flash of memory dissolved her concentration. She had regrets too.

He laughed into her eager mouth. "You're a bruja, a witch. I can't get enough of you."

Suddenly the doorknob rattled and someone pounded on the door. "This door is not supposed to be locked!"

Lauren and Luis jumped apart, and Luis staggered a step to the door. He waited a second for Lauren to pull down her T-shirt before he slid back the bolt. A young woman burst in and halted face to face with Luis. Her eyes bugged open and she covered her mouth. "Dr. Hernandez! Excuse me."

"That's okay, Jenny. Poor Lauren here was

locked in for a second, and I had to see what the problem was. The bolt works fine now." He patted Lauren on the back and headed down the hall.

"Sorry," Lauren said, as she slipped past the woman without making eye contact. Just before she reached the door to the bunkroom, Luis showed up in the beam of her flashlight.

Passion lingered in his eyes as he laced his fingers with hers. "Take care of yourself."

Chapter Thirteen

Before dawn, the howlers' thunderous calls woke Lauren. She lay on her clumpy, sweaty bedroll and pulled herself out of the dregs of a nightmare. The man from the pyramid was chasing her through snake-infested ruins down endless temple steps. In darkness thick as tar, his rotting teeth and jagged fingernails slashed her neck. Lauren sat up and felt her pulse still pounding in her ears.

She was glad she hadn't told Luis of her panic at the top of the pyramid. It was crazy to think that evil man could be one of those who had attacked Luis and killed Ken.

The bed's sagging springs, the still air, and a symphony of snorers had kept her awake past midnight. The loudest noise came from Enid, blaring just a couple of feet beneath her. Sometime after three, Lauren's bunk shook, when Enid got up to go to the bathroom. She fell back to sleep right away, only to reawaken when Enid returned.

Despite her lack of rest, Lauren was eager to see the rain forest and the ruins in the daylight and hurried to get her chance in the shower. When she returned to the bunkroom, all of the others were stirring, except for Enid. Lauren pulled on her long-sleeved shirt, her khakis, and her hiking boots, grabbed her backpack and hustled down to the dining room in hopes of catching Luis alone. Unfortunately, he was seated with other staff members, so she picked a seat at the far end of the table and helped herself to the cold buffet of breads and fruit.

She listened to the staff discussing progress on a gravesite and cringed after Frank snarled at one of the women about a mislabeled artifact. Once she'd finished eating, she took her mug of coffee outside and found a flat rock to sit on near the beginning of the path. Ten feet away a half dozen parrots were competing for a cluster of flaming red blooms on giant stalks. Dazzling red, yellow, and blue feathered elegance dipped and soared as trills echoed into the shadowed woods. Now and then, a hummingbird snatched a turn at the blossoms and flitted away.

Lauren watched their desperate battle for food and thought about the vegetation Luis described the night before, vines that climbed trees to reach light and water, smothering their hosts in the process. From her mother she'd learned that other plants grow in harmony with species around them, giving off nutrients that nourished each other. Everywhere in life there were those that give, those that take, and those that share.

Like people, Lauren thought. Some support each other, some share whatever they have, and others choke off those around them.

By the time she returned to the dining hall, students were swarming the buffet and tables were filling up. Annetta clanked her glass and rose to speak. "I'm passing out a simple map of the dig site." Her eyes darted around the dining hall like the hummingbirds.

Lauren thought how lovely Annetta's face was and how stunning she would be if she washed her hair more often and cut it, rather than wadding it up in a bun on top of her head.

"The village was built on two levels along the Rio Bravo flood plain," Annetta began. "The larger plaza is on the upper plateau with the Castillo, or temple, rising above it. The lower plaza was the site of four large constructions, dwellings for priests and other citizens.

"We've assigned each of you to a work squad, but you can always trade with someone tomorrow if you wish. Dr. Mark Hanrahan's squad will be shoring up the temple steps where we had a cave-in. Dr. Luis Hernandez's squad will be excavating the staircase. In both places you'll either be digging, shoveling, or screening, especially near the stele we uncovered last season. Oh, for those of you who haven't done the reading," she said, and shook her head like a patient mother, "stele is a Latin term for a large stone or pillar carved to commemorate an event or an accomplishment of a ruler.

"My squad will be working on a grave. We've already unearthed terra cotta fragments covered with delightful decorations, a grand tibia, and a lovely pelvic bone. I'm hoping the rest of this elderly gent might give us some clues to his identity." With her laughter, her top knot began to come undone. "We're hoping to discover proof of his royalty. That would be quite exciting."

At a nod from Annetta, Enid stood. To Lauren's surprise, she introduced herself modestly, said they should call her by her first name, and then had Lauren stand too. "Throughout the day, as each of you takes your break, you may join Lauren and me for a chance to learn how a journal can be a useful tool in your work as archeologists. Remember, one doesn't have to be a poet to write with eloquence about an important life experience."

Lauren spotted the glint in Enid's eye that always preceded a flow of enthusiasm. "We hope to turn your academic experience into a valuable record of your inner growth as scientists," Enid continued. "We'll set up a work station of sorts near Annetta's dig site, which I'm told will be easy for you to find. If all goes as we hope, and with your permission, at the end of our trip we'll gather your thoughts into a book you can each keep as a memento of your burgeoning careers."

Amid the ensuing chatter, Luis stood and announced the work squads. Lauren was assigned to Annetta's team and hoped Enid wouldn't keep her from doing at least some of the archeological work. He pointed out the buffet table where they could assemble their own sandwich lunches, put them in bags, and label the bag with their names.

As the group swarmed around the lunch spread, Lauren made sure she was never more than two feet from Luis. When he slapped peanut butter on his bread, she stood next to him and spread jam on hers. After he split a banana from the bunch, she took one too and stuffed it into her lunch bag. Her hand rested on his fingers as he handed her a pen so she could label her bag, and their knuckles brushed as they placed their bags in the cooler that would be trucked to the worksite. Frustrated that he hadn't made eye contact, Lauren bolted for the screen door.

"Ms. Richmond?"

She stopped at the bottom of the steps and turned. "Yes, Dr. Hernandez?"

His sunglasses masked his eyes. "Great view."

She nodded. "I agree."

"From behind, that is."

"I agree." She laughed, and turned back to the path.

"We seem to be making progress."

"In what way?"

"We actually agree on a few things."

****

The sun was already a blinding ball, and the parrots had vanished. The group marched along the path behind Annetta, who pointed out rubber trees, a gum tree, an array of orchids, a monstrous nest of

179

termites, a bamboo thicket, and a cedar tree the size of a silo.

Lauren tried to pay attention to Annetta's narrative, but as long as Luis was near, she thought only of his magic hands and his soft, damp lips.

As the group filed through the gate, Luis pointed out the nearby latrines and suggested they refill their water bottles frequently from the water tanks.

Once they reached the work site, Lauren set her pack down for a moment to admire Luis as he strode over to the temple stairs. He halted to speak to one of the workers and whipped off his cap to scratch his head. While she was thinking how much she enjoyed looking at him in his threadbare long-sleeved shirt, frayed jeans and his uncontrollable thatch of hair, he glanced at her and waved.

For a moment, her ambitions, dreams, treasures, and all her fears fell away. The spell was complete when Luis pointed at her, touched his chest, and laughed out loud.

In her distracted state, Lauren had trouble locating her workstation. When she finally arrived there, she found Frank Jerome leaning on a shovel near a four-foot-deep pit surrounded by piles of rubble.

As soon as all the students had gathered, Frank introduced himself and handed out small shovels with picks attached. "Most of you will be working at the foot of the arch. When Annetta gets here she'll assign someone to work with smaller picks in the pit, next to what we hope is a royal leg bone. Ah! Here she comes."

Annetta trotted up panting and dropped her huge rucksack at the edge of the grave. "Well, I have to say, I just never seem to get used to that climb. Let's see now, you're all here, aren't you? You there, with that blue cap," she pointed to Lauren. "You're tiny enough. You come down in the hole with me, won't you?"

"Me? Sure." Ever since Lauren's grandfather had told her about King Tut's tomb, she had imagined herself discovering an ancient grave. Perhaps that dream was about to come true.

"Don't be too quick to volunteer," Frank said with a wink. "Annetta allows very few breaks."

"Ignore him, uh, what's your name again?" Annetta asked. "You're the one in the bunk next to mine. Is it Laurie?"

"Lauren."

"Okay, Laurie, have you got your water bottle? Good. Now I want you to climb into the opening just as I do. We must step with care." The woman was so agile she hardly disturbed the ground. "There, now pass me my sack. Next, step just there, no this way. That's right." She looked up at the other students. "Did you all see how you must watch where you step? Two more rules: as you work, if your pick touches anything harder than what you've felt before, stop and examine the area. Next, you must call Dr. Frank or me for a look-see, or we'll be quite upset."

In response to this announcement Frank clamped his legs together, turned his toes out, and bowed so low his nose nearly touched his knees.

"I must apologize." Annetta shook her head. "Whenever we have new visitors, Frank is compelled to entertain them. Oh, dear. Did I forget to tell you first names are fine with us? I just know you're going to love this job. I don't want to raise your expectations, but you'd be amazed to hear how many surprises our beginners have uncovered lately." She handed what looked like a dentist's pick to Lauren. "Here, Laurie, dear, take this pick. See the edge of that bone I'm working on? I want you to start there just picking away very gently. We might have a rib fragment, but I suspect there may be something else on top of it, so go gently now, scraping off the sand so you can get under that edge."

Using the small pick wasn't hard, but finding a comfortable way to kneel in the narrow pit was a challenge. To add to her discomfort, the pit was much hotter than the outside air.

Within an hour, Lauren's pick had found the edge of something hard. As soon as she pointed it out to Annetta, the professor scraped for a few minutes and discovered a jagged rock, but urged Lauren to keep working. Whenever Lauren stopped to sip her water, she observed the woman's gentle way of sliding the pick through layer after layer of thin clumps of soil.

After an hour Annetta began to half-sing, half-hum show tunes in a reedy soprano voice. Once she'd made her way through "Oklahoma" and moved on to "West Side Story", Lauren had to bite her lips to keep from begging her to stop.

"Annetta, tell me something," Lauren asked.

As "I Feel Pretty" died on Annetta's lips, her eyebrows made perfect arches. "What, dear?"

"Have you ever seen a Mayan codex?"

Annetta sat up and adjusted the chinstrap on her broad-brimmed hat. "You mean one that predates the Spanish Conquistadores?"

"Yes."

Annetta's nostrils flared. "I assume you know about the infamous Bishop de Landa, the book-burner. In one month, under his orders, priests destroyed five thousand idols and countless hieroglyphic rolls." She wiped the sweat off her eyebrows with the back of her hand. "I suppose that sounds like nothing, when you hear how he burned people alive or hanged them."

"Gruesome."

Annetta put down her pick and reached for her

water bottle. "I saw the codex in Paris. Documents as fragile as that are never on display, you understand, and of course, they're never allowed out of their special environment. I had a friend, you see, a special friend. Mmm, such a man he was!" Annetta winked. "I'm sure you know what I mean. Well, anyhow, he told me he'd show it to me after the museum closed that night. My, what a night that was! What I didn't know was he'd promised another woman the same thing. That turned out to be quite an unusual evening, but at least we got to see a codex as close as anyone could!" She covered her mouth and smiled. "Foolishly, I'd hoped to touch it. That's how naïve I was then. From that night on, I learned to delay payment until I'd received the goods, if you know what I mean."

Lauren chuckled at the image, but was grateful not to hear the rest of Annetta's tale of sexual bribery. "And what did it look like?"

Annetta adjusted her glasses and bit her lips for a moment. "It was behind tinted glass, of course, in an anaerobic container. Airtight, that is. To preserve the print, the light has to be dim, so one couldn't really examine the glyphs, unfortunately, but some of the colors were glorious. Others were a faded blur. The pages looked as if they would decompose if you blew on them. It was quite alarming to realize how fragile they were. I sometimes wonder if we scientists have our priorities straight. Those museums keep their prizes so locked up, scholars might wait a lifetime to examine them, yet never get the chance before they crumble to dust." She paused and laughed, "Or we crumble to dust."

Lauren went back to her pick work. "Are there other pre-Columbian codexes?"

"Yes. There's the one in Dresden, one in Madrid and the other, the Grolier Codex, is in a private collection somewhere."

"Have scholars been able to translate them?"

"To a certain extent, but there's still more to learn. Most of the information in the codexes, or codices, as Frank insists on calling them, concerns religious practices, astronomical tables and agricultural records. Later codexes, of course, also help us translate the glyphs we find on our work sites."

"Is it possible there are others still hidden somewhere?"

"You've been listening to Luis's legends, haven't you?" Annetta smiled as she shook her head. "It's doubtful. If you dug down in that spot you're working on right now, and you opened a casket that once contained a codex that old, all you'd find is a pile of ash. Nature's job is to recycle plant material, not preserve it."

Lauren poked the dirt with her tiny tool and remembered how her grandfather had mocked his grandfather for losing all his money in the stock market. Dreamers and gamblers went broke, he said, while planners dug in and built and rebuilt the world. Was Luis a dreamer?

As she wondered if dreamers and gamblers had more fun, her dental pick hit something that didn't give. "Here, look at this, Annetta. I feel something."

Annetta leaned over and poked her pick where Lauren's was. "Very interesting. You see this ridge here?" She gently scraped back the dirt and revealed a curved edge of something harder and a lighter shade than the dirt. "I think you've found a shell, Laurie, dear."

"What does that mean?"

"Oh, my, it's wonderful news. It's a large shell, as you can already see by the radius. The Maya often used a giant bi-valve as a mantle to honor an august leader." Annetta's chin bobbed. "Additional evidence that we may have a king beneath our knees." She patted Lauren's arm with her dusty glove. "When was the last time you knelt before a king, dear?"

Lauren was thrilled to think a few hours of work could be so productive. She wished her grandfather had lived long enough to hear that she was digging up the remains of an ancient king.

After Annetta left to report the news to the other professors, Frank took her place in the pit.

"Nice work there, Lauren," he said as he jammed the space with his gangly body. "We should be able to lift that shell in the next couple of days." Sweat streaked his face, and dark circles rimmed the underarms of his shirt. "Go ahead; keep working while I record the location on my chart."

Frank looked up sideways. "Last night I should have realized you're Luis's latest. Uh-oh, was that the wrong thing to say? Forgive me."

His words hit her like ice water. Luis's latest, that's exactly what she was. She shook off her grimace. "How about you?" she said and spread her mouth into her camera-ready smile. "Is Enid merely your latest?"

"I refuse to answer that one." He twiddled his pen and frowned. "I have to admit Luis has good taste. You're like the hymn, 'all things bright and beautiful.'" His smile looked as plastic as Lauren's felt.

"Very poetic. How often have you used that line?"

Frank chuckled. "Let me see. I should know this, since I keep a chart of my women and my most successful approaches. I register the time of year, magnitude of effect, difficulty of separation, and weight of personal history." He tipped his hat back and exposed his freckled forehead. "I confess a few years back, I used to include their G.P.A."

"You're kidding."

"I don't kid about important things."

185

"You kept records of your girlfriends' grade point averages?"

He closed his eyes and sniffed. "It's not hard. I'd check the student information we received before they even arrived." He looked out over the edge of the pit and frowned. "Uh-oh, here comes lover boy. Looks like he's searching for someone. Could it be you?" Frank nimbly hefted himself out of the pit and flashed his teeth at Lauren. "Time for a toilet break, Lauren. Here, give me your hand, step on that stone block and I'll ease you up."

Lauren glanced over in time to see Luis spot Frank gripping her arm. His grimace turned as cold as a stone stele. "Morning, Frank. Congratulations, Lauren. I heard about the shell. Let's hope we can get it out in one piece."

"Hey, Luis," Frank said and smirked as Lauren snatched her arm away from him. "We were just talking about you and your old girlfriends. Oops! Did I say 'old' girlfriends? I should have said 'former' girl friends.'"

Luis's cheeks flushed. "Watch out, Lauren. Instead of accepting himself as one of the top experts in pre-Columbian pottery in Mesoamerica, Frank has chosen the field of female seduction as the test of his worth."

Frank's nostrils flared. "Who else would I choose to compete with, Luis, but you, the best? Excuse me, Lauren. It's snack time."

Luis scowled at Frank's back. "That guy hates me and always has." He shrugged, put the cap back on, and stuffed his hands in his pockets. "Hell, you can't please all the people. You headed for the toilet?"

"Yes. I need to walk. My legs are cramped."

Luis's frown lines disappeared as he described how they would lift off the shell once it had been completely uncovered, and then study it in the lab at the University.

Lauren was brooding and couldn't concentrate on the details. How long, she wondered, did Luis see one girlfriend before he'd break off the relationship? She interrupted him. "Do you all keep track of your girlfriends the way Frank does?"

They stopped in front of the portable toilets and Luis frowned at Lauren as if he thought she was crazy. "What are you talking about?"

"Frank said he records their statistics, including the weight of their relationship, which I suspect means the extent of sexual involvement. He used to record their grade point averages."

"He was kidding. He's a leach."

"How'd he get here?"

"He has impressive credentials, no doubt about it, but he's lazy, he gets everyone else to do his jobs, and he has no people skills, not even with women, I hope you noticed." He sipped from his water bottle. "Your Enid seems to like how he dotes on her, though. What he's really good at is sucking up to the people in power."

"The other night at dinner he told me he hoped to be rich and famous someday."

Luis choked on his laugh. "He said that? Not too many rich and famous archeologists around. Go ahead. Enid told me to tell you she's waiting for you."

****

In her all-khaki outfit and her battered U.W.M. Panthers cap, Enid stood like a general on a low stone wall beneath a cedar tree, with the journaling students arrayed on a tarp spread below her. As soon as Lauren joined them, Enid ordered her to pass out composition notebooks.

"Do you all have a pen or a pencil? Fine. Now, have any of you ever kept a journal?"

Four women raised their hands. "That's quite

good. You can help the others learn this valuable skill. Remember, it isn't merely journalists, poets, or authors who need to keep notes on their observations. A scientist's discovery may depend on what's in front of his or her eyes, nose or even what's in the darkness behind her." Enid fell silent for dramatic effect.

"Now, the first thing you need to do is jot down details to help you describe your setting. We'll take five minutes to do this. Look around you and write what you see."

Lauren grabbed a notebook too, and recorded her observations from the morning in the grave pit. She was elated to uncover a piece of the past, a remnant of a people whose history had been buried for so long. She suspected such a thrill could be addictive and hoped she would be there when they lifted the shell from its tomb. When she glanced over where Annetta's group toiled, she caught Frank staring at her, and shot bad will at him until he looked away. She wondered what Enid saw in the creep.

The students shared their efforts, and the next exercise involved using a scent, a sound, a taste, or a texture to retrieve memories from the previous day. Once that was completed, Enid congratulated the students and announced their assignment for the following day was to record their day's work with the same sort of detail they'd used in the exercises.

After the class dispersed, Enid yawned and told Lauren she was returning to the lodge for a rest, and Lauren was free to rejoin Annetta in the pit. Even with a few more inches of the dirt removed, Lauren still couldn't tell the dark surface was a seashell.

While Lauren scraped gently along the rim of the shell, she heard the rumble of Luis's and Annetta's voices above her. After the voices faded, Lauren paused to sip her water bottle. She looked up to see Frank invading her space again and gritted her teeth.

"Poor Luis," Frank said and snorted.

Lauren kept her head down and ignored the comment.

"He insists on repairing the stairway himself, but he won't even set foot in the cave."

"The cave near the castillo?" She hadn't meant to say anything to the jerk.

"Yeah. It's next to the staircase. We didn't discover that cave until the whole wall collapsed. As soon as we finish the repairs, we'll have a chance to document its dimensions and make a plan to explore it."

"Has the cave ever been occupied?"

Frank shrugged. "You should have seen Luis's face that first day, when he had to go in there." He flipped up his glasses and rolled his eyes. "He's scared shitless of caves, did you know that? Just now he came over here to make Annetta go in and check on the braces they installed yesterday."

Lauren squeezed her hands into fists and pinned them to her sides, so she wouldn't slap that arrogant mouth. She twisted away from his eyes glazed with jealousy and scrunched down to work again. But Frank wasn't finished. He bent down next to her, so close she smelled the garlic on his breath. "Too bad your boyfriend is no Indiana Jones." His laugh repeated like a broken CD.

She wanted to jab her scalpel into his eye and slam his face into the clods at her feet. Instead, she continued picking away, letting him see only calm in response to his taunts. Poor Luis. His fear must be a terrible burden.

At quitting time, Lauren was one of the last to put away her tools. Although she was sweaty and exhausted, her back ached, and her stomach growled, she wished she could keep going until the shell was complete and the experts could tell her the identity of the man in the grave.

Dusk shrouded the rain forest, and shadows streaked the path. Lauren marched along in her sweaty boots, inhaling warm, rich scents, relieved to be alone in the quiet. Although she saw no one else when she entered the portable toilet, as soon as she sat down she heard men's voices.

"Donde esta la muchacha?" Where's the girl? a man had asked.

"Quien?" Another man answered. Who?

"La rubia, la misma con la mapa." The blond with the map.

"No hay ninguna muchacha por aquí. Eres tonto." There's no girl here. You're stupid.

Were they speaking about her? And about Luis's map?

As the sound of the voices trailed off in the direction of the gate, one of the men called the other "fucking estupido." Once she was sure they had gone, Lauren unlatched the door and stepped out.

"Lauren!" Luis's yell from down the path made her jump and grab her chest. He jogged to catch up with her. Lauren glanced where the voices had come from and glimpsed a figure ducking into the thick growth.

She grabbed Luis by the hand and began to run, pulling him along. "Who was on the path ahead of you just now, Luis?"

"No one. What's the matter?"

"Hurry. We have to see who came by here while I was in the john."

Luis loped along with her. "Why?"

"Shoot! They're gone. Are there other trails that lead from here?"

"Lots of them. What the hell are we doing?"

Lauren explained what she'd heard.

"Are you sure they said map?"

"Yes. They were talking about me."

"Well, I don't see anybody. Besides, I know everyone who works here, and none of them are the guys who attacked me. Which way did they go?"

"Toward the gate. You think I'm tonta, estupida, loca? They called each other those words."

"It doesn't make sense, Lauren. The guys who stole the map wouldn't come back here, unless—"

"Unless what?"

Luis held her close with his chin against her forehead. "I promise you, if the men who attacked me and shot Ken ever come near you again, I'll kill them."

"Luis!"

"I mean it, Lauren. It's me they were after and it's me they'll have to deal with."

In Luis's arms, Lauren felt ready for battle. "And I'll help you." She heard his laugh and pulled out of his hug. "You think I can't?"

"Oh, no. I know you could." He kissed her hair.

"You said the guys wouldn't come here, unless. Unless what?"

Luis shook his head, reached for Lauren's hand, and resumed walking. "I always assumed the map referred to the area on the other side of the hills, near my grandparents' village."

"Why?"

"Because my grandfather drew the map, and, if he'd ever visited here, he'd have told me."

"And he never did?"

Luis shrugged. "He said the people here were evil, that they stole from the gods and the dead. It's possible he was talking about this settlement."

"I remember you said looting was common."

"Yes. Even though my grandmother's family lived off the sites, my grandfather was a self-righteous man who got religion in his old age. He believed the mountain was holy and man must never enter it, especially not archeologists like me." Luis sighed and bit his lip.

They walked in silence toward the entrance. "Did people live in the caves?"

Luis nodded. "Between the second and ninth century C.E., or A.D., as they used to call it, the Maya built many cities near caves. Like other cultures, they believed caves linked the living earth to gods, to mythical creatures, and to the dead. They decorated them as we decorate churches, with the finest carvings and statues. It's likely they punished trespassers by using them in sacrifices in those caves."

Luis squeezed her hand and reached for the water bottle he kept clipped to his waistband. Lauren reached for his sweaty hand again.

"Have you ever tried to understand the origin of your claustrophobia?"

Luis acted as if he hadn't heard her and paused when they came to the curve in the trail where they could see the bunkhouse. "Let's walk down the road a bit."

Luis stared at his feet as they ambled down the dusty driveway toward the vans. "After I tell you what happened, you'll think I'm crazy, Lauren, but here it is." At the first van, he leaned against the door, stuffed his cap in his pocket, slid his sunglasses up on his head, and reached for Lauren's hands again.

The man continued to surprise Lauren. When he was teaching, he was serious and respectful. When he was amorous, he was eager, clever, funny, and gentle. On the night the men attacked him, his face had shown only fury. At that moment, as sweat beaded on his upper lip and his breath caught, Lauren felt her own stomach cringe with his fear. He was about to tell her what made him so afraid of caves.

"As I said, when they could afford it, my parents sent us down to visit our grandparents for the summer. To us city brats, it was the great adventure." Luis smiled. "Their village is tiny, twenty houses and an old church that's about to fall down. The hills around the houses are pockmarked with caves, some no bigger than a pup tent, but others wind for miles."

He glanced at Lauren and touched her lower lip with his forefinger. "We loved and feared my grandfather who ruled the family like Montezuma. At night he'd sit in his chair, his, and no one else's chair. We called it Montezuma's throne." Luis's cheeks softened into a grin. "When I was small, I cried when he spoke to me." Luis's smile vanished. "I'll never forget the time *el Señor*, that's what we called him, caught us in the caves. God, I thought he was going to pick us up by the feet and whack our heads off like one of his chickens."

"Why?"

"That cave is the darkest place I've ever been. Ever." He held her hand against his lips and closed his eyes. "People got lost in there."

Lauren's stomach blipped. "Lost, like forever?"

Luis sighed. "One summer two kids disappeared. They were about my age, maybe thirteen." His voice was so low Lauren had to lean close to hear.

"Men from the town tied ropes around their waists and tried to track them in and out of the torturous twisting caverns. That went on for days as they worked each tunnel."

She saw the answer on his face. "They didn't find them?"

"No."

Lauren put her arm around him and rested her head on his chest. His heart raced.

"I got really sick after that, so sick I was in bed

for two weeks with pneumonia. Mom had to fly down and bring me home. I went crazy with guilt."

"Guilt for what?"

"My parents didn't have the money for her trip, so everyone in the family suffered because of me. We ate nothing but bread and beans for months."

"It wasn't your fault you got sick."

Luis's eyes were rings of darkness. "But it was. One night when they were searching, I sneaked out of my grandparents' house to watch. It poured that night, the way it does in the summer. Sheets and sheets of water flowed from the sky. I didn't care. I had to stay there until they found those boys. By dawn I was cold, shivering so bad I couldn't stop. It was my fault."

"You know that's not true."

"Before that, caves had never bothered me. My cousins and I even got lost a couple of times ourselves, but we were lucky. As scared as we were, still we couldn't stay away from their mystery. All that ended for me when those boys vanished."

Luis touched Lauren's cheek. "This may sound dumb, but it wasn't until that night, as I watched the men searching for those kids, that I realized I could die. That everyone dies. I freaked. After that, I'd go to the cemetery and read the names of dead people. I was going to be just like them some day, dead, buried, feeling nothing. The realization trapped me, paralyzed me, and made me helpless in my body. I was going to lose my life and become nothing, and there wasn't anything I could do about it. I had horrible dreams."

"We all fear death, Luis. It's human to have doubts about the afterlife. The Maya thought they knew what was next after death. Christians do. Muslims do. And we won't really know until our time comes."

"Being unsure wouldn't be so bad, Lauren, if it

wasn't for the dreams."

"You still have them?"

Luis closed his eyes and nodded. "Sometimes I dream I've found the grave of the high priest deep inside a cave. I carry his golden bones and jewels out into the sunshine. The whole town is there watching me. But I'm not triumphant, I'm terrified."

"That's an exciting dream. Why should it scare you?"

He looked over her shoulder into the darkening forest. "When I come out of the cave and see the people, the sun disappears and the light flickers and fades into night. And then an enormous god rises from behind the crowd in a spectacular feathered cape."

"Like judgment day in a scary movie." Lauren hoped he'd laugh at that. "Have you ever figured out what's making you feel so guilty?"

He shook his head. "All I know is that dream still gives me the shakes."

"You haven't entered a cave since then?"

He swallowed. "No, and I don't intend to." The fear lingered in his eyes, though his mouth was soft as he leaned down and kissed her. "Lauren, you can help me forget all that." He unbuttoned the top of her shirt and kissed her neck. "Want to read what I'm thinking right now?"

She smiled, relieved that his fear had ebbed. "I always want to read your mind."

His cheeks were tan again and the hand that caressed her breast was cool and dry. "Good. If you check out what I have in my pocket, it'll be easy," he said, as his nostrils flared.

"I haven't fallen for that line since I was fifteen."

He laughed softly. "Fifteen? A guy said that to you when you were only fifteen? Jeez, I don't think I should be consorting with a woman like you." He moved her hand down his chest to his pants pocket.

"Feel it?"

She pulled his hips against hers. "Yes, I'm feeling it."

"No, I'm serious. Reach in my pocket."

"Car keys?"

"Yes. And what might we do in the privacy of a big back seat?"

"You're kidding."

He kissed her lips so hard she tasted blood. "I don't kid about this problem I have around you." He let her go for a minute, unlocked the van, and pulled open the door. "Top or bottom?"

She climbed in and slid across the seat. "Both."

He chuckled, jumped in beside her, and closed the door. "Both?"

She lay back and pulled him on top of her. "It's been way too long. "

Chapter Fourteen

The rise and fall of Luis's chest roused Lauren from her nap. The sky blended into the rest of the darkness. Luis's bare shoulder was beneath her cheek. Her arm encircled his chest, and her legs were tangled in his. She kissed his stubbly chin. "Even in the dark, I can see what a lovely man you are."

Luis groaned.

"That groan, Luis, tells me everything." She felt his head nod.

"You are my goddess, Lauren," he whispered. "I will worship and protect you."

"Your goddess wants to know how long we can stay here."

"Until dinner."

Lauren played with the hairs that curled over his ear. "I think we may have missed dinner."

Luis lifted his wrist to his face and checked his watch. "We have twenty minutes 'til they ring the dinner bell, plenty of time to get cleaned up before that, which I have to do, since the woman from the regional permitting board arrives right after dinner." They both shifted and sat up.

"What's that about?"

"Just government stuff. She has to inspect the cave before she gives us a permit to begin excavations." He pulled on his shirt and handed hers over. "Sorry you have to put this on again. Where're your lips?" He lingered into the kiss. "Mmm. Nice. Will you meet me later?"

"Where, when?"

"This meeting shouldn't take long. You know that giant cedar tree near the curve in the path? Meet me there a half-hour after dinner."

Lauren had trouble getting her shirt on right. "It's so dark out there."

"Bring your flashlight, and you'll be fine. I always take mine. Get going."

"Where are my underpants?"

"I'm not telling."

"Not fair. I don't have enough to give away as souvenirs."

"Okay, here." He waited while she finished dressing. "You go first and I'll follow."

"That sounds familiar."

Luis chuckled as she stepped out of the van.

Whoops of laughter competed with the howlers as Lauren neared the bunkhouse. At the top step, she looked back toward the forest that appeared so innocent in the daytime and so menacing at night.

Their lovemaking had been more than sex, more than passion. She'd felt the power of his body and of his fear. It was odd to think that her friend Ken now knew the answer to the big black, death question, and her parents and her grandfather did too. People always said they hoped the dead were at peace. She hoped they could feel love.

Luis had told her he wished he could have protected her from the evil men. She wished she could protect him from the horror he felt in a cave.

Lauren took a quick shower, changed from her work clothes to clean jeans, and reluctantly joined the crowd gathered on the porch. She found herself next to Rocky. He slung one arm over her shoulder and the other over Val's, and Lauren was instantly on guard. The few times she'd seen Rocky drunk he'd been nasty. By the sway of his body and the glaze in his eyes, he was on his way.

"What are we celebrating, Rocky?" Lauren asked, when he released her long enough to pass a beer to Val and kept one for himself.

Rocky spoke breathily into her ear. "Sexy women."

Lauren raised her glass. "Great, here's to sexy women."

"Like you and Val." He reached for his own bottle and tipped it up.

Val pressed her chest to Rocky's as they clanked bottles. "Here's to a cold beer after a hot day," she said.

Rocky grinned. "And a hot woman after a cold one!"

Val giggled and winked at Lauren.

"How about this, Rocky?" Lauren said with a frozen grin. "Here's to kind thoughts for an old friend." Before Rocky had a chance to respond, Lauren backed away and pushed through the crowd to the dining room. Behind her, she heard Enid's stern voice calling her name.

Still in her work fatigues, Enid stood at the foot of the stairs with a glare magnified by her bifocals. Despite the shocking pink scarf she had tied over her hair and the splashes of rouge on her cheeks, she looked so haggard Lauren grasped her wrist. "Enid, are you sick?"

"Of course I'm sick. Why do you think I left the dig so early? I needed you. There was no one here to help me."

"Is it your stomach?"

"I have an iron stomach. It's the heat. I've been flat on my back all afternoon. The least you could have done was to bring me something cool to drink."

Lauren gave her a guilt-filled hug and immediately regretted it. Enid liked men to touch her, not women. Embracing her was like cuddling a stone.

"It's too late for false sympathy, Lauren. What I need now is food—and some whiskey, though I suppose they don't serve that here." She folded her hands on her stomach and sighed. "Go find me a beer. I'll save you a place at dinner."

Relieved to escape from Enid's self-pity, Lauren threaded her way back to the porch against the flow into the dining room. As she grabbed a beer for Enid, she felt a heavy hand on her shoulder and turned. Rocky's eyelids drooped so low, he looked like he was nearly asleep.

"Sorry, Lauren. What I said there? That was unsportsmanlike." He lunged, but Lauren dodged his intended kiss, which landed on her ear. "She, you know, Val? She's going to help me get over you."

"I hope so, Rocky. I care about you."

He backed up and shook his head. "Not where it counts, though, eh?"

In the dining room seated next to Enid, Lauren watched Rocky load his plate with chicken, rice and beans and then slump into the chair next to Val. Lauren asked herself how she'd become such an expert at guilt. When Rocky flicked his sad, sagging eyes at her, Lauren looked down at the skinny breast of chicken and beans she'd loaded onto her plate and picked up her fork. Through dinner Enid talked poetry to the student seated on the other side of her, while Lauren relived the 'van action,' as Luis had called it, and wondered when they'd get another chance to make love.

During dessert, Lauren watched Luis appear in the entrance to the dining room and scan the tables until he saw her. His smile turned her on all over again. He shrugged as if to say, can't help making love to you, and then pulled out a chair next to Annetta. She watched him listen somberly to the woman and noticed his hair was still wet. By the looks of the wayward thatch, he hadn't bothered to comb it afterward.

Enid had to ask twice for more cookies from the buffet, before Lauren responded. She was glad for the excuse to walk past Luis. When she returned to the table with a plate in her hand, Enid was staring at her with her mouth open. "Lauren," she whispered, "I didn't believe what Carlos said, but it's true, isn't it? You and Dr. Hernandez are having an affair."

Lauren reached for a cookie and laughed. "Carlos told you that?"

"I saw how that man looked at you just now, as if you were his, his—"

Lauren looked over at Luis and grinned. "His lover?"

"Yes!"

Lauren chewed and swallowed her cookie. "And you, of all people, don't approve?"

Enid slapped her chest and laughed. "Of course I approve. It's just that I didn't think you had it in you, so to speak." She covered her mouth and laughed again. "Oh, dear, this is news."

"It's not news, Enid. Please. I don't want you talking about this to anyone."

Enid's eyebrows rippled in disappointment. "Of course I wouldn't."

"Of course you would. That's what you do, but this is me, Enid, your assistant, your gofer, your slave. If you mess with my relationship with Luis, I won't be able to work for you, and you'd hate that."

Enid bit her lips and nodded. "My lips are sealed."

Lauren had to acknowledge she was hoping for the impossible. "Think of me as that character in your poem, was it Helene, the woman who fell in love with the doctor and died of heartbreak?"

"No, dear, that was Marjorie. After her horrible stepmother revealed her past, the poet left her, but she didn't die, Lauren. She fled to Bangkok. Be a darling and get me some coffee."

As Lauren crossed the room to fetch coffee, a woman appeared in the doorway and glided over toward Luis, who was still seated at the table.

She was gorgeous in a too-much-of-everything way. Her shorts were too tight and too skimpy. Her lips were too plump and too scarlet. Her eyes were too wide. Her teeth were too white. Never mind how ridiculously too tight her shirt was.

"Luis!" the woman cooed, as she leaned down and kissed him on each cheek. "I'm delighted to see you."

Lauren stared as the woman messed up his hair.

"Your hair is just as wild as you are," she said.

Lauren realized her mouth was open and she was blocking the doorway, so she closed her mouth, poured a cup of coffee, and put one foot in front of the other until she was seated again next to Enid.

She'd been thinking of Luis as a part of her life, but that woman proved how wrong she was. For a long time, Luis had lived in another world, a world away from Lauren. Would she ever feel truly close to him?

"Don't make me laugh, Luis," the woman said, as she bent down far enough that everyone at the table got a generous glimpse of her cleavage. "You'll make my mascara run!" When she shook her head, her mass of mahogany hair shimmered.

Lauren tried to shift her eyes elsewhere, but the show was on, and all around the table diners tuned in. Luis's eyes sparkled. His chuckle was low, as the woman slithered into the empty chair next to him.

Enid put down her coffee mug and leaned toward Lauren. "Who is that slut with Luis?"

Lauren had to drink some water before she could answer. "Some cave inspector."

"Hmm. More like a very good friend."

Lauren watched the woman pick a few bites off Luis's plate with her fingers and nodded. "Too good, I'd say."

Enid squeezed Lauren's wrist. "The bastard. You must make him pay." Enid rose and threw her napkin at her dessert plate.

"Where are you going, Enid?"

"Sleuthing."

Lauren got up to follow her, but Enid had already rounded the table and was marching toward Luis and the slut. "Luis, is this another one of your archeologists?" she called in her most charming tones.

Luis pushed back his chair and rose. Without a glimmer of guilt, he flicked a quick grin at Lauren. "This is Marcella Rodriguez, an old friend. Marcella, this is Dr. Enid Godwin, our poet in residence."

Enid pumped the woman's hand. "And you're here for—"

"Permits," Luis answered. "Marcella is with the Mexican government. We need her to approve our permits each time we excavate a new area."

Enid frowned and finally released the woman's hand. "Ah, a bureaucrat."

"I am honored to meet you, Dr. Godwin." The woman leaned her chest against Luis's forearm and smiled. "How wonderful, Luis, to have a distinguished lady at the dig site. Luis and I are very old friends, Dr. Godwin. Very old friends." Her long fingers crept up Luis's neck. "Come, Luis. Business first, pleasure later."

Luis elbowed her arm away and looked over the woman's shoulder at Lauren. "This won't take long, will it, Marcella? All I've got is a half hour."

"But, Luis, that hardly gives us time to catch up," Marcella said, as Luis steered her out of the dining room.

Lauren followed, but Enid intercepted her in the

doorway. "Did you see that, Lauren? She was all over him."

"Yes."

Enid glared at Lauren and shook her head. "Anyone could tell he cares for you, Lauren, but he's a man with a reputation. You must be honest and strong, dear, or he'll break your heart."

Lauren gritted her teeth. "I intend to defend my territory, Enid, and I refuse to flee to Bangkok. See you in the morning."

Enid caught Lauren by the wrist. "Just a minute, dear. I'm going up to bed right now, and I'll sleep so much better if you give me a quick neck massage. Come up in ten minutes. That cot is killing me."

Lauren felt trapped. Enid would never let her get away quickly. She glanced at Luis ambling into the bar with that woman's arm around his waist. She stood in the hallway and pretended to read the schedule posted on the bulletin board. Now and then, she glanced at the far end of the porch where Luis and the woman were huddled together on a crowded couch. The woman laughed too much. Luis never put his hand on any part of her, which was a good sign, though Marcella clutched his fingers once, rested her hand on his knee twice, and played with her hair in between. Lauren had read somewhere that playing with your hair was one of the top five ways to show a man you wanted to sleep with him.

The only time Luis laughed was when he looked up and caught Lauren watching them. The sound was like a caress, intimate and sexual, as if he'd taken her into his arms and kissed her deeply.

Was Enid right, she asked herself. Was Luis in love with her?

When her watch told her fifteen minutes had gone by, she waited to catch Luis's eye. He finally looked her way again, and she pointed upstairs and mouthed Enid's name. Luis winked and nodded.

While she played nurse to Enid, she thought about the wink and the nod, another intimate gesture, just between lovers, a sign that he was hers and she was his. At least for now.

The minutes became an hour, and Lauren grew frantic. Luis must be waiting for her on the path and would soon give up on her. Worse, he could be so enraptured with Marcella that he'd forget to meet her at all.

With Enid spread-eagled on her bunk, her eyes cooled by a damp cloth and gentle snores finally emanating from her mouth, Lauren fled.

Luis was no longer on the porch, but Marcella was, leaning against the bar, clanking her beer bottle against Rocky's. On her way out Lauren let the screen door bang behind her.

She strode along the path inhaling damp and fertile air. Luis would come soon, she assured herself. The monkeys were quiet, so she would be able to hear him before she saw him.

Enid's words brought back her doubts. If Luis dumped her and broke her heart, would this love affair be worth that pain? So many questions made her head hurt. Where the hell was he?

Lauren strained her ears for his voice. Maybe he'd been in the bathroom when she came down the stairs and was already back lounging on the porch with Marcella's chest in his face, while Lauren paced around in the dark, being bitten by an insect making a strange sort of growling buzz.

From the direction of the ruins, Lauren heard sounds of the nightly nature walk. She strained her ears, but all was quiet again.

Maybe Lauren had misunderstood Luis. Maybe he was waiting for her at the gate to the ruins. The generator would turn off in about forty-five minutes. Did she dare go farther down the path and call him?

Anything was better than stomping around there doubting her lover. Lauren decided she'd be safe enough if she simply walked along the route the nature group used each night. She had her flashlight. She knew the way, at least in daylight.

The howlers' complaints erupted so suddenly that Lauren jumped and dropped her flashlight. In a panic, she fell to her knees and scrambled around the dust and twigs until she found it beneath an outcropping of something prickly. She flicked on the light to be sure it still worked and stayed in her crouch until her heartbeat slowed. If the damn monkeys would shut up, she'd be able to think straight.

The noise stopped. The silence was abrupt, as if the whole rain forest held its breath to listen for Luis.

Her heart banging away, Lauren stood. Ahead of her, the gate clanked. Maybe Luis had gone in to check the grounds. She neared the entrance and saw a beam of light flickering beyond the trees to her left. Then there was darkness again.

"Luis?" She called his name quietly, so she wouldn't rouse the monkeys. No answer. Where would he go? Another beam blinked ahead, and she hustled to catch up to it. Her hiking boot caught on the uneven path, and she tumbled to her knees. One knee hurt like hell, so she flashed the light to see if she'd cut herself. She noticed a blood stain on her pants and other drops on the rocks, but none on her knee. Had an animal died there? Had someone else had an accident?

The gate stood open. To her left was another glimmer of light. Who else but Luis would be walking there at that hour?

A man shouted. Lauren held her breath. It was Luis's voice. Or was she crazy?

No, it was Luis's voice, and he wouldn't shout,

unless something was wrong. Her pulse raced in her throat as she stepped through the gate.

Surrounded by blackness and silence, she wasn't sure which way to go. Should she go back and get help?

Ahead, and to her left, she heard another noise, a groan. Feeling her way with her feet, Lauren inched toward the sound. She thought she might be on the path to the caves, but Luis would never go to a cave at night.

Luis would never go into a cave at all.

Lauren flicked on her flashlight and noticed the path narrowed before curving to the right. She flicked it off and waited to let her eyes readjust to the darkness.

She was breaking all the rules. She was alone. She had no protection from snake or insect bites. Hell, she didn't even know where she was going. Worst of all, no one else knew where she was.

Her boot hit something—another rock, maybe. She stopped to shine her light on it and picked up a large flashlight exactly like Luis's. Nearby were gashes in the sandy earth path. Signs of a struggle.

She had no time to get help. If she'd waited for help that night in the parking garage, Luis might have been killed.

Someone had followed Luis. Or had waited for him. She moved along as quickly as she could with an occasional flick of her flash to keep her on the narrow path. The rumble of male voices told her she was closing in on them, whoever they were.

After Lauren nearly bashed her nose on a rocky outcropping, she made herself move more slowly. Ten feet above her, the flashlight revealed a series of layered rocks jutting like steps up a wall. At the top was a shadowed opening that might be the entrance to a cave, Luis's nightmare. Now her nightmare too.

With her first step, the rocks shifted. She

toppled and turned her ankle and scraped her elbow as she fell. She hoped the cut wouldn't attract bloodthirsty vermin.

The next few stairs held her, but the upper ones were nothing but loose gravel. She found a toehold on a stable outcropping, grabbed the trunk of a sapling and hauled herself up to the level area in front of the mouth of the cave. She stood still and heard nothing, not even the rustle of a palm branch.

Lauren flicked on the flashlight again and drew back in horror. Serpents with bulging eyes and swollen tongues and feathered monsters with horns and fangs ogled her from high on the walls surrounding the opening. The faces were harmless, she assured herself.

What she was about to do, however, could be fatal.

Before she entered, she had to think everything through. Did she dare use the flashlight inside? What if the ground dropped away after the entrance? What if there was a pool of water inside?

To move safely she needed the light.

A whooshing, flapping sound gusted toward her, like hundreds of people clapping with gloves on. She froze, as the sound grew closer. In an instant, the sky above her whirred with swooping birds.

Not birds, but bats. She swung away from the opening and flattened herself against the painted wall of rock.

Something or someone had scared them into flight. Once they had evacuated, Lauren crept inside and listened again. The cool air stank, like excrement, guano, maybe.

She stood in a small cavern with a ceiling just a few inches above her head. There were no pottery shards on the floor, no carvings or drawings on the walls, nothing that hinted that the space had ever been inhabited.

There seemed to be no exit. She turned to leave, and then realized all those bats must have come from a larger space beyond that cavern. In the far corner, she found a hole not more than four feet square. Her light revealed a narrow corridor beyond. Like Alice down that hole, she followed.

There the walls were unadorned too, but the corridor was easy to follow. As it widened and rose at a steep angle, her footsteps made a different crunching sound. Ahead of her was another opening. She turned off the light, listened, and heard nothing. She glanced into the dark behind her and wondered if she'd ever see daylight again. Her arms were cold.

With her light back on, she crept through the opening, scraping her elbows along the way, and found herself on a shelf of rock overlooking an enormous space. At least thirty feet above her yawned a ceiling covered with colorful carvings of frowning heads. Below her water glimmered. When she inched closer to see more, the ground gave way, and she fell, tumbling and skidding. The flashlight flew out of her hand and splashed before she did.

She came up sputtering, terrified that her voice had echoed like a burglar alarm. She couldn't see. The water was slimy, cold, and too deep to stand. Keep your head, she told herself, and splashed around for a ledge. In two strokes, her hand touched rock. With a giant kick, she managed to pull herself out of the water and onto a shelf of rock. Luis's flash was gone, but, amazingly, the flashlight from her pocket still worked. She found herself on an island surrounded by water.

When she sat down to catch her breath and dry off somehow, she heard men's voices. If they saw her, she'd be trapped. She stretched out as flat as she could and listened.

Beyond the cavern, a man was complaining about bats in Spanish. Another man said something about ghosts, as a light beamed around the walls of the giant room. "Nadie." Nobody. The light flicked out and the footsteps retreated.

Lauren stashed the flashlight in her pocket again and forced herself back into the slime to swim over to where the man had stood. The water smelled putrid, like the mice that lived and died in her damp basement back in Milwaukee. She shrugged off thoughts of what kind of animal life might live in the water, or might have died in it. Her foot found a foothold, and she climbed out of the pool.

Exactly like the time in the parking garage, she heard the sound of fists and knew someone was being beaten.

Lauren smelled kerosene before she saw the wavering shadows cast by the lamp. Dripping in her soggy clothes and shaking with chill, Lauren used the light to pick her way over piles of rubble through a tunnel into the next chamber, and then turned it off. She must not stumble, and she must not let them see her. She tucked herself behind a jut of wall and decided she had to take a peek.

From the direction of the flickering light of the kerosene lamp, she could tell the occupants stood around the wall to her right, but she couldn't get a good look without exposing herself. Before she dared to move, she looked down to be sure of her footing. In the shadow, she saw a skull. And another one. And a rib cage.

The entire area around her feet was littered with human skeletons.

"How many times do I have to tell you? I don't know where the treasure is! How would I? You had two sections of the map. I only had one."

It was Luis!

"Speak in Spanish! Are you ashamed of your heritage?" a harsh voice growled.

"I am ashamed of you. You lie and cheat and

kill, and for what? To despoil your ancestors' history."

"What a joke. You are the great archeologist! Stealing from others is your job. Fito, hit him until he speaks in Spanish!"

"Que?"

Lauren heard the smack and had to hold onto the cold wall to stay on her feet.

"You can beat me till I'm bloody. Face it Gorge, someone got here first. Somebody else has the treasure."

Lauren inched closer, carefully avoiding the bones of people who had been buried there, or more likely, had been sacrificed. Again, she tucked herself into a niche along the wall and dared to take a quick look. She saw Luis, barely twenty feet away, stretched out on a shelf of rock. His cheek was bleeding, and his arms were stretched awkwardly behind his back.

When one man bent over him, Luis heaved up his body and kicked him in the groin. The man swore, bent double for a moment, and then slapped Luis twice until he lay still. The other man stopped pacing back and forth and barked at him to stop.

She must surprise them. She felt around her feet for something hefty to throw. The first thing she touched was shaped like a jawbone, which gave her the shivers. At last, she grasped a heavy rock small enough to fit in her hand and a skull she could grip with the other hand. She leaned through the opening, tossed the skull, and ducked back into her niche.

"Vaya!" The pacing man must have ordered his buddy to investigate.

A nearby crunching sound told her to make her move. She raised the rock above her head and cocked her other fist close to her side. As the man bolted through the passage, she struck, bashed his head, jabbed his gut, kicked his legs, and stomped on him as he fell. Once he lay still, she ducked back into her niche to wait.

The other man yelled something. His voice sounded quite near. She must time her next attack perfectly.

The second man was smarter than the first. He called to his partner, waiting, staying away from her. She waited too, barely breathing. Then the footsteps crunched away. Where was he going?

The kerosene light went out, and it became so black she thought her eyes were closed. Where was he? What was he doing?

She knew he'd drawn near again by the crunch of stones and bones. As long as the light was out, she was safe. But so was he.

A frigid hand grabbed her neck, threw her to the ground, shoved her face into the bones, and knelt on her back. She kicked and screamed, but couldn't get away. Choking on dust, she refused to lie still until the man turned his flashlight on her.

Even though the light blinded her, she knew the two men were the muggers who had killed Ken. Barking at her to shut up, the man tightened his grip on her neck until she stopped kicking, and then hauled her to her feet, twisted her arms behind her back, tied up her hands, and dragged her through the passageway into the huge cavern. The man gave her a shove, and she fell on her face.

Lauren had screwed up. She hurt everywhere. Her mouth was bleeding, her arms were numb, she was colder than she'd ever been in her life, and her head hurt so much she didn't want to move even her eyes.

She was about to die. For all she knew Luis was already dead. His efforts to find the treasure were wasted.

The odor of kerosene invaded her sinuses and

burned the back of her throat. She coughed and felt something move next to her. Someone whispered her name. "Lauren, tell me you're okay."

She turned toward Luis's voice and could just make out his face in the lantern light. "I can't see you. Are you hurt?"

"Shh." He breathed the words into her ear. Something warm touched her shoulder. "If they hear us, they'll be back over here. My hands are tied, but I just touched you with my elbow. You're all wet."

Lauren twisted her body until her mouth was near Luis's face. "I fell into a pool."

"Are your hands tied behind your back?"

"Yes. They're going to kill us, Luis."

"We won't let them. Can you slide your feet through the ropes until your hands are in front of you?"

"I'll try. Must have bashed my shoulder. Can hardly feel my hands." She broke out in a sweat as the pain shot through her shoulder and up her neck. She bit her lip and continued inching her arms down the backs of her legs to her feet. She didn't want to die in that cave.

"One leg's through."

"Shh. Here comes Fito. Look out. He's pissed that you got the drop on him." Luis stifled a laugh. "You kicked him in the balls."

Lauren heard his footsteps and felt his presence above her. Fito yelled something about beating her bloody as soon as she was conscious again.

Lauren opened her eyes enough to watch him trudge back to the far side of the cavern. "Is that a pyramid over there?"

"Yes. Be careful. Fito just glanced this way. This chamber must have been a holy place. There're some serpent heads that are still intact, and they look a lot like the drawing on the map. Lauren? I think we're in the treasure chamber."

"You found it?"

"No. Gorge and Fito did. Turns out there were three pieces of that map. Gorge and Fito had one, stole one from someone, then stole mine. Some other bastard figured it all out for them."

"Then where's the treasure?"

"Not here anymore."

"It's gone?"

"Guess so."

"Someone got here first?"

"Apparently."

"Are you okay in this cave?" When he didn't answer, she asked again.

"I'm sweating like a pig, but at least I can breathe now. They knew about my phobia. They hoped I'd tell them anything to get out of here. Did you get your wrists in front of you yet?"

"Uh-oh, my other leg is stuck. There." She blew on her hands to warm them.

"I'll turn over so you can untie me."

Lauren forced her numb stubs to work on his ropes. On the other side of the cavern, the glow of the lantern highlighted two men methodically moving back and forth. "There're so many knots. Who's the guy who figured out the map?"

"Don't know."

"Are these the guys from the parking garage?"

"Yes."

"And they think you already found the treasure?"

"Yep. How are you doing there with my rope?"

"Can't tell."

"I'm out," he said, and rolled over to face her. "You're wonderful. Here, let me undo your knots, and then you can put your hands behind you again, so they think you're still tied up. Think you can run as soon as I get a chance to jump them?"

"Let's both jump them. They won't expect that."

214

She'd seen what they had done to him in the garage, but she blotted out the image of a bloody battle and prayed her legs would work when she needed them.

"Once they're down, Lauren, you go where I go, no matter what."

Lauren touched his lips with her fingers. "Don't die, Luis." When he said nothing, she inched closer to him. "How do they know you, Luis?"

"Later. Be ready."

Lauren sucked on her bleeding lip and watched the moving shadows. After one of the men swore, the sound echoed like a chorus through the chamber, and Luis's breath came in puffs, as if he was trying not to laugh.

"They've been digging up carvings and pottery they found over there near one of the pillars that braces the cave, but Fito's in bad shape, thanks to you, and it's taking longer than they thought."

Lauren watched one of the men lift the lantern and stride toward them, with the other man limping along behind. Giant shadows danced on the walls. Lauren closed her eyes and wished she had another rock in her hand.

The first man's boots stopped at her feet, and he settled the lantern on nearby stones with a clatter.

"How's your pretty lady, Cousin Luis?"

The man's boot thumped against her back. Lauren bit her tongue and kept quiet.

"Que malo, Fito, la señorita es muerte, eh? You think we killed her, Cousin? You don't want to die like that, do you? Eh, Luis?" The man stepped closer to Lauren. "You asleep or weeping for your sweetheart? Do I have to kick you, too, for the answer?"

Luis groaned. "My arms are so numb I can't move."

"If you tell us where the treasure is, we'll untie your hands so you can dig it up for us."

"What?"

"You can't move? You can't even hear?"

Terrified the man would attack Luis again, Lauren stole a glimpse of him as he bent down over Luis.

In a flash Luis sprang up shouting, head-butted the man to the ground and leaped on top of him, bashing him with his fists. The other man, Fito, yelled and reached for his pocket. Lauren leaped up, threw her body at Fito's knees, and took him down. As he fell, he kicked her in the ribs and sent her spinning. Deafening shots rang out. Rocks rained down from everywhere.

"Cave-in! Run, Fito!" Gorge screamed above a torrent of noise.

Dust filled the air and the world went black.

Colliding rocks rumbled into the cavern. Luis shouted her name. Lauren felt him tug her away from the cascading ceiling. They stumbled through the dark, fell, and hauled each other up to scramble again. Lauren was sure they would slam into a wall of rock or be smothered under the rubble, but somehow they kept moving.

For a moment the debris stopped pelting them, though the noise continued, ugly and terrifying. Lauren's ribs ached with every breath.

"Keep moving," Luis yelled. "The whole cavern could collapse." He yanked her by the arm. "Damn! All I have is my little flashlight."

"Here," Lauren said and shoved hers into his hand. "I found yours on the path, but lost it back there."

Luis flicked it on and focused it on a narrow shadow in the wall of rock. "Come on. This way."

They stumbled into the next tunnel, and dust rolled after them. In a panic, they raced toward the blackest tunnel. Luis's light picked up the reflection of a small pool.

"Quick. Let's get some water while we can." Luis squatted next to the pool, unclipped his water bottle from his belt, and handed it to her.

Lauren's hand trembled as she gripped the bottle. "I can hardly swallow, my mouth is so full of grit."

"Finish it." He rested his light on the ground, dug into the pocket of his cargo pants and pulled out a small tin box. "Here, take a couple of these." He handed her two painkillers, popped two in his own mouth, and swallowed. "Maybe I can refill the bottle here." He rested his light on the ground, cupped his hand into the pool, and sipped. "The water's okay." He filled his bottle, drank, and then refilled it once more. "Let me clean that gash on your head. Is your lip still bleeding?"

Lauren sat cross-legged on the rough stones and tried to hold her head up with her hands. "How are we ever going to find our way out?"

Luis focused the light above her left ear and pulled his kerchief out of his pocket. "I'll get us out," he said, as if he performed miracles every day. "First, I have to stop the bleeding. Then I have to warm you up. Here, lie down in my lap."

Surrounded by Luis's warmth, Lauren closed her eyes and tried to believe that a man who battled panic attacks the second he stepped into a cave could possibly save them both. His gentle hands dabbed coolness on her cuts. Waves of pain scrambled her thinking. She felt him tug her arms out of her sleeves.

"Sit up now, Lauren, so I can get your wet shirt off over your head and then try to unhitch your damn bra."

For a moment, Lauren couldn't remember where they were. "You're good at that, Luis." She heard another rumble. "What if all these caves collapse?"

"We won't let them. Show me—are you hurt

anywhere else? Here, put this on."

She struggled to make her fingers work on the buttons. "Your shirt's so warm, Luis, and it smells like you, but won't you be cold?"

"I'm fine in a T-shirt." He tied his kerchief around her head like a bandana. "Let's go."

Once they each had another long drink, they were back on their feet and moving again. Luis grumbled when they had to crawl through a low passage. "Hope those bastards add their bones to the rest back there."

"I wish I had knee pads. These rocks are murder."

"Keep going, Lauren. You okay?"

"Talk to me, Luis. Keep my mind somewhere else. Tell me: who are they?"

"Gorge and Fito, two guys from around here. Here, we can stand up now, though you still have to watch your head."

Lauren tried not to stretch her sore ribs as she stood up. "Luis, I have to tell you something before we die."

Luis pulled her along. "I refuse to die in a cave, Lauren. Driving my Jeep too fast? Yeah, it's possible I'll die that way. In a fight in a bar when some guy calls me a Spic? Yeah, definitely possible. But, not here. Not today."

Lauren laughed and wondered if they were both crazy. "How about getting beaten up for flirting with that so-called government official?"

Luis stopped and turned to touch her face. "Come on. You thought I was interested in Marcella? No way."

"You have your reputation. Women flock to you. You flock them."

"A good pun, but a bad lie. She and I had our time, I admit, but that was long before the mystique of La Bella Lauren."

Lauren wasn't going to let him change the subject for long. "I understand that you are the kind of man who needs lots of women."

"Lots of women?"

"You taught me about passion. You taught me to live. Ouch!"

"What happened?"

"I stubbed my toe."

"Save this informative chat for later, Lauren, when I can look into your gringo eyes and watch your imagination grow. Now we focus on getting the hell out of here."

They wound their way through twisting tunnels, until Lauren's hands, knees, and shoulders were scraped and bloody, and she was positive they'd been moving in circles. Blood kept dripping from the cuts on her forehead and her lip. Her feet ached in her soggy shoes and socks, and she yearned to rest. In every cavern, Luis's light flashed on layers of rocks, sparkling walls of crystal and towers of candle-like rock formations, and each time he located another opening for them to follow.

They squeezed single-file through a corridor and entered a large domed space. Luis froze and whistled. He flashed the light around slowly, once, and then again. "Whoa! Look at the size of this place! You could hold a soccer match in here. The ceiling's nearly five stories high. This must have been a ceremonial cave. Look," he said pointing his light at a wall of cascading sparkles. "Have you ever seen anything like that?"

"What is it?"

"A wall of limestone. Looks like a frozen waterfall, doesn't it? Over there is where they must have performed their bloodletting. Sit down and rest for a minute while I find a way out of here. Be careful where you step. There's a pile of bones over there."

Lauren flashed her light along rows of stalactites and stalagmites that supported the ceiling. Some of the formations were carved into long, twisted faces, while others appeared to be eerie, emaciated statues. In the center of the space stood a rock shaped like a table. Next to it was a pillar of stone three times the size of the clock that had stood in her grandfather's hallway when she was a child.

Lauren picked her way over the shambles of rocks and dodged the pile of skeletons until she could get a closer look. The table-like stone turned out to be a reclining statue of Chac Mul, the Mayan rain god she'd seen in photos, with his passive staring face at one end, his bent knees at the other, and his stomach as the resting place for offerings.

One pillar appeared to be the remains of a broken stalagmite carved into the wizened face of a frightened old man. His eye sockets were empty, his nose long and pronounced, his cheeks lined, and his lips sagging in agony.

Death. That's what Lauren saw when she peered into those sockets. "Luis?" She needed to be near him.

"Yeah?"

She scrambled over to the far side of the sanctuary and found him scanning the walls with his flashlight from the rugged floor to the high domed ceiling. At the end of a circle, he motioned her to follow him back to level ground near the eerie face.

Luis rubbed her aching shoulder. "How's your head?"

Everywhere she looked, she saw death. "It hurts. I want to get out of here."

Luis touched her cheek. "Did I tell you what a tough woman you are?"

Lauren was sure Luis was pretending to be

optimistic. "Did you find a way out?"

He shrugged. "If we could scare up some bats we'd find our exit right away."

"How do you know this isn't a dead-end?"

"The air's still pretty fresh. It has to get in here somehow." He flashed the light to the ground. "Our field team would go crazy with those pottery shards. Look, there's a bowl fragment right here." The light lingered on a triangle of pottery painted orange and blue. "The ancient Maya always made sure they had more than one way out. That's the good news."

Lauren's eyes followed his flashlight beam as it climbed the wall and halted above them.

"It's possible the gap up on that ledge is the exit—very possible. There might have been a stairway from here to there." He reached for her hand. "That climb is going to be tough, though. Let's rest first. This is as good a place as any."

"What if this cavern collapses too?"

"The other one caved in because Gorge and Fito were excavating near one of the inner walls, and then the idiot shot off his gun. I warned them they could cause a cave-in, but of course, they didn't believe me. Hey, you're still really cold."

They both sat down on Chac Mul's stomach. Luis pulled Lauren against his chest and began to massage her arms. "This should help." His cheek settled against hers. "Tell me, how in hell did you find me?"

"When you didn't show up to meet me, I went hunting I saw lights ahead of me. I thought I heard you yell, so I followed the sound. Then I found your flashlight on the ground near the cave, and knew you were in trouble."

Luis kissed her forehead. "Nice work."

"If I'd gone back for help we wouldn't be stuck here." Lauren stifled a sob. "I screwed up." She listened to Luis's heart beating. "How did these guys know about your map?"

Luis blew air through his lips. "Gorge's mother is married to my cousin, the bad one in the family, El Malo, as my grandmother always calls him. The parts of the map were distributed around the family, so he got one, I got one, and then last summer someone broke into the third cousin's house and killed him. Now I know why. For his part of the map."

Luis brushed her hair off her forehead. "The treasure should have been in that cavern where you found me, right there with all those bones."

"What is the treasure, Luis?"

His arms dropped to his knees. "You got me."

"How do you know that stuff they were loading up back there wasn't part of the treasure?"

Luis sighed and leaned his cheek back against hers. "I don't, but I know my grandfather, and he knew what was valuable. He or his brothers must have found something so rare they were afraid to keep it themselves."

"So they made a map to guide you to this valuable something?"

"I guess so. At some point, someone must have found it and moved it, or sold it, or destroyed it." He sighed and kissed her shoulder. "Here, curl up against me."

Luis took off his shoes and put them under his head as a pillow, and Lauren smoothed off Chac Mul's tummy and resettled herself against Luis's chest. "Luis?"

"More questions, Lauren?"

She felt his lips on her forehead. "Is there anything else you want to tell me?"

"Like what?"

She touched his cheek. "You know."

"Like a list of women I've made love to?"

Lauren didn't answer.

"Was that the wrong answer?"

Lauren turned away and got a cheek full of dust. Reluctantly she rolled back against his shoulder. She imagined herself whining, could you pretty please tell me you love me before I die? Still, Luis was silent. What was he thinking? Did he really believe he could get them out of the endless black maze?

No, he was as scared as she was, but somehow had banished his panic.

"I need to know what you're thinking, Luis, but I'm afraid of what you'll say. Tell me lies, if you have to, but talk to me."

Luis caressed her cheek and tucked her head beneath his chin. "Here's the truth, Lauren. I'm scared. Caves freak me out, but I can do this, because I have to." He paused. "And because you're with me."

Lauren bit her lips to keep from crying. "Thank you."

Luis stopped her with his finger on her lips. "Listen. I've never met anyone like you, Lauren Richmond, a woman so beautiful, a woman so nosy and annoying, a woman who won't let me go. Now sleep if you can."

In the quiet depths of the dark, Lauren listened to Luis's steady breathing. She was on the verge of sleep, when he kissed her gently, sweetly.

"I dragged you into this, Lauren, and I'll get you out of it." His voice grew hoarse. "I couldn't stay away from you, you know. I tried," he said and yawned. "I really tried."

****

"Lauren?" Luis's voice woke her and set her heart pounding. "We should get going to keep our bodies warm."

The glow from his flashlight blinded her for a moment. Every muscle complained as Lauren stood.

"Okay."

"Drink first. No, don't turn on your flashlight. We have to save the batteries for movements only. How do you feel?"

Lauren knelt to drink and then stretched her arms and legs. Her neck snapped like popcorn. "Warmer, thanks to you, and sore." She wasn't going to admit her knee throbbed and the gash on her elbow was bleeding again. They were alive, so far. She reached for his mouth, remembering his words as they fell asleep. "Are you okay, Luis?"

Lauren waited for him to reassure her again that he was fine, that he was sure he could get them out, but he hadn't heard her question. He stood next to her, not saying a word. She assumed he was worrying about how to get out of there. Maybe he was even more terrified to think ahead than she was. Maybe his plan was risky, but Lauren didn't dare ask him.

"Okay, let's go." Luis flicked on his flashlight and led her over to the wall of rubble. "You light my way up, and then I'll light yours. Just keep your light on me."

Feeling for sturdy handholds among the loose rocks, Luis clambered about eight feet up and rested for a moment. He moved his hands along the narrow ledge, found solid rock to grip, and hoisted himself until he could stand at the top. He flicked on his flashlight and motioned her to follow.

Lauren stuffed the flashlight into her pocket and began slowly. She had luck at first, but when she neared the top, with Luis's hand in reach, the gravel beneath her feet gave way and she cascaded halfway down, scraping her elbows, inhaling dust.

Luis flung himself over the edge. "Lauren, quick, grab my hand."

With every wiggle, she sunk more deeply into the wall of sand. "I'm up to my knees in this stuff."

Before she finished the sentence, she sank up to her thighs. She began to panic. "I'm trapped, Luis!"

"Here, I'll haul you up."

"I can't move, Luis. The gravel keeps shifting!"

"Come on, Lauren, stretch. If I come any nearer to the edge, I'll spill even more of this crap on top of you. Reach. You're almost there. Okay, I've got you."

Luis's firm hand hauled her onto a flat boulder.

"I was drowning in gravel. Luis, please, get me out of this place!" Her heart galloped against her ribs. She couldn't catch her breath.

"Take it easy, Lauren." He held her close and whispered. "I know what you mean. You're scared. I am too. We can do this. Together we can find our way."

He helped her drink some water and held her until her breathing slowed. "Do you still have your flashlight?" Lauren nodded. "Good." He pointed it in an arc around them. "Wait," he shouted and steadied the beam on a figure sitting in a niche in the wall next to them. "Get a look at that!"

"It's beautiful!" Lauren let him pull her onto her feet.

"Typical pottery figure of a woman, about two feet high, Pre-classic, I think. See how she differs from the figures you've seen at our excavation?"

Lauren realized Luis was trying to distract her. She nodded. "Her face is round and sad. How long do you think she's been here?"

"Close to two thousand years," Luis said. "Looks to me like others have worshipped here more recently than that. See how the rock walls are carved like a cathedral? Early seventeenth century, I'd guess. In this part of the peninsula, the Maya evaded the Spanish conquest by going underground. There would have been a pool in the middle there for sacrifices. And more bones."

Lauren shivered. "Like all the bones I saw

before I bashed Fito."

"We Maya share a long history of violence."

"Your grandfather would have disapproved of our intrusion here."

Luis's laugh echoed eerily. "My grandfather would have disapproved of a lot of things you and I have done." He slipped his arm around her waist. "Hey, what's this?" He reached down to sift the sand at his feet and picked up something that glowed under his flashlight. "Here, a souvenir for my lady."

Lauren fingered the cool stone Luis placed in her palm. "Is it jade? It's so smooth."

"An amulet to get us out of here." Luis flashed the light around the other walls and then along the floor of the ledge. "If I ever get the guts to come back here, I intend to excavate this cavern, Lauren. Let's keep moving."

They trod single file through a corridor carved into the cave. Sometimes it rose. Sometimes it fell. Eventually they entered a small room with no outlet, except for a low tunnel. Lauren wanted to cry or scream. "Luis, we have to go back."

Luis bent down and directed his light into the tunnel. "There's a larger opening at the other end, probably a room."

"We'll never fit."

"You can make it, for sure, but my shoulders might be too wide. Let's drink some water first, Lauren."

The two drank as Luis shined the light on the impossibly narrow tunnel. "I say it's doable."

"There's no other way out, besides that narrow passage?"

"Not that I can find. Start out on your hands and knees and then just inch along like a worm."

"It's so narrow. What about your problem, Luis? Will you be okay?"

"I just won't think about it. I'll go first."

Lauren held the flashlight as Luis crawled through the first five feet of the passage. Then he had to inch along on his stomach by pushing with the toes of his hiking boots. Watching him and worrying about him made her feel like throwing up. The tunnel was impossibly long and narrow.

"Come on, Lauren. I'm almost through."

She couldn't answer him. Frozen in fear, she gaped at the tiny space.

"Are you coming?"

Drenched with sweat, Lauren crawled along on her hands and knees. Luis was at least three feet ahead of her. She hurried to catch up to him, before her terror became panic. Don't panic, she told herself. Don't think about panicking, she told herself. It was mind over matter, she told herself. There wasn't enough air. Lauren's bleeding elbows stung. Her hip landed on a sharp rock.

"Ouch! I can't see, Luis. I can't breathe. Oh, God, don't leave me like this. There's no air. No air."

"Stop talking. Breathe in slowly. Then breathe out, slowly. Count with me. Are you counting? Inhale, one, two, three, four, exhale, one, two, three, four."

The blackness closed in. One, two, three, she counted and inhaled. One, two, three, she exhaled. The blackness receded. Inhale, exhale.

"I'm almost out, Lauren. Are you right behind me?"

"Yes." One, two, three, she counted. One, two, three.

As Luis lunged, his upper body cleared the passage, but his boot kicked away the corridor wall and thick, wet clods of clay and stone covered Lauren's head and shoulders. The flashlight went out. Blackness surrounded her.

"Luis!" she shrieked. "Luis? Help me. Oh, please!" She stabbed away at the clumps with her fingers and pressed forward with her toes.

She tried not to think about being buried alive, about being stuck in that airless shaft, lost and alone, like the boys Luis had known. How long before her air ran out? Still she forced herself to inch her body forward. When her fingers broke through the stony muck, she wanted to cheer, but she had no breath. Her shoulders were wedged in the narrowest part of the passage.

She rested her head on the stones for a moment to listen for Luis and heard nothing but dripping water. "Please be okay," she begged, but there was no answer.

Lauren pulled with her hands, shoved with her toes again, and wiggled her shoulders until the top half of her body was free. The bit of light she glimpsed ahead gave her hope.

She scooped clumps of stony clay from around her waist and hips and shoveled them into the cavern ahead of her. The air was plentiful again. The sliver of light was her guide. After another lunge, she wiggled free and tumbled into the cavern.

Lauren didn't see Luis beneath the rocks until his hand moved. "Luis." She touched his face.

"I'm stuck." His voice sounded far away.

Lauren found his shoulders and moved her hands down his body. "There's a chunk of something across your thighs. I'll try to move it. Keep talking."

He coughed. "Can't feel my legs. You were right. We're going to die here."

His toneless voice terrified her. "No, that rock is jammed, that's all. I can pry it up. Can you help?"

He gasped and coughed again. She shoved at the slab, but it wouldn't budge.

"Forget it, Lauren. Wait! I can move my leg!"

"Okay, now the other. Can you push as I pull?"

"There's crap in my eyes. Jeez, the thing is heavy."

"It's moving, Luis. Push!"

"It's almost off. There, it's off, thank God. Whoa!"

"What's wrong?"

"My knee. Must have wrenched it when I went down."

"Can you stand? Can you walk?"

"I thought I was done, Lauren. I thought we were both going to die. You find the flashlight?"

"I found something better." She pointed to a crack of light ahead of them. "Look."

"Daylight! Lauren, you're amazing. Did I ever tell you that?"

"Not enough."

"Let's get the hell out of here."

The corridor narrowed again and then grew steep. Trickles of water made walking slippery. Sweat poured off Luis's cheeks as they trudged up the incline. The corridor turned and opened into another cavern where a pale light penetrated an opening thirty feet high in the wall of rock.

"This is it!" Luis's joyful words echoed. "See how those ribs of rock are shaped like the vaulting in an old cathedral? This was our hideout when we were kids."

"No kidding?"

Luis took her hand and led her across a narrow bridge of rock over a deep pit. "The entrance is ahead."

Once they rounded a boulder the size of a car they emerged through a gash in the rocks into humid, fresh dawn air. Luis groaned as he crouched and breathed deeply, and then grinned at the valley below. He stood and pressed his dusty lips to hers.

"That's twice now, Lauren."

She was dizzy for a second and needed his arm around her to stand. Luis leaned on Lauren's shoulder as he limped down the side of the hill.

"Twice what?" she asked.

His smile blazed down on her. "You saved my life twice, Lauren Richmond."

"No, Luis. You saved mine."

Chapter Fifteen

Lauren and Luis followed the orange glow of dawn down the stony mountain path. Below, a dirt road zigzagged through the valley. Lauren tried to block her ache for water, food, and sleep and forced herself to focus on staying upright and placing one foot in front of the other. When she stopped for a moment to rest, she saw the first curve of the sun emerge from behind a cloud. They were alive and free from the darkness at last.

A small stone church with a wooden bell tower huddled in a boulder-strewn niche against the mountain. Plastic bottles and bags dotted the roadside. A rooster crowed and set off a cacophony of barking dogs. Lights glowed in the windows of concrete block houses. Condensation dripped off their tin roofs. Along the road, a creek dribbled through a stand of scruffy trees. Farther down the road, they passed more houses rimmed with gardens, weather-beaten sheds, or fenced-in chicken roosts.

Finally, Lauren asked where they were going.

"To my grandmother's house, down this road and then to the right."

"How far?"

"Another three blocks. Can you make it?"

Lauren nodded. Talking took too much energy.

Larger than its neighbors, Luis's grandmother's bright pink house sat alone at the end of a short spur off the main track. On either side of the pink front door, sea-blue curtains billowed from the open windows.

Soon after Luis banged the iron-knobbed knocker, a thin young woman in a loose T-shirt and tight jeans opened the door. With a yelp, she gathered Luis into her slender arms and hugged him so hard he stumbled. She stepped back, brushed her thick dark hair off her face as a smile burst across her face. "Baby Luis, I hoped you'd come!"

"Maria, what are you doing here? Has something happened? Is Abuelita sick?"

Like Luis, the tiny woman had tan skin, dark eyes, long lashes, and graceful hands. She bit her bottom lip and led them by the hand into the house.

"We don't know what's wrong with her. I just got here yesterday. Mom's coming next week. We're taking turns. Didn't the other girls reach you? Of course not." She threw up her hands and shook her head. "You're impossible to reach, Luis, as always. It's so early, how did you get here? Wait! You're hurt." She raised her eyebrows and stared at Lauren. "What the heck happened to you two?"

"There was a cave-in near the dig site, Maria. We were trapped in it. We need to sit down."

They entered a small living room so crowded with Victorian chairs, couches, and tables, it might have been a furniture showroom.

The woman reached for Lauren's hand again. "I'm sorry. I didn't mean to be rude." Her grip was warm and dry. "How did you get here?" Maria grabbed her hair and pulled it back from her face. "You were trapped? I don't understand any of this."

"We just got out of there, crawled out, to be accurate, and ended up here." Luis put his arm around Lauren. "This is Lauren Richmond." His eyes had a glint of amusement as he watched his sister. "Lauren, this is my oldest sister, who I thought was still in Chicago. What we need is water, food, and some rest before we go back to the research site."

"I don't believe it. You, in a cave-in?" The woman's skin grew pale as she hugged her chest. "I thought you'd never go back in any cave, anywhere. You're lucky to be alive." She moved a stack of books off the couch, and piled them on the coffee table. "Here, sit and I'll get you some water." She trotted toward the back of the house.

Luis and Lauren slumped onto the couch. When Maria returned with two mugs of water, they slugged them down and asked for more.

"I'm warming some soup and bread," she said from the doorway after she'd refilled their mugs. "What in the world induced you to enter a cave, Luis?" The young woman's lips spread into a thin line.

"It's a long story, Mari. We're fine, thank God. Lauren came down here with my class to work on the site for a couple of weeks."

Lauren nodded.

Maria perched on the edge of a large overstuffed stool. "So you're in grad school?"

Lauren shook her head. "I run my own business. One of my clients is a professor on the trip too."

Maria bent forward to kiss Luis's forehead and frowned at Lauren. "And maybe you're also my brother's special friend?"

Luis smiled. "Let's say she's a very special friend." Luis rested his hand on Lauren's thigh. "Tell me about Abuelita."

The woman wound her thick hair into a ponytail, twisted a band around it, and shrugged. "We don't know. She stopped eating. She stopped talking. All day long, all she does is sit in the chair Papa made for her." Her dark eyes flashed the way Luis's did when he was annoyed.

Luis and his sister had similar profiles as well, Lauren noticed, especially the same curved lips, wide mouth and beautiful teeth.

"The neighbors, you know, the couple that does her shopping for her? Well two weeks ago, they noticed she hadn't eaten any of the food they brought over, so they started taking turns eating meals with her, until she refused to eat all together." She wiped a tear on the sleeve of her T-shirt. "I tried to call your cell and the other number at the research office with no luck. Such a bad phone system you have there." She rose and turned toward the hall. "The soup should be ready. I'll get the doctor over here. You should bathe and rest, but not until you tell me what happened in the cave."

"I should call the dig site so they know we're okay," Luis said, but didn't move.

Lauren didn't have the strength to offer help, but gulped more water, settled back against the couch and closed her eyes. In what seemed like seconds, Maria returned carrying a tray of bread and bowls of soup with the heavenly aroma of onions, peppers, cheese, and garlic.

Maria watched them eat for a while, before she refilled their bowls and sat down again on the stool. "Now it's your turn." Her mouth pinched tightly. "What made you go into a cave? "

"I should go say hello to Abuelita."

"She can wait. Make your call and then talk to me."

Luis stood up slowly and nodded. "By now, they probably think we're dead. Then I'll call the local policía too."

Maria followed him toward the back of the house. "You need the police? Luis, you're driving me crazy. Did someone die in the caves?"

While Luis made the calls, his sister bustled back and forth between the kitchen and the living room with a frown rippling her forehead. Lauren stood to help her, but she waved her back. "Lie down until the doctor comes."

Lauren slid back on the couch. "To tell you the truth, I hurt everywhere, but what I need is a bath. I'm filthy. I even have dust in my ears."

"Of course." Maria covered her mouth as she smiled. "I have a surprise for you. Besides being a clever teacher, my grandfather was a man of many talents and too much energy, as my grandmother used to say. Come on." Lauren struggled to keep up with her down the hall and past the kitchen where Luis was speaking in rapid Spanish. They continued out the back door and into a flower garden surrounded on three sides by a rail fence. "*El Señor*, or Papa, as we liked to call him, was determined to have a fine bathroom for 'los gringos,' as he called his grandchildren. So he built the bath house, laid the ceramic tiles, assembled the pipeline and the pump to feed it."

Maria paused next to a shed made of the usual tin-roof and concrete blocks and pointed at Lauren's dust-covered clothes. "I have some things you can change into after your bath. I'll leave them here on the step." She opened the door and stood back.

Lauren entered the bathhouse and laughed out loud. "Wow! The tub is big enough for four, isn't it? I don't know what to say. It's beautiful!"

Luis's sister nodded. "*El Señor* would have enjoyed the look on your face just now." She pulled a bar of soap from her jeans pocket and dropped it into the soap dish on the rim of the tub. "You can leave your clothes in the bin there and I'll have them clean for Luis next time you visit."

"Thanks," Lauren said, "But I think you can throw them out."

"When you finish you can rest in the bedroom we passed just inside the back door. I'll let you know when the doctor arrives." Just before she closed the door behind her, Maria poked her head back in and bit her lip for a second. "Luis will kill me for saying this, but you seem like an intelligent woman. Maybe you can teach my brother to let his heart rule him instead of his ego."

Lauren was just climbing out of the tub when Luis entered the bathhouse buck-naked. "Don't leave," he said with a tired grin. "I need you to scrub my back."

His body looked as battered as Lauren's, with bruises and scrapes on his elbows, knees, and shins. They were quiet for a while as Lauren sudsed his back and shampooed his hair. "Who did you talk to on the phone?"

"Everyone: Enid, Frank, Annetta."

"What'd they say?"

"The cave-in was huge. Dust poured out like smoke. I don't know if we'll ever be able to get back in there."

"What happened to Gorge and Fito?"

Luis shook his head and shot Lauren a look of evil satisfaction that made her shiver. "No way could anyone have escaped such destruction. It took awhile for them to figure out that you and I must have been in there."

"Didn't they notice we were missing last night?"

"No, not until this morning when Enid kicked up a huge fuss. She took charge, apparently, and divided everyone into groups to search for us. Some of them are still out there. Frank had just returned when I called."

"Where were they looking?"

Luis closed his eyes and slid closer to Lauren so their bodies touched. "In the ruins, I guess." He rolled his head back and forth on the edge of the tub. "As if I would get lost in my own ruins."

"Or in your own cave." Lauren closed her eyes too. "I'm getting out before I drown." She eased out of the tub and handed Luis a towel when he followed. "Is someone coming to get us?"

Luis nodded. "They're picking us up in the van. It'll take them a couple of hours to get here. They have to drive all the way back to the airport to connect with the road that goes this way. Time for sleep."

She turned him around so she could dry his back with her towel. "Your hair is worse than ever." She tried to comb it with her fingers and gave up. "Sleep. What a wonderful idea."

When she was done drying his back, he took the towel from her. "My turn." He began to rub her breasts and then her belly and thighs. "You missed some vital spots. If I could stand up any longer, I'd find them all."

Clutching the clean clothes Luis's sister had left for them, they limped to the bedroom, stretched out and huddled beneath the cool sheets. "I was afraid for you, Lauren."

She shook away the memory of her panic in the cave. "I lost it, Luis. I thought we were both going to die."

"It made me realize what you mean to me."

Lauren wanted to answer him, but Luis covered her mouth with kisses.

****

When Lauren awoke, Luis's space on the bed was empty. She dressed in the borrowed clothes, a soft cotton shirt and a pair of baggy jeans, and forced her stiff body to follow his voice into the next room.

Bundled in a thick sweater that swamped her body like a blanket, a shapeless dark skirt, and a pair of ragged slippers, Luis's grandmother resembled a wrinkled bird-like version of her granddaughter. Luis sat on the single bed in the darkened room and held her shriveled hand, while she rocked forward and backward in a creaky chair.

"*El Señor* was a special man to all of us, Abuelita. He's the reason I love what I do."

The old woman said nothing.

Luis kissed her hand and touched the top of her head. "You know I love you. You are part of my heart. That's what you always used to say to me. Part of my heart."

Still the woman's face showed no emotion.

"Without you and Papa I would never have learned to appreciate my heritage."

She lifted her gnarled hand toward Lauren. "Who's that woman who gapes at us?" she said in English.

Luis looked up at Lauren and laughed. "Hey, she does talk, and in English as well. Abuelita, I want you to meet my girlfriend, Lauren."

The woman stared at Lauren. "Girlfriend? She speaks Spanish?" Her mouth hung open, revealing her yellow teeth.

Luis tipped his head. "A little."

"None of them speak Spanish. Ah, come here, girl." Her voice was scratchy, as if she needed to clear her throat. "Sit." She pointed a shaky finger toward a spot on the bed next to Luis.

Before Lauren obeyed the command, she bent down and kissed the old woman on her papery cheek. "I'm glad to meet you, Mrs. Hernandez. Luis told me how much he loved visiting you and your husband every summer."

The grandmother shook her head stiffly. "La mapa. That's what brings him here."

Lauren bent lower to understand the words. "Excuse me?"

The old woman stretched her hand to Luis's knee. "Luis. He wants me to talk about la mapa."

"Yes." Lauren turned to Luis and nodded. "Everyone wants you to talk."

The woman pointed her finger again at Luis. "He wants to hear about Papa's map."

Lauren sat down next to Luis and grinned.

"We'd love to hear about a treasure map, wouldn't we Luis?"

"Hah!" she said and turned to Luis with a squint. "I promised my man not to tell."

Luis's red-rimmed eyes begged her. "Abuelita, Gorge, and his buddy Fito tried to kill us last night, when we couldn't tell them where the treasure was, so, please, tell me about Gorge."

The woman's fingers danced to her mouth as she closed her eyes and poured out a jumble of Spanish and English. Luis had to translate now and then as she went along.

A very bad boy from the time he was able to walk, Gorge was the stepson of her drunken cousin. As the woman spoke those words, the creases around her mouth deepened. "Terrible, malo," she said with a shake of her head.

Many months earlier the bad boy who was now a bad man had visited her, asking her about a treasure map. The old woman told him her husband's map was a fake that his brothers had made to sell to tourists at the dig sites. With her wide eyes and her clasped hands, Abuelita acted out her ignorance for Luis and Lauren, emphasizing that no matter what the muchacho malo had wanted, she did not intend to help him.

The woman rocked forward and backward with her eyes closed and hummed with each breath, before she took up the story again. When he was a teenager, the boy had run off to Mexico City, and turned rotten like a fruit left under the tree, rejected by parasites and buzzards. The boy's stepfather was a sweet man who let his wife boss him. The mother gave the boy money they should have spent on their future. The old woman's hand shook as she pulled at her chin and shrugged.

Lauren lost the thread of the story after Luis attempted to get his grandmother back to the subject of the map. When the old woman closed her eyes for a moment, Luis reached for her hand. "Tell me, Abuelita, what happened to that treasure?"

As they waited for her answer, the old woman slumped back in her chair and closed her eyes. "Tu sabes todo," she whispered through her dry lips. Her chin rested on her chest. "You know all," she repeated in English. "The story is in the sunshine, rotting in the ground no more." Soon a snore bubbled from her lips.

Solemnly Luis stood and kissed his grandmother on the forehead. "I'll come back soon," he whispered and touched her knotted, arthritic hand.

Luis's sister stood in the hall outside the door. "I heard her, Luis. She actually spoke to you! What did she say? I didn't dare go in there, for fear she'd go mute again. That's what the doctor called it. 'Mute.' What was she talking about?"

Luis shook his head. "I asked her about that cousin, Gorge. Remember what a bastard he was?"

His sister closed her eyes for a moment. "Luis, please, he's a relative."

"She knew what I wanted her to tell me, Maria, but she danced around it. She's a stubborn woman."

Luis and Lauren followed Maria down the hall until she halted and faced Luis. "How come she would talk to you and not to me?"

Luis winced and put his arm around Lauren. "Actually, Lauren was the one who got her going. Until she arrived, Abuelita just stared through me as if I was the window next to her bed."

"Hmm. Well, the doctor's waiting for you in the living room."

Lauren sank into one of the well-worn upholstered chairs and watched a skinny young man with a huge mustache and a worried face examine Luis's cuts. After Luis explained how he'd injured his knee deep in the cave, the doctor crossed himself and mumbled something about the curse of las cavas. Lauren gave up trying to follow the conversation and closed her eyes.

Sometime later, the doctor nudged Lauren gently, rousing her from another nap, and examined her forehead, knees, hands, and arms. He warned in Spanish that she should hold still while he cleaned and stitched the cut on her forehead and on her elbow, and then attended her other gashes. He checked her blue-black ribs for fractures, her eyes for signs of concussion, and then patted her cheek as if she were a child.

"Estas bien, señorita, y bonita también. Viva Luis, el rey de las muchachas!" he said, and got up without observing her reaction to his words.

Lauren translated the first part as, "You're fine and pretty too," and the next part as "Long live Luis, the king of the girls," an apt title, Lauren thought, and snuggled back against the cushions.

She must have been asleep for half an hour, when persistent banging sounds jolted her awake. Before Luis's sister could answer the door, it burst open, and a short, round man in a crisp navy shirt and wide pleated pants strode into the room. He shouted Luis's name, stuck a dark, stinky cigarette into his mouth, and pumped Luis's hand so hard Luis staggered and nearly lost his balance.

Once the man sat down on the couch next to the doctor, who was eating a bowl of soup, Luis began to describe their ordeal. Luis's sister entered the room carrying beer for the visitors and then settled in the chair next to Lauren. The round man puffed on his cigarette, took notes on a pad of paper propped against his stomach and interrupted often.

With a shake of her head, Maria whispered to Lauren. "That's Diego, the local police. He thinks he's Sherlock Holmes. Dr. Hermano is the new young doctor. Abuelita says he knows nothing, but he's harmless." She shrugged. "I think he's pretty good. They think of themselves as Sherlock Holmes and Dr. Watson." She sat up tall and scrunched up her lips. "Every summer when we all were little, Diego would come over to play with us. He preferred to be the boss." She shook her head and sniffed. "Obviously, he hasn't changed."

With the conversation as her lullaby, Lauren began to doze again, but sat up after Luis swore.

"What? You saw him? Here in town? Where?" Luis's eyes were like black bullets.

Lauren couldn't follow the Spanish. She wondered who was here in town and why Luis was upset. In a haze of blue smoke, the men hunched over the coffee table plotting something peligroso, very dangerous. The doctor mentioned Gorge twice, which set Lauren's heart vibrating in her throat. Was Gorge the one they'd seen in town?

The men stood and shook hands. After the farewells, the door thumped closed, and Lauren overheard Luis and his sister talking in low tones.

"I better wake her," Luis said. "We're meeting the van in the church square. I hope she can walk that far. She's pretty banged up. Let me know if Abuelita says anything about *el Señor's* treasure map. Anything at all, Maria."

Lauren opened her eyes and watched Maria shake her head and turn away. "I hope all the talk about that map won't set her off again, Luis. Abuelita has suffered enough from that curse."

Luis reached for his sister's arm, but she turned her back on him. "Come on, Maria. If *el Señor* hadn't wanted me to find something, he wouldn't have put my name on the map. Did you think of that?"

Maria whirled to face Luis. "People have died because of that treasure."

"I had never heard that story about *el Señor's* brother until today." Luis gripped her shoulders.

"Maria, tell me, you were here when *el Señor* died. Did he say anything about the map?"

His sister's nostrils flared and her hands became fists as she knocked his hands away. "No. But if he had, I'd die with the knowledge, before I'd tell you."

Luis reached for her hand again, but his sister stiffened her back and crossed her arms in front of her.

"Maria, two guys kidnapped me, beat me up, and threatened Lauren, all because of the map. We almost died for that treasure ourselves, when we didn't have a clue what it was or where it might be. Those men think we have it. If they're alive, we're still not safe, until we find out what happened to the treasure."

Maria spread her hands in front of her. "I don't know anything, and I don't want to know."

Luis clamped his mouth shut, looked down at his watch, and turned to Lauren. "You think you can walk as far as the church?"

Lauren stood up and stretched. "Sure. I'm much better, thanks to you, Maria."

Maria took Lauren's hand. "I hope you have a safe trip from now on." She glanced over at Luis. "Maybe we'll meet again, Lauren, perhaps in Chicago?"

While Luis and his sister went through the motions of a hug, Lauren realized the question mark implied at the end of her sentence symbolized Lauren's relationship with Luis. Would Lauren see Luis's family in Chicago? Would she come back to this house again? Or would their love affair be nothing but a brief, violent adventure?

Dusky clouds huddled above the hills as Luis and Lauren walked along the sandy road. The air smelled of wet soil, manure, and fried tortillas. Two small boys with chocolate eyes and shy smiles stopped kicking a ball to stare at them.

On the main road, they passed four men in overalls. One of them called to Luis by name. Luis returned the greeting with a wave, asked him about his brother, and the two laughed.

Ahead of them, the church tower pointed up at the darkening sky. An old woman in slacks and a colorful blouse climbed the church steps and entered through the wide front door.

Though Lauren's swollen feet ached in her damp shoes and her knee throbbed, she noticed Luis seemed to be loping along without discomfort. "How come I hurt and you're fine already?" she asked.

Luis smiled and slung his arm around her as they walked. "Can't keep up with me, eh?"

His arm felt protective. "You and those men were plotting something back there."

"Not really."

"That's a lie."

"You're right."

"You don't want me to know about it."

"True."

"I'm going to drive you crazy until you tell me."

"You've already done that."

"Damn you, Luis! I'm an adult. What's happening?"

Luis halted and stuffed his hands in his pockets. "Here's the story, adult. The sheriff and I have a backup plan in case Gorge didn't die in the cave." He started strolling again. "That's all I'm going to tell you."

"Okay." She'd get him to tell her sooner or later. "Your sister was very nice to me. I liked meeting your grandmother too. She's a strong woman."

"And stubborn. She likes you. She called you my wife." He grinned and flicked a glance at her.

"Really? What did you say to that?"

He took her hand. "I said '*todavía no*.'"

"That means 'not yet.'"

244

"You do remember your Spanish. When I said goodbye to her, I promised we'd visit the church before we left town, but you don't have to come in with me. It's not exactly historic or beautiful, but she's proud of it, since my grandfather helped his father lay the new stone floor." Luis gave a dry laugh. "Not exactly new anymore. He was a teenager at the time."

Lauren guessed Luis was relaying information to change the subject. *Todavía no.* Did he really think they would marry some day, Lauren wondered, or was he humoring his grandmother?

"What did your grandmother say about the treasure?"

"You understood the part about my evil cousin?"

"Yes. She said something about brothers having a map and how one of them died."

"Right."

"Does your grandmother know what the treasure was?"

Luis shook his head. "She claims el *Señor* never spoke about it." He began to laugh. "I think she was lying."

"What's so funny?"

"She told me why she stopped talking to anyone."

"Why?"

"To get my sisters and my mother to visit her." He raised his eyebrows. "She said the daughter and the granddaughters should be with her more than twice a year." He grinned. "I am exonerated, since I visit her whenever I'm nearby."

"Did you tell your sister that?"

He shook his head. "No way I'm getting between those women. They'll work it out." He sighed. "Abuelita reminded me how secretive my grandfather was." He halted and looked up and down the street. "According to her, he was ashamed of something he did in his youth, but refused to tell her about it. In his later years, he felt so much guilt about whatever it was, he had trouble sleeping. My grandmother noticed, but said nothing until he started going to church again." Luis paused to flex his leg. "She told me she felt sad that her husband wouldn't trust her to love him no matter what he'd done."

"Did she find out what happened?"

Luis's eyelids drooped, and his mouth turned down. "After my grandfather died, one of his brothers finally told her the story. As the oldest brother, my grandfather was the one who enforced the rules, but one day, it was his idea to have 'an adventure,' as my grandmother called it. They disobeyed their father and played in the caves. When they got lost and scared, they circled through the passageways and finally came across something that excited them. Somehow, they carried it out of the cave and all the way home without anyone seeing them."

They arrived at the tiny square in front of the church, and Luis took Lauren's hand again. "This is where Frank said he'd pick us up." He looked at his watch and then down the street, empty except for the children and the men strolling home. "We still have time to visit the church, but you can wait here if you want."

"I'll come with you. Finish your story." She followed him toward the church steps.

"Anyhow, Jaime, the youngest brother,' *L'estrella*,' the star, they called him, had studied archeology and realized the value of their find." Luis's eyes sparkled. "He couldn't wait to show it to experts, but of course, that would get them all into trouble. The boys argued." Luis shook his head. "Abuelita said she heard they beat each other bloody, but I can't picture that. Eventually *el Señor* decided they must take their treasure back where they found it, since their fighting proved that those who stole from the ancient people were cursed."

"It's a thrilling tale," said Lauren. "And after they put it back, they made a map so they could locate it again someday."

Luis kicked the sand at the side of the road. "That's half the story. A few days later, Jaime, the youngest brother, disappeared."

"No!" Lauren gripped Luis's wrist. "He went back for the treasure by himself?"

Luis closed his eyes for a moment. "What a waste, eh? They searched for him for weeks."

"Such heartbreak. Your grandfather blamed himself. And none of the brothers ever told anyone what they found?"

"Not that I know of."

"So no one knows what it is."

"It must have been something astonishing." Luis spoke the words in a hush. "And it couldn't have been very big, because they managed to carry it out of the cave and then back in again."

"That doesn't explain why they made the map."

Luis paused at the foot of the church steps and stuck his hands in his pockets. "Maybe they weren't supposed to. Maybe they did it to spite my grandfather." His hands flew out of his pockets and into the air. "Maybe they hoped it would help them to keep searching for their brother, at least at first. Oh, I almost forgot." He pulled something from his pocket. "Abuelita wanted me to give you this, to protect you." Luis opened his hand to reveal a small silver cross on a chain. "Would you like me to put it around your neck?"

"Yes. It's beautiful." Lauren didn't want Luis to see her sudden tears. "How sweet of her. Thanks."

"It's a nice one. She said *el Señor* gave it to her." He fastened the cross, kissed Lauren on the cheek, and they climbed the steps. Luis pulled open the thick wooden door. "It looks good on you, but I think everything looks good on you."

With his words and his smile lifting her sadness, Lauren ducked through the door ahead of him. The church was as cold as the cave, and nearly as dark. The door creaked shut. Incense and mildew filled her nostrils.

Luis stopped at the bowl of holy water, bowed, and dipped his hand. Out of respect for him and for his family's church, Lauren copied him, and then followed him up the aisle toward the altar.

Sparse in its decorations, the church was built in a simple Spanish Colonial style. The windows were patched with wood, and the mismatched pews were ridged with wear. Luis sat down in a middle pew a few rows behind two women kneeling over their rosaries. Lauren continued forward and stopped at the side altar where tiny candles burned under a murky painting of the Virgin and Child. She knelt and folded her hands on the railing. The tightness in her chest from their night of fear gave way when she studied the dim figure of the young woman and her baby. The Virgin looked surprised at the tiny thing that had turned up in her arms. The baby was so much smaller in scale than its mother, he might have been kidnapped from another painting.

Lauren closed her eyes and thanked God for rescuing her and Luis from the cave. Then she prayed that no one else would ever come after Luis to find the treasure. After that, she had trouble concentrating, because her knees ached from the cold, hard stones. She opened her eyes.

Beneath the altar, she saw a large gravestone set into the floor. As she adjusted her knees, she whispered the words carved on the stone in front of her. "Salmos 32: 7," she read, and struggled through the rest. It was a Bible passage, something about a hiding place, about trouble and songs of liberación, deliverance. "Songs of deliverance," Lauren whispered to the sad Virgin.

She felt cold fingers on her neck and jumped. She hadn't heard Luis's approach.

"Let's head out. The van should be here soon."

Lauren struggled to her feet and followed Luis down the aisle behind the two women. The gray church with its meager decorations felt claustrophobic.

At the church door, Lauren tugged on Luis's arm and waited as the women shuffled out. "Luis, remember the Bible quote on the back side of the map?"

Lauren could tell by the glaze in his eyes that Luis's thoughts were elsewhere, as he swung open the door for her. A sweet garden smell filled the air. She paused on the steps so Luis would have to stop. "Did you hear what I said?"

Luis bumped into her. "What? No, sorry." He frowned and touched her shoulder.

"Do you remember what your grandfather wrote on the backside of the map?"

"The Bible quote? Um, sure, it was from Psalms, something about a hiding place and deliverance. Let's go. We should be out there where they can see us as they drive up."

"Luis! That's it!" Lauren turned and reopened the church door. "Come back in here for a minute. You have to see this!"

Luis grimaced. "It's a poor church, Lauren. There's nothing here to get excited about."

Lauren yanked his hand. "You must see this."

Luis took three steps into the church and halted. "I'm telling you we don't have time for this."

She twitched with impatience. "Up here, Luis, beneath this altar. Look!"

At the sight of the Bible quote, Luis's face transformed. "That was *el Señor's* favorite quote." He frowned, shrugged, and then a smile crept across his face and lit his eyes.

"It has to be a clue," Lauren said. "Translate for me."

Luis knelt. "'You are my hiding place; you will protect me from trouble and surround me with songs of deliverance.'"

Lauren thought Luis was bending low to examine the carving, until he grunted, and she realized he was hefting one of the large stones. "Hiding place, Lauren. That is definitely a clue. Is there anyone else in the church?"

"No." Lauren shook her head.

"Give me a hand with this."

"We shouldn't do this, Luis."

"You started it, so give me a hand."

The slab was thinner than it looked, and they managed to slide it six inches to one side, just far enough to see beneath it. Dust and a foul odor billowed out. Lauren coughed and turned away for a second, hoping she wouldn't have to touch any more bones, or even look at them.

In the dim light, they saw a small covered stone casket, but no bones. Luis reached in and tried to shift the cover. Lauren shivered, imagining the horrors he might encounter. His arm stopped, and he looked up at Lauren with a grin. "There's something here."

"What?" she whispered, afraid of his answer.

"We have to pull the slab out a little farther. No one's around, right?"

"Right."

"Good. Push there. A little farther. That's it." Luis flattened himself across the opening and extended his arm. "It looks old, carved of stone." He inched out the container, set it on the floor, and lifted chunks of the crumbling lid. When Luis knelt next to the box, he stared.

Lauren could see only shadows inside the container. "Is it a skeleton?" A chill tingled her arms. Behind them, a door banged and she looked up. "Luis, somebody just came in. We have to put it back."

Luis pulled folds of some sort of paper out of the box. "It's gold, Lauren."

"Golden paper?"

Luis nodded as he gently fingered the cover of the mass of papers and grinned. "Golden paper," he whispered, "black with mildew, but look what's underneath. Lauren, is anyone coming this way?"

Lauren peeked around the pillar. "It's two more women, but they're sitting way in the back."

Luis's eyes glistened when he lifted a few pages more as if they were as fragile as glass. Folded like an accordion, the sheets appeared to be made from bark.

"Is it a codex?" Lauren whispered the word as if it was holy. Across the strange parchment tiny drawings were segmented into boxes like cartoon squares. Some featured characters similar to those on the carved steles at the dig site. Others were rows of glyphs like the Mayan numerals she'd seen in the books she'd studied.

Luis's eager eyes found hers, and he sat back cross-legged. "Lauren, it was a dream, a long shot at best. But here it is, a codex rescued from the flames of the Inquisition."

Lauren wanted to see more, but Luis had already returned the pages to the crypt. "What are you doing?"

"Are the women still here?"

Lauren looked behind him. "No. We probably scared them away."

"Good. Help me get the slab back."

Lauren was bursting with questions. "You're going to leave it here in the church?"

"It's the safest place for now. It's fragile. God knows how it survived in that crypt."

Just as they bent down to fit the stone back where it belonged, the side door to the church swung open, and a skinny-faced priest wearing a black robe and a worried frown scurried toward them. "Buenos noches, Señor. Se puede ayudar?"

"The women must have blown the whistle on us, Lauren," Luis whispered. He strolled over to greet the priest and stood so that he blocked his view of the side altar. "Soy Luis Hernandez, hijo de Carlos Hernandez."

The priest nodded, pointed out the door, and started to say something, but Luis interrupted him. He began to explain he was an archeologist and had found something special beneath the church floor, but again the priest interrupted him and pointed to the church door. He asked if Luis was expecting someone to come for him. Luis nodded. Then the priest said something about men with guns, and Luis gripped his hand and asked him where they could hide. The priest pointed to the door on the other side of the altar.

"Go," Luis said with a wave of his hand toward the door. "Vaya." The priest tugged on Lauren's sleeve, scurried past the altar, and motioned her to follow him into an office the size of a closet.

Lauren expected Luis to come with them, but he didn't. She heard the thump of the church door and the rumble of men's voices. When the priest crept over to the doorway to listen, she joined him. The new voice sounded familiar. The priest cracked the door open so they could see into the sanctuary.

Luis stood with his arms crossed and his back to the side altar, his gaze steady. Frank marched up the aisle with a sneer on his face as if he'd smelled a bad smell. The two men reminded Lauren of cowboys facing off in a gun battle.

Luis pretended to laugh. "We took a little side trip last night, Frank. Thanks for coming to get us."

"Where's Lauren?" Frank said.

Luis took a couple of steps away from sad Mary, which made Frank turn his back on the doorway where Lauren and the priest stood. "Who else came with you, Frank? "

Frank's hands rose up over his shoulders. "Enid was in high gear bossing everyone around, so I got in the truck and sped over here without them." He shrugged. "It could take them forever to get organized. You're hurt. You need a doctor?"

"Already saw one. Tell me about the cave-in, Frank. Was there any damage to the ruins?"

"You wouldn't have believed the noise, Luis. It woke up the whole camp. Of course, we haven't had a chance to assess the effect on the work sites yet. Were you in the cavern when it collapsed? How did you get out?"

"We ran the other way, into the cave."

"Whoa! Gutsy. You were lucky. What were you doing in there, anyway? You're the guy who hates caves."

"Somebody jumped me, dragged me in there."

"Why would anyone do that? We thought you and Lauren were all alone in there, you know, sharing some quiet time." Frank emitted a dry laugh.

"So did anyone else escape from the cave-in?"

"Not that I know of, Luis. Guess they both died." Frank turned away from Luis and glanced at the floor. "What's going on behind you? A little excavating?"

Luis grabbed Frank's shirtfront and shoved so hard he stumbled backwards. "How did you know there were two guys in the cave with us, Frank?"

"What?" Frank said, and steadied himself on the pew behind him.

"You said you guessed they both died. I never mentioned there were two guys."

Frank turned away from Luis and bent down near the altar railing. "Good guess on my part. You think they're restoring this floor?"

"More likely it's just falling apart. Answer my question, Frank."

The side door creaked open and both men turned to watch Gorge limp toward them. In the pale candlelight, Lauren could see a bruise on his forehead, bloody bandages on his hands and a shotgun slung across his forearms.

Luis exploded. "Gorge, you bastard!" Luis shoved Frank into the pew where he lost his balance and crashed to the floor. Spanish spewed from his mouth as Luis slugged Gorge in the face and knocked him sideways.

Gorge scrambled onto all fours and then rose up with the gun pointed at Luis's chest. "I kill you good this time, Luis, and fuck your woman too. Where is she?"

"Shut up, Gorge!" Frank yelled.

Lauren heard the priest gasp behind her and turned to him with her finger on her lips. His eyes grew into enormous circles of white. "Gorge es muy malo." Halitosis wafted out with his whisper.

Luis shoved the shotgun away from his chest. "Keep talking, Gorge. Did Frank order you to beat me up in Milwaukee? Was it his idea to murder Lauren's handyman?"

Frank grabbed Gorge by the sleeve. "What's he talking about?"

Gorge hugged the shotgun and shook his head. "It was an accident. The guy tried to stop us when we were leaving her apartment."

Frank bent down for a moment and reached into

his pocket. "The man's obviously a fool, Luis." When Frank stood up, he held a revolver and pointed it at Luis. "Forget that. You tell us where the treasure is, Luis, and we can all go back to our jobs."

"Diablo!" the priest murmured.

Luis shook his head. "I doubt the university will employ you, once it gets out that you've stolen Mayan artifacts. I told Gorge and Fito the truth in the cave, Frank. I didn't know what the treasure was or where it was."

"Is that why you're here in the church, to pray for answers, or did the map lead you here? Quick, look around, Gorge. Luis, I can tell by your face I'm right. There under the floor," he pointed, "is that the treasure your grandfather hid?" The words shot out like pellets, "Not in some cave, but right here in the family church?"

The priest gripped Lauren's arm so tightly, she moaned with pain. "Aquí," he whispered into her ear as he handed her a large candelabra and made a motion that she should use it like a baseball bat.

"Gorge, go turn the bolt on the front door." Frank pointed the gun at Luis's chest. "Luis, haul it out of there now!"

Luis shook his head. "I'm tired, Frank. I had a really tough night. You do it."

Gorge smashed Luis across the face. Luis staggered back, and then ran head-down at Frank, and butted him to the floor.

Lauren started into the sanctuary, but the priest pulled her back, signaled her to wait, and then crept into his office. Lauren turned back in time to see Frank struggle to his feet and lean against the rickety railing next to the sad Virgin. "Gorge, get down and help him lift that thing out of there. Now!"

Gorge looked down at the shotgun in his hands. For a moment, Lauren thought they'd shoot each other and Luis too, until Gorge reached to help Luis stand up. Scraping sounds told her they were removing the heavy box from beneath the altar.

Holding the crumbling lid above his head, Frank stood up in front of the Virgin and shouted, "Tesoro!"

It was hard to tell which came first, the bang of the side door, the explosion of Gorge's gun, or Enid's shout of outrage at the scene before her.

In seconds the front of Enid's white blouse turned a sickly pink, her eyes fluttered and she collapsed to the floor just inside the door. Luis swore, kicked Gorge's feet out from under him, and they both went down. Frank slugged Luis in the back, pulled him off Gorge, and banged Gorge's head on the stone floor until his blood splattered into the open vault.

Finally jolted into action, Lauren flung herself through the door and swung the candelabra in an arc that included Frank's head.

Frank ducked, lunged for the stone box, hefted it against his chest, stepped over Gorge's body, and charged down the aisle. Lauren hurried to Enid, when a horrendous clanging filled her ears.

On and on the flood of sound assailed her senses, jangling the air and shaking the rafters of the sanctuary. Before the clanging stopped, Lauren found a pulse. "Luis, what should I do? Her heart's beating, but there's so much blood. Help me!"

Luis stripped off his shirt, folded it, and pressed it against Enid's bloody chest. "The doctor's probably outside the church somewhere. Hold this right here, and I'll find him."

Enid's face had grown pale by the time Luis and the skinny young doctor hurried through the side door, dragging his backpack full of drugs and bandages. In the dim candlelight, Lauren nestled Enid's head in her lap and held her limp hand, while the doctor examined the wound and wrapped a bandage around her shoulder. Lauren glanced up at the sad Virgin and prayed Enid would live to brag about the day she rescued Luis and Lauren from murderers.

"Go after Frank, Luis!" Lauren whispered. "He has the codex."

Luis squatted next to Lauren and gripped Enid's hand. "He's going nowhere. The sheriff recruited a bunch of the guys in the village to follow us. By now the bell has attracted everyone else in town, and they're all itching to beat Frank to a pulp."

Luis was correct. When he and Lauren followed the stretcher carrying Enid through the doorway into a sunset-pink evening, headlights from a dozen trucks and a rusted bus lit the churchyard. Men, women, children, dogs, and a flock of turkeys competed with the clamor of the bells.

In the center of the square, the priest pointed a shaky shotgun at scowling Frank, while the policeman clanked on the handcuffs. At their feet, in the glare of a dozen flashlights, stood a cracked and crumbling box. Inside it were the remains of the legendary lost codex, a treasure rarer than a king's crown.

"What the heck was that awful noise?" Lauren asked Luis, when the sound finally stopped. "That can't be a church bell."

"The call of Santa Maria Pequeña." Luis's lips spread with pride. "A gift from a Spanish conquistador who tried to grow sugar here. The peal is still so harsh the town uses it only as a fire alert." Luis winced and leaned on Lauren. "I think I better go sit down somewhere."

"That jerk beat you bloody." Lauren pointed at the vehicle parked under the tall palms behind the church. "The doctor is taking Enid to the hospital. You should go too."

He shook his head. "The hospital is an hour from here." He gripped her upper arms and pulled her to his chest. "By the way, I beat him bloody too. Check it out." His nostrils flared and his eyes sparkled.

Lauren touched his face and kissed the cut on his chin. "I was afraid you'd die."

"Ditto." He kissed her sweetly and then held her until they both began to breathe with a steady rhythm.

"I need to go with Enid, Luis."

Luis nodded. "And I have to stay here and figure out what to do with the codex." He reached for her hands. "Lauren, there are so many things to talk about and no time to do it." He spoke into her hair. "Without you, I wouldn't have made it out of that cave." Then he kissed her hard on the lips, as if he weren't sure he'd ever kiss her again.

"I'll see you soon, won't I?" Lauren asked, doubt tearing at her chest.

"I'll be in touch."

Once the doctor and the ambulance driver had loaded Enid into the back of the town's emergency truck, Lauren climbed in next to her and the vehicle pulled away. Lauren held Enid's hand and watched as the doctor attached a monitor, checked the IV drip, and then sat back against his seat and combed his mustache with his fingers.

Lauren finally put together a sentence in Spanish so she could ask the doctor how the patient was doing. He nodded, said she'd be fine once they removed the bullet, and added something about cleaning the wound.

Lauren glanced back at the church courtyard. In the center of a circle of villagers, Luis huddled over his prize. After a few miles, Lauren felt her body going slack and was nearly asleep when Enid spoke. "Lauren? Lauren, dear?"

"I'm here." Lauren squeezed her hand.

"Where are we going?"

"To the hospital. The doctor says you're going to

be fine."

"Frank shot me."

"He's a bad man, Enid."

"How could I have been so foolish?"

"You saved our lives. He was going to kill us all." Her own words shocked her. How did her world become so dangerous?

"Well, at least I was some good." She shuddered. "I have regrets, Lauren. I haven't treated you well."

"Not true. Thanks to you, I can support myself with my own business."

Enid closed her eyes and shook her head. "I have a cruel tongue."

Enid lay so still, Lauren thought she'd drifted back to sleep, until she felt Enid's hand tighten around hers. "You need to understand something, Lauren. Though your parents made each other jealous with their flirtations, when they were together, they were one, truly and beautifully one."

The doctor leaned over to check Enid's pulse. "Buenos días," she said and blessed him with a weak smile.

"Buenas noches, Señora."

Enid nodded. "Lauren, my lips are getting thick. Must tell you this about your parents. After the divorce, they realized they were useless, like broken dishes. I wrote a poem, one of my best, about them. Never published. Too painful to see in print. I knew their lives would end in ruin and grief." Enid licked her lips, as her breathing slowed. "I promised myself I'd take care of the remnant of their love." Enid closed her eyes and nodded. "That's you, Lauren. It's even documented, dear." She winced. "You know I've been frugal. In case I don't survive this adventure, I want you to know you're my heir."

Lauren smoothed Enid's forehead and struggled to keep from crying. "I don't know what to say, Enid. Thank you." She kissed her cool cheek.

Two hours later, alone in the darkened waiting room at the hospital, Lauren stretched out on the ripped vinyl couch. Waves of deep sobs ripped through her chest. She cried for her parents who had squandered their love, for the little girl they had left behind, for the grown woman she'd become who mocked their affection. And she prayed for Enid, the new Enid who was trying to fill in for her parents.

Then she cried quietly for Luis, the man she loved, the man she might lose to fame and fortune.

Chapter Sixteen

Four days after the dramatic discovery in the church, Lauren and the doctor eased Enid up the steps and into the hospital plane. They paused when they heard an engine sound and turned to see a dusty van motoring across the grass airstrip.

Lauren waited for the driver to jump out, hoping it was Luis. It was. He left the van door open and jogged over. The flash of his smile made her laugh. "Look at you, the hero of archeologists around the world!"

Luis grinned wider. "You saw CNN?"

Lauren nodded. "On the hospital's television."

"Did you hear me mention your name?"

"Yes. That was—" Luis interrupted her sentence with a kiss. She laughed into his chest while he covered her head with more kisses.

"Don't go back, Lauren. I need you here to share this."

"I wish I could stay." Lauren touched the new scar on his cheek and brushed back his hair. "I have a business to run. You look exhausted."

"I feel great—so excited, I hardly sleep at night."

"You need me next to you."

His eyes turned serious and he clasped her hand. "I want you next to me."

"You know where to reach me. When do you think you'll come home?"

"To Milwaukee?" Luis rubbed his nose with the back of his hand. "Hard to say." He bit his lip. "We're short-handed with Frank in jail, and now there's a foundation that wants to help us build a structure to house the codex and fund the research."

"That's wonderful!" Lauren had the feeling she'd remember that moment for a long time. "So how long will that take?"

Luis shook his head. "Who knows?" He cupped her face. "God, I never thought I'd feel this way, Lauren, happy and sad, all at once. I have to take a sabbatical. I haven't even told the university yet." He scratched the stubble on his cheek and kissed her again. "I want to make love to you right here. Tell me you'll come visit me if I get stuck here. Say yes."

"Yes, when I can." The pilot tapped her on the shoulder, and Lauren had to push away from Luis's last kiss. She climbed the steps to the plane and looked back to wave at him standing alone, watching her.

"I'll call you every week," he yelled and crossed his heart with his hand.

Lauren laughed. "I'll believe that when it happens." She blew him a kiss and then took to her seat next to Enid.

****

As usual, January in Milwaukee was cold. Cloudless, sunny days were always the coldest, with temperatures hovering in the teens. The news was full of weather alerts, wind-chill warnings, and stories of elderly people dropping dead shoveling snow.

Lauren felt like she lived in her own wind-chill warning. Snow piles towered defiantly in the corners of her alley. Crusty, grit-covered chunks of ice rimmed the streets and sidewalks.

Lauren got home and found a note from Julie taped to the inside of her apartment door, informing her that three days earlier she'd departed on a Caribbean cruise with a guy she met at a theater party for singles. She'd be gone for a week, but had completed all the work for January before she left. Julie had even sorted the mail and stocked Lauren's refrigerator.

One week later, Lauren was in bed proofing an annual report when the phone rang. It was after midnight. It had to be Luis.

"Lauren?" Luis yelled over the noise of a crowd. "Can you hear me?"

"Where are you?" Her heart banged so hard it hurt. "It sounds like a bar."

"It is a bar." He laughed. "I'm in Mexico City. I'll be here at least another week. The police inquiry is muy despacio—very slow."

"How are you?"

"Fine, fine. What?"

"I didn't say anything, Luis."

"Sorry! There's a group of us here and I can hardly hear, but at least my cell phone works. My grandmother took good care of me, of course. One of my cuts is infected, but it'll be okay. How are you? Any headaches?"

"No. I'm tired, bogged down with work." She wanted to say only heartaches, but didn't. "I miss you." As soon as the words were out, she wished them back. She wanted to sound supportive, not pathetic.

"I miss you too. How's Enid?"

"She's doing okay. The bullet broke one rib, but her lungs are fine, and there's no infection. She needs some help now that she's home, so she hired two handsome young male nurses to take turns in the evenings. I take dinner over every night, and some of her students have signed up to come during the day."

"I'd fly there tonight if I could, but now we're into plans for a museum to house the codex. It's very exciting. We got government support right away. A big donor visited yesterday to see the codex for himself, a young guy, friend of Marcella's who owns a phone company. Hey, you wouldn't believe how helpful she's been."

"Who, Marcella?"

"Yes. Her uncle is a commissioner of something. We hope to build the museum in Santa Maria Pequeña, near the church, but it will be affiliated with the National Archeological Museum."

A chill crept into Lauren's lungs. "Great. That's great. That will take awhile, I guess."

"The University granted me a leave of absence until next fall."

"Then of course you'll be gone all summer." With Marcella.

"Lauren? Can you hear me?"

"Yes."

"I think of you every day."

"I'm glad." Her tears were making her voice change.

"Yes, señor, si. Lauren. I should go."

"Wait, Luis? You have to tell me how Frank got mixed up with your cousin Gorge and Fito."

Luis groaned. "The story is Gorge and Fito got jobs on the dig right after I left last summer. One night when Frank was down there, he overheard Gorge bragging about his family's treasure map and figured out the connection to me. Hey, Lauren, I have to go. I'll call you again as soon as I can. Adios."

Luis hadn't spoken the word love, though he did mention Marcella. Face it, Lauren scolded herself, it was time to get back to reality. Luis wouldn't miss her for long. After the phone call, Lauren knew she'd never be able to sleep, so she clumped down to her office to deal with the batch of bills she had left for last.

New mail teetered on top of the old bills. One bill was from the maintenance company she'd hired, another reminder of Ken's death. The next envelope was from one of her tenants informing her that he and his wife had decided to make Florida their permanent home and would be selling the condo, which meant more chaos in her life.

Lauren studied the next envelope without touching it. It was from the publishing company where she had submitted her latest novel six months before. She felt the envelope. It was too thin to be good news, so she stood up and held it over the wastebasket, daring herself to throw it out without reading it.

In a flash, Lauren remembered the elation she felt as she and Luis marched out of the cave into the dawn. She was a survivor, and survivors could face discouraging words from one hot-shot New York editor. She opened the letter and had to sit down.

The editor wrote to congratulate her. Lauren's book of short stories, the fabulously intelligent person informed her, was just what they were looking for. What's more, they had selected her work as one of "The Hot Three by the Hottest Young Three," and it would be rushed into print.

The staff was working on a promotional tour, something they rarely did, the letter writer explained. The publisher would sponsor three women authors as they traveled to bookstores and lecture halls around the U.S., giving readings and signing books. As soon as Lauren was under contract, she would be one of the "Hot Three."

Lauren was thrilled, but very confused. She hadn't sent those short stories to anyone. They were still sitting somewhere in her file drawer. She pulled open the drawer, and then remembered she'd been unable to find the file before the trip to Mexico.

The only way the editor could have received those stories was if someone else had mailed them. For a moment, she suspected Julie, but dismissed her as too honest to be the culprit. Enid, however, was truly sneaky and definitely nosy enough to steal the stories from Lauren's desk and contact one of her buddies in New York.

Enid called before seven the next morning and woke up Lauren. "Please, Lauren," she squawked in her morning voice before Lauren had even said hello, "I can't stand it any longer. Don't you have some news for me? Don't be mad, dear. I did it for your own good."

Lauren tried to sound offended. "How and when did you find those stories? I wrote them just for fun, just for me."

"And they are that, just for fun. Others will enjoy them as I did."

"So tell. How did you happen to steal them?"

"Oh, dear, such a strong word. Let's see; was it the day I took you to lunch, you know, at the University Club? No, not that day. Oh, well, I came into your office for something. What was it? Oh, to make a phone call, I think. Anyhow, I pulled out a drawer to find your phone book, and there they were. I read one or two and admired your voice, your descriptions, and especially your love scenes. Oh, Lauren, I didn't want to stop reading, so I snitched them. And then, I just decided to give my old pal Henry a call."

"I thought he'd retired from publishing."

"He did, but he still has clout, dear. He read them and passed them on. Aren't we thrilled?"

"We are, Enid. Thank you."

"How much are they offering you?"

****

Julie dropped by Lauren's apartment on her way home from the Caribbean trip. The two sat on Lauren's couch eating a pizza while Julie raved about her new love, Philip, a CPA whose mathematic genius was superseded only by his ability to recall forty years of movie titles and their stars. Lauren was overjoyed for her.

Eventually Lauren described her own trip, beginning with her misery on the airplane. Omitting several dramatic or intimate moments, she drew the layout of the dig site and quoted from Annetta's lectures on the ancient cities of the Maya.

Julie sprawled on the floor with her head propped on three pillows and finally cut in. "You haven't mentioned Luis."

"You can't believe how lush the dig site is, with monkeys chattering above as you work."

Julie sat up and leaned on her knees. "Come on; tell me about you and Luis and the treasure."

"I don't know what to say about him."

"And why's that?"

Lauren shook her head.

"He's out of the picture?"

Lauren stretched. "Want some ice cream?"

"I'm not leaving until you tell all."

Julie begged for details about how Lauren and Luis had escaped from Gorge and Fito and from the cave-in, and barely breathed as she listened to the description of the discovery of the codex in the church and the grisly shooting of Enid.

"What a plug for Luis's research! And for that Hottest Chicks deal," Julie said, after Lauren finally stopped talking."

"It's the 'Hottest Young Three', Julie, and it's Luis's story to tell, not mine."

"Did you and Luis make any future plans when you left?"

"He's going to call me, and he hopes I'll visit him." She felt a tear slip out and roll down her cheek.

"And has he called?"

"Once." Lauren dodged Julie's glance. "He's busy with his exciting new life." She picked up the pizza box and headed to the kitchen with Julie trailing her. She tried to stuff the box into the garbage bin. "I have to go to bed."

"I don't get this," Julie said. "He's called once since you saved his ass again?"

"He told me the police inquiry was taking a long time and that his plan to have a museum in his grandmother's town funded by a big donor is moving along with the help of Ms. Marcella of the cleavage." When the pizza box wouldn't stay in the can, Lauren slammed the cupboard shut and kicked it.

Julie put her arm around Lauren. "So based on that, you discount other factors, the evenings together, and the demonstrations of love."

Lauren panted from her exertion, pulled a Kleenex out of her pocket, and blew her nose. "I knew he was like this. I saw all the signs. I thought maybe he could be my fling, and then I could let him go without—"

"Without him breaking your heart, deserting you the way your parents did."

"No more amateur psychology."

Julie removed the pizza cardboard, flattened it, and carefully slid it into the garbage bin. "I've learned a lot in the last few weeks. You have too."

Lauren slumped on the kitchen stool. "What have you learned?"

"Love controls you. You don't control it. Lauren, Luis is your man. You love him. He's tough, independent, smart as hell, motivated. He's everything you've avoided for years. In other words, he's perfect for you."

"He doesn't love me."

"You don't know that."

"He wears awful clothes."

"Exactly. You can't even begin to shape him up."

"He never gets his hair cut."

"Ditto above."

"He's an amazing lover."

"Whewee! Now we're getting somewhere! You need a plan."

"What kind of plan?" Lauren stood and began to shake a can of cleanser over the sink.

"The apartment is now cleaner that it's ever been."

"I've been working on it."

"But your suitcase is still sitting in the living room, full of clothes."

"I haven't gotten to that."

"It's full of the clothes you wore with him. Or," Julie said and snickered, "took off with him."

"Julie!"

"Time to go on the offense."

Lauren scrubbed the sink so hard she shredded the sponge.

"Get a great haircut, maybe some highlights, some new clothes, so you'll be ready for your big book tour. And when he comes back, well, by then we'll figure out how you can drive him crazy."

"He said he wanted me to visit him this summer."

"So go down there."

"I have to wait until he asks me."

Julie stood up, yawned, and then shook Lauren's hand. "Perfect plan."

In the dark of night Julie's pep talk faded and the black cloud settled around her. Luis was lost, never to return to Milwaukee or to her. She would let him go, turn herself into the Hottest of the Hot Young Three, and crank out another book.

****

After two months and a mere three more phone calls from Luis, Lauren ran her best time against the April wind off the lake and came home to find a message on her voice mail. "It's Luis." He spoke so quietly, Lauren had to press her ear to the phone to hear. "I miss you. There are so many things I want to tell you. They're planning a special event to announce the donor's gift. They hope the publicity will attract more donors. I want you to be there with me, Lauren. I'll call back when I know the date." He paused, and Lauren could hear a woman's voice in the background. "Yeah, I know. Okay, Marcella, I'll be right there. Lauren," his voice grew soft again, "I have to go, but hey, I almost forgot the reason I called. Congratulations! The secretary at the university told me about your book. Wow! That's great! At last, I'll get to read your fiction." He laughed. "I'll be thinking of you. I'll be in and out of this office for a while, so please call me here." For the first time he left her a number to call.

****

I'll be thinking of you, he'd said. Lauren listened to the message over and over. Maybe she'd been wrong about Luis. Maybe he did care about her. She pulled out her checkbook to see what she could cut in order to afford another trip to Mexico and sighed. Perhaps Enid would lend her the money. She picked up the phone and dialed the number Luis had left, but it rang and rang and rang.

When she returned to the office after her hair appointment, a shopping bag of clothes was on her desk with a note from Julie. "The editor called," it read. "Your book tour begins in Chicago in mid-August. P.S. These clothes are a must for the 'Hottest Chick Writer' in America today." She had attached the bill.

The phone rang and she snatched it up, hoping it was Luis, so she could hear his invitation in person.

"Lauren, guess who?" came the melodious voice.

"Enid? Where are you?"

"Monaco, dear. This sabbatical has been glorious, new images, new vocabulary, even new men!"

270

"That's great, Enid. I'm glad for you."

"And my wound has healed perfectly. I confess I relish describing how I rescued my dearest companion and was shot by the villains. However, you take the prize for your PR stunt. I read about the book tour in the *Times*. I'm very happy for you! So fortunate they mentioned your heroics in the Mayan jungle. Catchy stuff!"

Lauren laughed. "That was the editor's idea. Might as well get something out of that night of horror, right?"

"And Rocky? Are you at least friendly by now?"

"He's called me a couple of times. He says he likes the archeology class so much he's signed up for another semester. Julie's sister heard he's dating the young grad student who's teaching it. I ran into him at the grocery store one afternoon, and he was with Val, you know, the woman on the trip with us? They looked pretty cozy. I'm happy for him." Though Lauren felt Rocky's absence every day, she meant what she said.

"Of course you are, Lauren. You are a generous friend." Enid cleared her throat and paused. "By the way, dear, can you tell me what's going to happen to Frank?" Her voice had dropped to a murmur.

Ever since the trip, Enid had shown a tenderness Lauren had never seen. She hoped the woman could handle the rest of the story. "He's in jail and will likely be there a long time, although, according to Luis, his lawyer has tried to claim it was Luis's idea to steal the codex."

"Oh, dear." Enid sighed loudly. "It's difficult to admit one's most egregious mistakes, especially where passion is involved."

"I agree, but we'll all survive." After a pause, Lauren added, "I'm glad I can count on your friendship, Enid. It means a lot."

"Indeed, dear, to both of us. I'll be in touch."

Chapter Seventeen

Luis called once in May and twice in June, each time around midnight. Each time Lauren was either at her desk or lying in bed listening to the music from the summer festivals at the lakefront, wishing she could sleep. His stories about the progress he and his team had made on preserving and restoring the codex, as well as his tales of government interference and ineptitude, enchanted her and made her long to be at his side.

It wasn't until his tales ended and they spoke about each other that she grew nervous. She considered asking him straight out whether his feelings for her had changed, whether his new mission gave him little time to keep in touch, or whether he'd found another lover. "And you?" she asked him in June, setting up her next query, "Are you okay?"

"Great!" he answered. "I'm living my dream."

"Your life is perfect?"

"Close," he answered, not understanding what she was truly asking—or dodging it. "Close to perfect, like your life. You must be thrilled to have your book published."

"Thrilled," she answered, wishing she could add, "Except you're not here."

Luis didn't let that conversation go on for long, before he announced he missed her and hoped she'd visit him, never quite getting around to when that might happen. The distance between Mexico and Milwaukee seemed to grow.

Lauren ignored the tug of late spring and then summer activities, as she worked without breaks, without lunch and with little sleep—-first to finish corrections for publication of the book and then to get ahead on her clients' projects.

One night after she finally made time for a long shower, she found a message on her voice mail from Luis saying he'd definitely be delayed. There were problems with the museum plans, and government authorities were attempting to appoint other archeologists to work on the codex. He neglected to mention he missed her.

In August, she'd be on the tour and wouldn't have time to think about him. At least, that's what she kept telling herself, until Julie came up with a plan. Lauren must call Luis and tell him what a bastard he is. That would definitely bring him to her side, Julie said. She'd already tried it with Philip and it worked like a charm. She and Philip planned to move in together soon.

Late one night after dinner and drinks with Julie and Philip, Lauren tried the number Luis had given her. He answered.

"Lauren! I can't believe it!" he said, with obvious enthusiasm. "How are you?"

What could she say? Miserable. Dying of loneliness. Sex-starved. Furious. "Busy," she answered. "And you? I'm amazed I could reach you. How's the project going?"

"Great!"

"No problems with the government authorities?"

"Not anymore."

"The word around here is you got your tenure, and soon you'll be named head of the department at the university."

"I thought I told you that already. The tenure part's true, but the department head is still a long shot," he said with an easy laugh. "Can you come?"

"Where? When?" She held her breath and waited for his answer.

"To the announcement event in Mexico City. We're going to unveil a copy of the codex and show slides of the new facility being built for it. The president of Mexico is coming! Don't tell me you didn't get the invitation."

"No, I didn't."

"You won't believe it, Lauren; I deciphered one whole section of it. We've been able to control the decomposition enough to examine it carefully, and I can't describe how exciting it is to read. I hope you'll be here for the big night."

"That sounds great, but when is it, Luis?"

"A week from Saturday. You should have gotten the invitation weeks ago."

"Oh, but that's right before I go on my book tour."

"Book tour? I forgot about that. I'm happy for you." He didn't sound happy.

"I never got the invitation, Luis."

"Knowing the mail in this country, it'll probably get there in December." Luis's voice dropped. "I miss you, Lauren. I want you to come."

"You what?" She dared him to lie again.

"I really want you to be here with me." Luis's words were soft, as if he hoped someone else wouldn't hear.

"If you had wanted me to be there, Luis, damn you, you would have called me, instead of me calling you. Even if every phone in a thousand miles didn't work, you would have crawled through a cave or climbed a mountain, but you wouldn't have just mailed me an invitation that never arrived. Forget it. None of that matters anymore."

"Lauren, wait, it's not like that."

"Luis, I'm paying for this call, and I'm going to talk until I hang up. Next time you get stuck in a cave or kidnapped, or mugged, I hope they beat your charming, arrogant, philandering brains out."

Five minutes after she hung up the phone rang again. "Lauren, I'm sorry. My world is crazy, I admit it. I haven't had time to do anything but work and fall into bed. Please come, even if it's just for one night. Please."

"One night?" Julie hung her dripping raincoat on the coat stand, wiped her running shoes on the doormat, and slumped into her desk chair. "What's wrong with giving him one more night? Wait a minute. When did he call you?"

Lauren paced back and forth in front of the window. "I called him around midnight, after you left last night."

Julie pointed at Lauren's silk pants and white blouse. "That's what you were wearing last night. You never even went to bed, did you?"

Lauren grimaced and resumed her pacing. "We're not talking about my sleeping habits. The attic roof is leaking, and it's going to cost me a bundle. I have a thousand dollars worth of reasons not to go down there for one night."

"Money is not a factor here. You deserve to be sure. Enid, the queen of love affairs, will gladly give you the money for an airplane trip."

"But I have to get ready for the book tour."

"So? A little romance before the tour would be good for you. Juice you up a bit."

Lauren leaned her knuckles on Julie's desk. "Juice me up? Give me a break. If I go, I'm going to tell him it's over."

Julie smiled. "Sounds like you already did that. How about letting him do his magic again? I'm betting the guy loves you, Lauren, whether he can say it or not. Hey, a delivery truck just drove up. I'll go see what he has for us. Maybe it's the invitation."

Lauren was upstairs in her bedroom pulling on

her jeans when Julie burst in holding a large envelope over her head. "Ta-da! It is the invitation from Luis, with an airplane ticket wrapped around it. He wants you! May I say I told you so?"

****

Lauren wound her way through Mexico City International airport customs, through the welcoming area teeming with families, and out onto the sidewalk where Luis told her to meet him. He wasn't there, of course, which didn't help her stomach.

She paced, wishing she had ignored Julie's advice to wear her new four-inch heels. Already a blister throbbed on her little toe. Her nerves were a mess. Her palms were soaked, and her heartbeat thrummed in her throat. A drop of sweat trickled from her scalp down her neck and into her bra.

The air was like a steam bath and felt like rain. She peeked out from the overhang to check the sky, but the gauzy light wasn't from hovering clouds; it was just Mexico City's usual mist of pollution. Lauren waved off two taxi drivers and wondered if she should go back inside and try to reach Luis on the pay phone.

"I am your driver, señorita." Lauren heard the words behind her and shook her head without turning around. "No, gracias." The tap on her shoulder made her jump.

"Señorita Richmond?"

The young man with slicked-back, jet-black hair and a cool hand flashed a wide smile full of bright white teeth. "I'm Luis's nephew, Enrico. He asked me to take you to the hotel and then to the ceremony. Pleased to meet you."

"Nice to meet you too. I thought Luis would be here."

The young man nodded and looked down at his feet. "He was getting into the car to come pick you up, when something happened and he had to go speak to somebody." Enrico pointed. "Please, this way."

As they climbed into the front seat of a dusty blue van, Enrico chattered about how he had decided to study archeology at the University of Chicago even before he was ten years old, because he had followed his Uncle Luis around the ruins near his great-grandparents' home. Lauren recognized the glint in his eyes as he described the small cache of pottery bits he had found beneath a boulder. The kid was already hooked.

"Tonight will be very special, Señorita Lauren. The president of Mexico will be there shaking my uncle's hand. We'll all get to meet *el Señor* Juan Cordero Villalobos, the guy who has promised two million dollars to build a laboratory and museum for the codex. " Enrico shook his head. " We were with him last night, very late last night. He's thirty, I think, younger than Luis, but already rich—and very funny after a bottle of wine, lots of bottles of wine."

"Luis must be happy to have a member of your family here."

"Are you kidding? We're all here."

"All six sisters?"

Enrico nodded. "Along with my parents, my uncles, and eight cousins. Even my grandmother arrived today."

"How is she? I met her the last time I was in Mexico."

"Grumpy, but fine." Enrico took his eyes off the hoards of traffic to nod at her. " We've all heard about your great adventure. Luis says you saved his life many times over. Even Marcella admires you, and she doesn't say nice things about anyone."

"Really? I barely met Marcella."

"The sisters suspect she wants to be part of the

story, anything to get her close to Luis, if you know what I mean."

"I know exactly what you mean. So what's her job?"

Enrico shrugged. "She has some sort of connection to Cordero Villalobos, as well as to the government. Whatever it is, she likes to be in charge." He laughed. "The Hernandez family isn't easy to boss around. Let's see, what was I supposed to tell you?" Enrico glanced at her. "Oh, what you're wearing is fine, so you don't have to change. Luis said to say that, but I'll tell you the other women are wearing like, uh, prom dresses, so you can change or not, as you want." He shrugged. "Okay, so next, Luis will meet you in your room at six, and we will leave for the museum as soon as you come down the elevator." He glanced at his watch. "Here's the hotel. You have approximately twenty minutes."

Enrico beat out the bell captain to open the car door for Lauren. "Here's your room key. The bellman will bring your luggage. By the way," he paused as a grin spread across his lips, "Luis was right. You are different from every other woman."

For the first time since Lauren had accepted Luis's invitation, her stomach felt fine, thanks to Enrico.

As soon as she entered her spacious hotel room, she pulled open the closet door to see if Luis's clothes might be hanging there already. Except for hangers, the usual extra blanket, and the ironing board, it was empty. During her two-minute shower, she analyzed the significance of the rooming arrangement. If Luis hadn't planned on having her stay with him, maybe he'd invited her to the event so he could say goodbye gracefully. Was it possible she'd actually hurt his feelings when she yelled that she hoped someone would knock his "charming, philandering brains out?" She tried to picture Luis with hurt feelings and failed. The guy wasn't built to feel emotional pain.

Lauren stepped into the cocktail dress Julie described as "appropriately form-fitting with a whisper of cleavage."

Earlier that morning, as Julie circled the airport driveway, she had reminded Lauren her mission was a scrimmage in a battle to the death for the man she loved. When Lauren had asked Julie who the enemy was in this battle, her answer was simple. "Luis. He wants you, but he'll have to change his life for you, which means he might have to stop seeing sexy broads like what's her name."

"Marcella." Lauren said the name out loud, as she put on her lipstick and checked her image in the full-length mirror on the back of the hotel room door. Her watch said Luis was already five minutes late. Maybe Enrico got it wrong. Maybe she was supposed to meet Luis in the lobby. She lifted the phone and asked to be connected to Luis's room.

A woman answered. Assuming she had misdialed, Lauren hung up and punched in the number once more. When the woman answered again, Lauren felt her shoulders sink. Of course, Marcella was there. "May I please speak to Luis?"

"Who's calling?" the silky voice asked.

"You tell me your name, and I'll tell you mine."

The silky voice chuckled. "Aha, this must be Lauren. He's right here."

In less than a second Luis spoke. "Lauren! You don't know how glad I am you're here. We're two floors above you. I'll be right down to your room. Don't move."

Lauren had to sit down and bite her lips to keep her tears from messing up the mascara Julie had said she had to wear. "'We're two floors above you,'" she mimicked him aloud. The silkiness of the woman's voice was proof she was the one who was sharing a hotel room with Luis—or wanted to. Lauren strode back to the bathroom, rechecked her face and hair, and prepared to meet them both.

Luis stood outside her door by himself, his dark eyes luring her into his arms. He held her, kissed her gently, touched her lips, and then kissed her again. He smiled and sighed. "You're here. You're finally here."

Lauren brushed his chin. "You shaved, really shaved. You actually have smooth cheeks."

He gripped her hand against his face. "You like it?"

She nodded. "I liked it before. And your hair is combed. I'm not used to you looking so distinguished."

Luis shook his head. "Me? Distinguished?"

"And you're wearing a suit. You look older, more mature."

Luis reached for her hands. "And you look like a movie star." He squinted down at her. "Where'd you get that fancy dress? Have I ever even seen you in a dress before?"

"From Julie the shopper. She tried to get me to wear earrings that hung down to my shoulders." She reached for his lips. "Sorry. I got lipstick all over you." When Lauren tried to wipe off the remains, he clutched her fingers and kissed them too. "Luis, I've never seen you in anything but jeans."

"Not true. You've seen me without jeans." He kissed her again and then just held her. "I'd like to stay here and talk." He stepped back. "About me getting my charming, philandering, arrogant brains knocked out, or was it arrogant, charming, philandering brains?"

"Okay, so I was angry. At least you should understand how it's been all these months. How am I supposed to know what you're thinking?"

"I didn't mean to neglect you. Everything

happened so fast after you left that I've barely had time to eat or sleep." He dropped her hand and his smile faded. "Alone or with anyone."

Lauren stepped back and shrugged off his light apology. "Okay. So I'm insecure and jealous, two bad things. With all your family here, will it be possible to have time alone?"

"Of course. You only have one night, unless I can talk you into flying down to the village with us tomorrow. I know, I know," he said as Lauren shook her head, "you leave in two days for your authors' trip, which is very cool. I went online and got the schedule. We'll come back here as soon as the dinner is over."

"There's a dinner too?"

Luis nodded and sighed. "After the reception we have to take Cordero Villalobos to dinner."

"A small dinner?" Her time with Luis was shrinking.

"It was supposed to be, but Marcella thought we should include the head of the museum and his wife, and somebody from the city government, and then someone else from the government bureau. God, it's going to be boring. Maybe Marcella will let us slip away early." Luis led her to the door.

"Does she work for you or do you work for her?"

"Good question." Luis turned and shook his head. "Lauren, I have to warn you about tonight."

"What do you mean?" Lauren's heart thumped again.

A smile lit his lips. "You're going to have to deal with my sisters—all of them at once, but it's too late to back out now. They're out there circling like sharks, waiting to eat you up."

Lauren picked up her purse and walked ahead of Luis through the door. "They can't be that bad. What have you told them about me?"

"Nothing. That's been my defense all my life," he

said as he followed her into the hall. "Tell them nada." Luis strode ahead and punched the elevator button.

"Maria was nice to me when we were at your grandmother's."

Luis shook his head. "Maybe, but altogether they form a force more intimidating than the Inquisition."

Lauren laughed. "Come on. You're all grown-ups."

He shrugged. "Jeez, this elevator is taking forever. Marcella will be furious."

"I suppose she'll be with us the whole evening."

Luis nodded and watched the elevator start to open.

"So, tell me, what does she do?"

Luis winced as they squeezed into the crowded elevator. "Marcella does everything I hate to do. She organizes interviews, coordinates the fund-raising activities, and writes all the request letters."

Lauren smiled at the elderly couple next to them as a flutter grew in her stomach. "So she's just an employee, right, all business?" She hoped she sounded light-hearted.

He didn't nod. Nor did he shake his head. He simply tipped it and frowned. "It's complicated." They stepped out of the elevator. "There's Enrico, who's in love with you, by the way. Love at first sight, he called it."

Lauren followed Luis through the lobby and out the revolving door, trying to recall how she felt when she met Luis. Had it been love at first sight for her?

The front passenger door of the van opened to the curb. Luis ducked his head in first and seemed to be having an argument with someone in the front seat. After a minute, he stood up and held the door while Marcella eased across the seat. Revealing her legs up to her thighs, she stepped onto the sidewalk, turned and stuck out her hand. "You must be the heroic Lauren Richmond. I don't think we've met. I'm Marcella Rodriguez."

Lauren pictured herself at a battle station, squeezed the hand as hard as she could and hoped to see the woman wince. "But we did meet, Marcella, at the dig site." Lauren smiled as if she was delighted to remember the incident. "Don't you remember? You practically climbed into Luis's lap, you were so glad to see your old friend."

The smile froze on Marcella's face. She stepped back and scooped a handful of dark, luscious hair off her shoulder. "Well, I'll just go in the next car, Luis."

Lauren hurried into the front seat of the van, before Marcella could order her out again. In the two rows of seats behind her, one of the sisters whooped and the rest started to clap.

"Bravo!" yelled the sister sitting behind Enrico. "We've been trying to get her to buzz off all day. Here you show up, Lauren, and she's outta here."

Lauren turned to see Luis's reaction, but he was staring at the stack of papers Marcella left behind and chewing on a fingernail.

"Don't worry about him, Lauren." It was Maria, the oldest sister. "He's nervous about his speech. Too bad he didn't catch the way you brushed right past her. Maybe he'd get some balls and tell Marcella to buzz off for good."

Based on that outburst, Lauren already liked the sisters. In the fifteen minutes it took to drive to the museum, each sister introduced herself, complimented Lauren on her outfit and her hair, and then pestered Enrico about his driving. Adarita asked Lauren if she was blind or crazy to have anything to do with their brother.

When they threatened to tell her why no woman should go near him, Luis finally looked up from his papers and pretended to cover Lauren's ears. As they waited in line for the parking service, Olivia, the self-declared youngest and most spoiled sister, cleared her throat and in a low voice said how grateful they were that Lauren had saved their brother's life.

"Okay," Luis whispered to Lauren as they climbed out of the car, "I don't know how, but you've made it through the worst. All you have to do now is dodge the sisters the rest of the night."

Lauren looked up beyond the skyline and tried to find a star to wish on. She had won a skirmish, perhaps, but she had a feeling her troops weren't as fresh as the opponent's. She needed some luck.

On the sidewalk, she stopped to admire the modern building ahead of them. "Wow!" Lauren slid her hand into Luis's. "This is the Museum of Anthropology? It's stunning!"

Luis tucked his papers in his pocket and led her up the steps, with the sisters keeping up on either side and Enrico trailing behind. "The best part is what's inside. We're gathering in the Maya room, which is even more impressive than this courtyard."

The sisters spotted Marcella waiting at the entrance and heckled Enrico for driving so slowly that she could beat them. He tried to defend himself, saying he wasn't a resident Mexicano, and that the doorman had sent him the long way.

Once they entered the Maya hall, Marcella and Luis disappeared into a crowd and didn't reappear until the director of the Museum stood at the podium, in front of vivid murals depicting Mayan life.

Surrounded by Luis's family, Lauren waited for the ceremony to begin. Off to the right of the podium, Marcella posed with her chin high and her arms crossed, like a queen among the lowly. Next to her, Luis, pale, but distinguished-looking in his suit, chewed on his lips and shuffled his feet.

A man with thick lips, a movie-star tan, curls cascading over his collar, and wearing a shimmering gray suit and cowboy boots, strutted up to Marcella and puffed out his chest. One of the sisters poked Lauren and giggled into her ear. "Get a look at that guy. Thinks he's something, doesn't he? He's the one who's donating all the money for the building."

With some translation help from the sisters, Lauren listened as the museum director introduced Dr. Luis Hernandez and related how he had found the codex. Before he finished, a slide show of the codex and drawings for the building played on a giant screen above and behind him. While the sisters murmured that he should have mentioned Lauren's part in the discovery, the director explained the historical connection of the codex to the impressive collection of artifacts in the room.

Luis's voice wavered when he began to speak about the exciting plans for the new home for the codex, but grew stronger as he read the long list of accomplishments of Cordero Villalobos, and then called him to the microphone.

Villalobos hugged the microphone like a rock singer and spoke so long Lauren's toes went numb in her hellish heels. Once he finally stopped talking, press and photographers swarmed the podium, swallowing Luis in the process.

The Hernandez gang grabbed glasses of champagne and hovered around a tray of hors d'oeuvres until Marcella marched over to tell them they should hurry over to the restaurant, so they wouldn't lose their reservation. She added that Luis and Cordero Villalobos would join them later.

At the restaurant Lauren's eyes drooped with fatigue, her feet swelled beneath the table, and Luis's grandmother asked to be taken to the hotel to go to bed. The sisters, their children, and spouses toasted Luis and each other. The invitees from the government were quite happy to join all of the toasts and add some of their own. When the champagne disappeared, Maria announced they shouldn't wait for Luis, Marcella, and Villalobos any longer, and told the waiters to serve their dinners.

After two hours of Hernandez family stories, Lauren whispered to Enrico that she would take a cab back to the hotel. He insisted on driving her. He ditched the van at the hotel curb and walked her to her room. At her door, he took her hand and frowned. "Lauren, I speak for my aunts and my mother. We are honored to meet you." He looked down. "I love and admire my uncle Luis, but—" He shook his head. "But we're afraid he's lost his way." He blushed after Lauren kissed him on the cheek.

At dawn, when Luis still hadn't shown up in her hotel room, Lauren called a cab and left for the airport to catch the earliest flight home.

In Milwaukee, there were three messages from Luis on her answering machine, apologizing for his absence and explaining that he and Marcella had to spend the entire evening renegotiating the building details and settling the donor's gift.

Julie went online to read newspaper commentaries about the museum event and found a photo of Lauren standing with the sisters. The caption read, "Forgotten heroine?"

Chapter Eighteen

The publisher's representative introduced the three authors to each other in the bar of the Ritz Carlton Hotel in Chicago. Lauren was surprised how quickly she grew comfortable with the women. Monique was a redhead, Laramie a brunette, and Lauren had made herself even blonder than before, which pleased the publisher's representative. The photographer liked how well they photographed together and started calling them "Charlie's Devils."

The schedule included three bookstore visits per day. Monique and Laramie announced they intended to use their free moments to do what they loved best, shop in the malls.

The three writers sat at a folding table set up in the center of a large bookstore in a suburban mall. Bookcases surrounded them on three sides. In front of them were twenty rows of chairs, all full.

Monique was narrating her favorite scene to the mostly female crowd. Lauren noticed movement among several women standing in the rear. She watched a bearded man in dark glasses and a lime green sport coat squeeze between two women.

As soon as the man removed the sunglasses, Lauren recognized the eyes, the amazing eyes, and the smile she saw each night in her dreams.

What the hell was he doing there, she asked herself, and fumed. Where had he found that awful green jacket and the hideous flowered tie? Lauren fingered the necklace she'd made out of the jade Luis had found in the cave and glared at him, wishing he'd disappear, when she realized the shop manager had introduced her. She gave her reading like a zombie on autopilot.

After the question session had gone on for a while, Luis raised his hand. Before Lauren could stop her, Monique called on the bearded man in the back.

"Ms. Richmond, Lauren," he said grinning at her, "I have a question for you."

Lauren looked around for an exit, but bookshelves blocked her escape. "Okay," she said. It came out as a croak.

"Will you marry me?

The women around him were the first to giggle. In seconds, the rest of the crowd laughed and didn't stop until Monique began clapping.

Luis never moved. He stood still watching Lauren with an expression she couldn't decipher. Was he sad? Was he sick? Was he crazy?

"Thank you, bearded one," Monique announced, smiling with toothy delight. "Since we're all single women up here, we hope you'll bring two more guys just like you to our next book signing. Pretty please!"

The audience applauded her, and Monique turned to Lauren. "Lauren, aren't you going to answer this poor man?"

Lauren was about to bolt. "No."

"No, you won't answer?" Luis asked, "Or no, you won't marry me?"

"No, I won't marry you."

The women in the audience began murmuring.

"Then will you have dinner with me?"

"No, thanks," Lauren answered quickly, and tried to clear her hoarse throat. "Monique, don't you think it's time to begin the book signing?"

The shop owner stood up quickly and instructed members of the audience to form a line with their books open to the title page. As people made their way to the front of the line, Lauren kept track of Luis. For a moment, he stared back at her, looking puzzled, and then slipped behind one of the bookcases. Lauren hoped he was on his way back to Mexico—or even China.

When the women arrived at their hotel, there was a note waiting for Lauren. "I'm here. Please call me. I have to see you. All my love, Luis." He left a phone number.

Luis's writing was surprisingly neat, bold, dark and all in caps. Lauren's chest hurt as if it had been kicked. "All my love." He'd actually put that in writing.

Luis had no idea what love was. She couldn't risk going near him again, when even a touch of his hand would mean the end of her resolve to move on.

In St. Louis, when the three authors arrived at a bookshop, Luis was seated in the front row wearing an orange T-shirt under the disgusting lime green sport coat. His beard had grown and his hair stuck out on one side as if he'd slept on it wrong. Lauren felt an urge to smooth it back.

The minute he saw her he jumped up, and before she could dodge him, he gripped her shoulder. "Lauren, I have to talk to you."

"I'm busy, Luis." She shouldn't have said his name. She clamped her mouth shut.

"Lauren, I'm in agony."

She noticed then his eyes were rimmed in red. She tried to shrug off his hand.

"Agony? You have to be able to feel to be in agony. Goodbye, Luis." She stood tall as she strode to the table where the others were seated.

"Isn't that your mystery man, Lauren?" Monique asked with a giggle.

Lauren nodded. "I wish he'd go away. Monique, don't call on him, please. It's embarrassing."

"Are you kidding? He's hot!" Laramie said,

giving Luis a wave. "Maybe he'll ask me to marry him this time."

At the end of the presentation, Laramie called on the man with the beard again.

"Thank you, Laramie," he began. "You know what I'm going to ask, don't you?" Luis said without smiling. "Lauren, I love you. Please, marry me."

Lauren shook her head and hoped to get away without speaking, but Laramie wouldn't let her. "Come on, Lauren, you could at least go to dinner with the poor guy after he's followed you across the country. Monique and I could come along as chaperones."

Lauren faked a smile and threw up her hands in apology. "The only mystery men I like are the ones in my books."

At that, the women in the audience clapped, while Luis sat motionless with his eyes on Lauren and his hands in his pockets. During the book signing, Lauren saw the shop manager corner Luis with a notebook and pencil in her hands.

Monique poked Lauren. "What's with that guy? Do you know him?"

"I used to."

"Really?" Monique watched Lauren autograph a book for a second. "Wait a minute! Is he the guy who found that Mayan thing? Hey! You two had something going, didn't you?"

Lauren didn't answer. She was worrying about what Luis was telling the bookshop manager.

"Hey, Laramie, did you hear that? Lauren had an affair with that guy. Isn't this great?"

The next day the story appeared in the local newspaper. The day after that it hit newspapers around the country. Luis hadn't revealed his name, only that he'd been in love with Lauren for months and realized it was time to tell her before it was too late.

"Too Late for Love?" and "Hot Author Has Mystery Lover!" ran the headlines.

The publishers were delighted. Lauren suspected they helped spread the story to ensure a better turnout at the bookshops. No one could have dreamed up a better gimmick.

Lauren knew the truth. One of the Hot Three had a mangled heart, but that headline wouldn't sell books.

When Luis didn't show up in Pittsburg or Philadelphia, the audiences were disappointed. Several held signs addressed to the mysterious stranger that read, "If Lauren won't marry you, I will."

The next week Lauren scanned the audience for him at each bookstore and then vacillated between relief and worry. She hated being embarrassed in public, but then fretted that he might be sick. He hadn't looked good at all. Had he given up on her?

Crowds at the book signings grew. Some even followed the three to the airport in hopes the mystery man would show himself and propose again.

Late one night at their hotel in Louisville, as Lauren was trying to fall asleep, the phone rang. She almost didn't answer it, fearing it would be Luis, but it turned out to be Julie.

"Lauren! I heard about you and the mystery man on the news. It's Luis, isn't it?"

"It's awful."

"Awful? It's great. He's figured it out!"

"Figured what out?"

"That he loves you. Congratulations."

"I'm not going to marry him."

"Of course you should ignore him for awhile. That's a good plan. Oh! I almost forgot to tell you what my mother decided."

"Don't give me any more of your mother's diagnoses."

"But she's right. She says you were stunted from the grief of your mother's death and your dad's coldness, but now you've overcome it. You've taken the risk and leaped for love. Remember we agreed he's the man for you."

Chapter Nineteen

Lauren had never been to Atlanta. After three weeks of touring with the other women, enclosed in windowless malls, eating food wrapped in paper, staying up watching digital clocks meld away the minutes in beige motel rooms, with very little exercise, Lauren was desperate for a change.

She'd read that the Milwaukee Brewers were in town to play the Braves. The minute the women had checked into the hotel, she strode over to the concierge and blew some big bucks on a good seat for that evening.

It was a hot night, perfect for a baseball game. Lauren took a cab to the ballpark, hoping she'd get there in time for batting practice. Her legs felt free in the chic orange linen shorts Julie had insisted she buy. The bright pink sandals Monique and Laramie had bought her at the latest mall made her feel like a kid on the first day of summer vacation.

Her seat was perfect too, close enough to home plate to observe the curve of each pitch and right on the aisle where vendors could reach her. Her hot dog smothered with pickles and mustard tasted unbelievably wonderful. The beer was even better. With a shadow of sweet sadness, she thought how her grandfather would have loved to have be there with her. Baseball, he'd told her many times, was his escape. At a stadium, he always said, there were no wars and no credit crunches. There were no bills. There were no demanding clients or endless questions.

There were no bearded men asking Lauren to marry them.

In fact, there was no one else in Lauren's row. She studied the lineups posted on the giant screen as batting practice wound down. The grounds crew smoothed the infield and outlined the batter's box. Lauren leaned back in her seat and felt her shoulders settle where they belonged, her teeth unclench, and her abs release.

People stood for the National Anthem and removed their caps. Lauren sprang up too, when a man arrived in the aisle and tapped her shoulder. Lauren stepped forward to let him by. The band began. The man squeezed behind her and stood in front of the seat next to hers.

Lauren avoided making eye contact with the guy, because she didn't want anything to intrude on her delicious escape. Clutching her oozing hot dog and her sweating beer cup, she sang lustily along with the high school chorus clustered on the field near home plate. The man next to her joined in. At the end of the song, Lauren bent down to move her purse out of his way, and he spoke.

"Your hair's different. I like it."

"Luis!" His beard was gone. His eyes were unbelievably dark. He stood too close. "What are you doing here?"

"Following you. I read your book. It's very good."

Luis looked wonderful, and he looked awful. Lauren put her beer in the cup holder and reached for his hair. "Don't you ever comb this?"

Luis pulled her hand to his lips. "When you marry me, I'll start."

His rough hand was warm, gentle. She snatched her hand away. "I'm here to watch the game, and by the way, I hate you." His eyelashes were even longer than she remembered.

"No, you love me and I love you. I don't want to

make you cry ever again."

"You don't love anyone, and who said you made me cry?" She shoved his arm off her armrest.

"Correction: I tried not to love anyone. You made that goal impossible."

"You're with someone else now, the woman with the big boobs."

He touched her cheek and smoothed her hair. "I can forget about you and Rocky, if you can forget about Marcella."

"Rocky is a friend, that's all. I told you what happened that night was a mistake."

"There hasn't been anyone else for me since I first saw you." He stroked her ponytail. "I forgot how soft your hair is." He inhaled and whispered, "And how good you smell. By the way, your boobs are perfect."

His breath tickled her ear. "What about your codex?"

"Lauren." He turned her chin toward him, but she twisted away from his fingers. "Next to you it's a wad of rotting paper." He rested his arm on the back of her seat. "I love you. I never thought I'd say that to anyone, and now I want to tell everyone."

"At the book signing. Well, that was obvious and very embarrassing."

"It's scary how much I love you. It's terrifying to be without you. Marry me. Please. I'd kneel, but there's no room."

"You had your chance in Mexico." She halted and bit off tears. "You just can't come running here and tell me you've changed."

"But I have."

"What would change you in a month?"

"Abuelita died."

Lauren's chest sunk with Luis's voice. "Oh, no."

Luis covered his mouth and nodded. "I was at the dig site, and I was supposed to have dinner with her the night before. But someone called and had to see me, so I postponed the drive. And then—" His breath came out in small gasps. "It was too late."

Lauren rubbed his shoulder. "I'm so sorry."

Luis shook his head. "I got there in time to hold her before they took her away, and I saw myself the way I was in Mexico City. Consumed with the codex. Like a dictator, it was ruling my life, tearing me from my family, closing my heart against the woman I love."

"Pretty words, but what did you do about it?"

"I gave my assistant the job of overseeing the construction project and the fund-raising. I hired another archeologist to take Frank's place, and I flew home to ask you to marry me."

"But I wasn't there."

He nodded. "I'd been so buried in my own life, I had forgotten you wouldn't be there."

"I was just fine, Luis. Some days I hardly thought of you at all, and then you showed up at the bookstores and messed me up again."

"I want to make love to you every day. I want to touch your cheeks, your lips, your eyes, every day."

"Luis, I can't sleep because I can't stop thinking of you."

"I want you to reach for my hair at least once a day and tell me what a slob I am. I want to hear your thoughts. I want to share mine with you." He kissed her nose. "I even want you to correct my grammar." He flashed his teeth and laughed.

"You're going to break my heart again."

"Never. I'd be breaking my own heart too."

They kissed through the first pitch and again between innings.

"Luis?"

"Yes, Lauren?"

"If you cheer loudly for the Brewers, it would help your cause."

Luis clapped, whistled, and yelled so much for each Milwaukee batter that the Atlanta crowd around them began to jeer. During the seventh inning stretch while everyone else sang, they kissed again, and two guys in the row behind them booed.

"Okay, Luis," Lauren said, pulling Luis's collar so his face was next to hers, "you've proven yourself, so I may decide not to hate you."

"Because you love me?"

"We'll see."

Luis dug his hand in his ragged pocket. He held up a large jade stone set in gold. "My grandfather gave this to my grandmother, and she left it to me. It's guaranteed to banish jinxes. As proof, I haven't lost it. Please, put it on your finger."

In the midst of another kiss, Lauren's heart exploded with joy. The stadium's roving camera found them, and their image filled the giant screen. Everyone applauded, even the guys two rows behind them.

About the author...

A.Y. Stratton grew up in Glenview, Illinois, moved to Milwaukee, Wisconsin, when in high school, and attended college in New York, majoring in English literature. A.Y. and her husband live in a suburb of Milwaukee.

As a child A.Y. had trouble sleeping. She made up adventures starring as the heroine and imagined the stories she would write some day. Once her children were older she began writing free-lance for local periodicals, including a regular baseball column for the website of her beloved Milwaukee Brewers.

A.Y. became hooked on ancient ruins the moment she stood among the spirits of the sacrificed virgins at the top of the Pyramid of the Sun at Teotihuacan near Mexico City. Eventually she visited other ruins in Mexico, Guatemala, Belize, and Honduras, where she conceived the idea for *Buried Heart*.

Visit A.Y. at www.aystratton.com

Breinigsville, PA USA
05 April 2010
235538BV00003B/5/P